VERNON DOWNS

WORLD GONE WATER

GARDEN LAKES

WE'RE SO FAMOUS

Jaime Clarke is a graduate of the University of Arizona and holds an MFA from Bennington College. He is the author of the novels *We're So Famous, Vernon Downs, World Gone Water* and *Garden Lakes*; the memoirs *Bookmarked: The Great Gatsby*, and *Typical of the Times: Growing Up in the Culture of Spectacle*, which is the basis for his microcast, *Typical*; editor of the anthologies *Don't You Forget About Me: Contemporary Writers on the Films of John Hughes, Conversations with Jonathan Lethem*, and *Talk Show: On the Couch with Contemporary Writers*; and co-editor of the anthologies *No Near Exit: Writers Select Their Favorite Work from Post Road Magazine* (with Mary Cotton), and *Boston Noir 2: The Classics* (with Dennis Lehane and Mary Cotton). He is a founding editor of the literary magazine *Post Road*, now published at Boston College, and co-owner, with his wife, of Newtonville Books, an independent bookstore in Boston.

By the same author

Vernon Downs: A Novel
by Jaime Clarke

"*Vernon Downs* is a gripping, hypnotically written and unnerving look at the dark side of literary adulation. Jaime Clarke's tautly suspenseful novel is a cautionary tale for writers and readers alike–after finishing it, you may start to think that J.D. Salinger had the right idea after all."

–Tom Perrotta, author of *Election*, *Little Children*, and *The Leftovers*

"Moving and edgy in just the right way. Love (or lack of) and Family (or lack of) is at the heart of this wonderfully obsessive novel." – Gary Shteyngart, author of *Super Sad True Love Story*

"All strong literature stems from obsession. *Vernon Downs* belongs to a tradition that includes Nicholson Baker's *U and I*, Geoff Dyer's *Out of Sheer Rage*, and—for that matter—*Pale Fire*. What makes Clarke's excellent novel stand out isn't just its rueful intelligence, or its playful semi-veiling of certain notorious literary figures, but its startling sadness. *Vernon Downs* is first rate."
—Matthew Specktor, author of *American Dream Machine*

"*Vernon Downs* is a brilliant meditation on obsession, art, and celebrity. Charlie Martens's mounting fixation with the titular Vernon is not only driven by the burn of heartbreak and the lure of fame, but also a lost young man's struggle to locate his place in the world. *Vernon Downs* is an intoxicating novel, and Clarke is a dazzling literary talent."
— Laura van den Berg, author of *The Isle of Youth*

World Gone Water: A Novel
by Jaime Clarke

"Jaime Clarke's *World Gone Water* is so fresh and daring, a necessary book, a barbaric yawp that revels in its taboo: the sexual and emotional desires of today's hetero young man. Clarke is a sure and sensitive writer, his lines are clean and carry us right to the tender heart of his lovelorn hero, Charlie Martens. This is the book Hemingway and Kerouac would want to read. It's the sort of honesty in this climate that many of us aren't brave enough to write." – Tony D'Souza, author of *The Konkans*.

"This unsettling novel ponders human morality and sexuality, and the murky interplay between the two. Charlie Martens is a compelling anti-hero with a voice that can turn on a dime, from shrugging naiveté to chilling frankness. *World Gone Water* is a candid, often startling portrait of an unconventional life."
– J. Robert Lennon, author of *Familiar*

"Funny and surprising, *World Gone Water* is terrific fun to read ... and, as a spectacle of bad behavior, pretty terrifying to contemplate." –- Adrienne Miller, author of *The Coast of Akron*

"Charlie Martens is my favorite kind of narrator, an obsessive yearner whose commitment to his worldview is so overwhelming that the distance between his words and the reader's usual thinking gets clouded fast. *World Gone Water* will draw you in, make you complicit, and finally leave you both discomfited and thrilled." — Matt Bell, author of *In the House upon the Dirt between the Lake and the Woods*

"Charlie Martens will make you laugh. More, he'll offend and shock you while making you laugh. Even trickier: he'll somehow make you like him, root for him, despite yourself and despite him. This novel travels into the dark heart of male/female relations and yet there is tenderness, humanity, hope. Jaime Clarke rides what is a terribly fine line between hero and antihero. Read and be astounded."

– Amy Grace Loyd, author of *The Affairs of Others*

Garden Lakes: A Novel
by Jaime Clarke

"It takes some nerve to revisit a bulletproof classic, but Jaime Clarke does so, with elegance and a cool contemporary eye, in this cunningly crafted homage to *Lord of the Flies*. He understands all too well the complex psychology of boyhood, how easily the insecurities and power plays slide into mayhem when adults look the other way." – Julia Glass, National Book Award-winning author of *Three Junes*

"Jaime Clarke reminds us that if the banality of evil is indeed a viable truth, its seeds are most likely sewn among adolescent boys." – Brad Watson, author of *Aliens in the Prime of Their Lives*

"In the flawlessly imagined *Garden Lakes*, Jaime Clarke pays homage to *Lord of the Flies* and creates his own vivid, inadvertently isolated community. As summer tightens its grip, and adult authority recedes, his boys gradually reveal themselves to scary and exhilarating effect. In the hands of this master of suspense and psychological detail, the result is a compulsively readable novel." – Margot Livesey, author of *The Flight of Gemma Hardy*

"Smart, seductive, and suggestively sinister, *Garden Lakes* is a disturbingly honest look at how our lies shape our lives and destroy our communities. Read it: Part three in one of the best literary trilogies we have." – Scott Cheshire, author of *High as the Horses' Bridles*

"As tense and tight and pitch-perfect as Clarke's narrative of the harrowing events at *Garden Lakes* is, and as fine a meditation it is on Golding's novel, what deepens this book to another level of insight and artfulness is the parallel portrait of Charlie Martens as an adult, years after his fateful role that summer, still tyrannized, paralyzed, tangled in lies, wishing for redemption, maybe fated never to get it. Complicated and feral, *Garden Lakes* is thrilling, literary, and smart as hell." – Paul Harding, Pulitzer Prize-winning author of *Tinkers*

We're So Famous: A Novel
by Jaime Clarke

"Jaime Clarke pulls off a sympathetic act of sustained male imagination: entering the minds of innocent teenage girls dreaming of fame. A glibly surreal world where the only thing wanted is notoriety and all you really desire leads to celebrity and where stardom is the only point of reference. What's new about this novel is how unconsciously casual the characters' drives are. This lust is as natural to them as being American-it's almost a birthright."
– Bret Easton Ellis

"Daisy, Paque, and Stella want. They want to be actresses. They want to be in a band. They want to be models. They want to be famous, damn it. And so…they each tell their story of forming a girl group, moving to LA, and flirting with fame. Clarke doesn't hate his antiheroines–he just views them as by-products of the culture: glitter-eyed, vacant, and cruel. The satire works, sliding down as silvery and toxic as liquid mercury." - *Entertainment Weekly*

"Jaime Clarke is a masterful illusionist; in his deft hands, emptiness seems full, teenage pathos appears sassy and charming. *We're So Famous* is a blithe, highly entertaining indictment of the permanent state of adolescence that trademarks our culture, a made-for-TV world where innocence is hardly a virtue, ambition barely a value system." – Bob Shacochis

"Clarke seems to have created a crafty book of bubble letters to express his anger, sending off a disguised Barbie mail bomb that shows how insipid and money-drenched youth culture can be." – *Village Voice*

"Jaime Clarke's novel *We're So Famous* follows Stella, Paque, and Daisy–three utterly talentless girls from Phoenix who share a near-horrifying affinity for Bananarama. But it's only after Daisy and Paque's unwitting connection to a double murder helps skyrocket their band, Masterful Johnson, to nationwide stardom that the story really gets going. Through a string of pop-culture references (Neve Campbell, Dennis Hopper, Jennifer Grey's nose job) and mishaps (an unfortunate lip-synching tragedy a la Milli Vanilli, movie deals, smack), Clarke keeps the satire sharp and his heroines clueless."
– *Spin Magazine*

"Darkly and pinkly comic, this is the story of a trio of teenage American girls and their pursuit of the three big Ms of American life: Music, Movies and Murder. An impressive debut by a talented young novelist."
– Jonathan Ames

"This first novel is plastic fantastic. Daisy, Paque and Stella are talentless teens, obsessed by Bananarama and longing for stardom. They love celebrity and crave the flashbulbs and headlines for themselves. The girls become fantasy wrestlers, make a record, get parts in a going-nowhere film, then try to put on big brave smiles in the empty-hearted world of fame. Sad, sassy and salient." – *Elle Magazine*

"*We're So Famous* smartly anticipates a culture re-configured by the quest for fame. The starry-eyed girls at the center of this rock-and-roll fairy tale are the predecessors of today's selfie-snappers. With biting wit and wry humor, Clarke brilliantly reminds us that we've always lived for likes." – Mona Awad

VERNON DOWNS

WORLD GONE WATER

GARDEN LAKES

WE'RE SO FAMOUS

SCREENPLAYS

BY JAIME CLARKE

PREFACE

Every novelist dreams of selling their work to Hollywood—and reserves the right to decry the results—even those of us who write books that don't intuitively translate to the screen. *How did they make a movie out of that?* is an old party game writers indulge in, their hopeful hearts filled with secret jealousy.

But the answer to how a film is made from what would outwardly seem like a plotless novel reveals the truth that every novel has a narrative structure a seasoned screenwriter can borrow, or choose to work against, or well-drawn characters that the hired gun can drop into circumstance. Hopefully both.

For these screen adaptations of the standalone novels in my trilogy featuring Charlie Martens—*Vernon Downs*, *World Gone Water*, and *Garden Lakes*—I was interested in something else entirely: a thematic adaptation of each that captures the essence of the novels while completely reimagining them plot-wise. The challenge was the catalyst for wholesale invention and between fits of despair and inspiration, I was able to find my through the material in a way that honored the books, but also reinvented them.

If nothing else, these are my best answers to that old writerly party game.

--Jaime Clarke (2024)

VERNON DOWNS, STARRING BENICIO DEL TORO

INT. RESTAURANT - DAY

ALEX, who bears a striking resemblance to Academy award-winning actor Benicio del Toro, and his ex-wife, KAREN, sit at a table in a fancy but mostly empty Midtown Manhattan restaurant.

ALEX
I killed it. I mean, I really knew it. But the whole time they're just staring at me. You know, like always. And you know what the director says?

The WAITER approaches with their food.

WAITER
Can I get you anything else?

KAREN
We're fine.

WAITER
(to Alex)
I hope you don't mind, but I'm a fan. I loved The Pledge.

ALEX
That's kind of you. Thank you.

WAITER
I actually used to work uptown at Tupelo. I used to see you there. The bartender said you lived nearby. It just closed.

ALEX
Yes. A shame.

WAITER
I could get fired for this, but could I have your autograph?
I always regretted not asking you at Tupelo.

ALEX
Sure.

The Waiter hands him a piece of paper and a pen.

WAITER
To Jared.

Alex signs it and hands it back.

KAREN
Aren't you going to tell him?

Alex gives a sheepish look.

JARED
Tell me what? I can get you anything.

Beat.

ALEX
I'm not who you think I am.

JARED
What do you mean?

KAREN
He's not the actor. He's an actor, just not Benicio.

JARED
(annoyed)
That's uncool.

He crumples up the piece of paper and walks away.

ALEX
You didn't have to say anything. It's harmless.

KAREN
It's not harmless. You're proof of that.

Alex shrugs.

ALEX
I seem to remember you not minding, when we first met.

KAREN
At Mary Cotton's party? That was a thousand years ago.

ALEX
But you thought I was him.

KAREN
Maybe for a minute.

ALEX
(teasing)
Was more than a minute.

Karen smiles.

ALEX (CONT'D)
Did you see his next movie?

KAREN
How would I know his next movie? I'm not obsessed with

him.

ALEX
Let's not...Let's just have a nice lunch.

Karen puts up her hands, surrender-style.

ALEX (CONT'D)
He's playing Vernon Downs.

KAREN
How are they making a movie about a writer? Sounds boring.

ALEX
Remember that piece in the Times that said Downs walks around New York just living his life under everyone's noses?

KAREN
No.

ALEX
It's based on that, I think.

KAREN
I've never understood why you like his books so much. The Benicio thing I get. But those books are pretentious.

ALEX
God, I would be perfect for that role. I'm actually a fan. Benicio's not even a fan.

KAREN
How do you know?

ALEX
Never heard him mention Downs in an interview.

KAREN
I wish you'd been half as obsessed about me when we were married. You know the kinds of books Benicio del Toro likes, but I'll bet you don't know what books I like.

ALEX
That's not fair. You don't read.

KAREN
My favorite movie, then.

ALEX
You always liked The Usual Suspects.

KAREN
(impatiently)
My favorite non-Benicio movie.

Alex thinks.

KAREN (CONT'D)
Doesn't matter.

ALEX
C'mon. Let's just have a nice lunch.

KAREN
Tell me what the director said.

ALEX
You won't believe it. I'm in the middle of the audition, I know it backward and forward and the director stops me and says—not to me but to the casting director—"If I wanted Benicio del Toro, I'd get Benicio del Toro." I

mean, what is that?

Karen looks at him, considering.

KAREN
Fuck it. We're not married anymore so I'll just say it: You
have to forget acting. I know it's not fair, but this happens
every god damn time. It used to kill me to see how it
would devastate you, but at some point you just doubled
down. It's like the more movies Benicio del Toro makes,
and the more awards he wins, the more auditions you go
on, as if to prove...to prove what?

ALEX
(angrily)
That's crazy. Not true.

KAREN
If only you'd doubled down on us. Who knows?

ALEX
Don't do this. I need your support. No one else
understands. I've got an audition uptown tomorrow and I
can't hear this.

Karen stands to leave.

KAREN
I told you this when we decided to call it quits: I still love
you, but this...thing...is mental. And you know it. And if
you don't know it, it's worse than I thought. And don't call
me every time you need fluffed for an audition.

ALEX
C'mon, sit down.

KAREN
I just can't anymore.

She leaves. Jared, who has been waiting, brings the check
immediately and sets it down unceremoniously.

EXT. MANHATTAN STREET - DAY

A DOORMAN holds the door for ALEX, who comes out
of an Upper West Side apartment building looking
distraught. He crumples a few script pages and tosses them
into the nearest trash can and starts walking.

EXT. MANHATTAN STREET - CONTINUOUS

Alex stops on a corner for a red light. He spies the
newsstand and saunters over.

NEWSAGENT
I thought you'd left already.

A MAN steps between them and buys a paper, giving Alex
a moment to think.

NEWSAGENT (CONT'D)
Change your mind?

Alex shrugs and smiles, unsure of how to respond. The
Newsagent slaps a pack of Big Red gum on the counter.

NEWSAGENT (CONT'D)
The usual?

ALEX
Changed my mind, yeah.

Alex pays for the gum and pockets it.

WOMAN (O.S.)
Do you have the new Vanity Fair?

Alex moves out of the way and the WOMAN approaches
the counter. Alex crosses the street and continues on his
way.

EXT. MANHATTAN STREET - CONTINUOUS

Alex is walking when a MAN and a WOMAN call out.

MAN
Excuse me!

WOMAN
Is it really?

FACES on the street turn to look at the commotion but
keep moving.

ALEX
I'm sorry, but—

MAN
Could we have your autograph?

WOMAN
We're huge fans.

ALEX
That's nice of you, really.

The WOMAN holds out a random scrap of paper and a
pen. Alex takes it and signs it. The MAN takes a picture
without asking.

WOMAN
I can't believe it.

She looks at the autograph to remember his name.

WOMAN (CONT'D)
Benicio del Toro, right. Wow.

MAN
She's too embarrassed to tell you, but she cried at the end
of Basquiat.

The Woman hits the Man playfully.

ALEX
No need to be embarrassed.

WOMAN
I love The Usual Suspects, too.

MAN
We both love it.

WOMAN
Right, true. True.

Alex smiles and nods and makes to go.

WOMAN (CONT'D)
Thank you for stopping. I just had a feeling you'd be real.
We met this other famous actor at a friend's wedding, and
Tom happened to be using the restroom same time as this
actor—

TOM
He doesn't want to hear this story.

Alex smiles as if to say it's okay.

WOMAN
And Tom tells him how much he likes this actor's movies, and the actor, this prick—excuse me—says, "I don't meet people in the men's room."

TOM
He wasn't a prick.

Alex is amused by the story but wants to get away. In the background a DOORMAN can be seen watching the whole exchange.

WOMAN
(gasps)
Oh, I forgot you were in that one movie together! I'm sorry.

TOM
Forget she said anything.
(to Woman)
Let's go. I'm hungry.

WOMAN
I'm so sorry. Thank you again.

Alex smiles as Tom and the Woman walk away. The Woman is fretting inaudibly.

TOM (O.S.)
You never said the name of the movie.

Alex takes a few steps forward, and the DOORMAN, who has been hovering in the background, opens the door to the building.

DOORMAN
Everything okay, Mr. del Toro?

Alex stops, confused.

DOORMAN (CONT'D)
We had a note that you'd left.

INT. BUILDING LOBBY - CONTINUOUS

Alex steps inside, the Doorman following.

DOORMAN
Let me get your mail.

The Doorman goes behind the desk and retrieves a bundle
of mail and hands it to Alex.

Alex sees the mail addressed to Benicio del Toro at the
building's address, including the apartment number.

DOORMAN (CONT'D)
I'll leave a note about the mistake, Mr. del Toro. Very
sorry about that.

ALEX
It's no problem, really. Crossed wires. It happens.

DOORMAN
Thanks for understanding.

Alex nods and walks through the lobby to the bank of
elevators, stops, and turns back.

ALEX
My keys...

DOORMAN
Ah. Left them upstairs again?

ALEX
Exactly.

DOORMAN
Give me a minute.

INT. ELEVATOR - MOMENTS LATER

Alex looks at himself in the mirror inside the elevator,
scrutinizing. He's wondering if he's going to go through
with it. He looks at the mail he's holding, including a copy
of the latest issue of a trade magazine. He instinctively
turns to the audition listings and scans them. The elevator
DINGS and the doors open.

INT. HALLWAY - CONTINUOUS

Alex looks at the mail again to check the apartment
number. He locates the correct door and inserts the key.

INT. BENICIO DEL TORO'S APARTMENT -
CONTINUOUS

Alex surveys the landscape. Takes in the modestly but
tastefully decorated apartment. The phone RINGS,
startling him. The answering machine picks up on the
second ring.

BENICIO DEL TORO'S RECORDED VOICE
Sorry I missed you. Leave a message and I'll return your
call.

There's a loud BEEP and then a CLICK when no message
is left.

Alex is drawn to the answering machine, which shows two unheard messages. He presses the button on the answering to listen to the messages.

AUTOMATED VOICE
Message one.

EMILY BLUNT (O.S.)
Benicio, I hope you haven't left yet. We have to talk about John. I'm worried about him. Call me.

AUTOMATED VOICE
Message two.

MALE VOICE (O.S.)
It's Barry. I know you're gone and that you're incommunicado but wanted you to know that I reached out to Downs through a backchannel—really had to call in a favor—but he said he wouldn't see you. So that's that. Call me when you're back.

A LOUD DIAL TONE plays, and Alex presses the button on the answering machine to stop it, but it doesn't. He lifts the receiver just as it gives a HALF RING.

DEEP VOICE (O.S.)
Hello?

Alex presses the receiver against his ear.

ALEX
Yes?

DEEP VOICE (O.S.)
del Toro?

Alex appears nervous.

ALEX
Yes?

DEEP VOICE (O.S.)
Downs here.

ALEX
(surprised)
Oh. Yes.

DOWNS (O.S.)
I heard you want to speak with me.

ALEX
I would—. It would be an honor.

DOWNS (O.S.)
I haven't even seen the script for this thing. Do I want to?

ALEX
(panicked)
Probably not. I mean, it's very good, but I imagine it's
hard to, um, read about yourself.

Alex grimaces during the silence that follows.

DOWNS (O.S.)
Hmm. Well, I can always sue, right?

ALEX
Can I just say how much of a fan I am? I really—. It's the
role of my career.

DOWNS (O.S.)
Yes, yes, okay. Well, how about coming over tomorrow

and we can talk. 425 Madison.

ALEX
It would be a pleasure

DOWNS (O.S.)
See you at ten.

Downs hangs up. Alex replaces the receiver. He spots a
matchbook bearing the name of the bar Maxwell Jay's in a
change dish.

INT. MAXWELL JAY'S - NIGHT

Alex enters and the BARTENDER gives a knowing nod.
The Bartender pours a Maker's Mark neat and sets it at the
corner stool. Alex sits in front of it.

BARTENDER
Nice to see you.

Alex lifts his glass in salute.

BARTENDER (CONT'D)
She was in here the other night looking for you. Like you
thought. I told her you were gone, like you said.

ALEX
Thanks.

A MAN in his late fifties waves down the Bartender. The
Man nods at Alex, as if in recognition. Alex nods back.
The Bartender sets the Man's drink in front of him and
moves on to another customer.

MAN
I'm sorry to bother you, but you're Benicio del Toro,

right?

ALEX
What's your name?

The Man moves a few seats closer.

MAN
Burton. Burton LaFarge.

ALEX
Nice to meet you, Burton

BURTON
I can't believe it. I've lived here ten years and have never seen a celebrity. Amazing.

Alex smiles.

ALEX
What do you do, Burton?

BURTON
I'm a writer. Unpublished so far.

ALEX
Just takes a lucky break.

BURTON
That's what I keep hoping for. At my age, though, who knows?

ALEX
What do you write?

BURTON
Novels, mostly. Dabble a little in screenplays. Had a play

produced off-Broadway.

ALEX
Congratulations.

The Bartender comes over.

BARTENDER
Excuse me, Benicio. You have a call.

Alex looks at the Bartender, confused. But then realizes
it's a ruse del Toro and the Bartender have worked out in
case del Toro needs bailed out.

BARTENDER (CONT'D)
Should I take a message?

ALEX
Yes, please.

The Bartender leaves.

BURTON
I take it this is your regular.

ALEX
It's a nice place.

BURTON
This might seem crazy, but maybe your being here is a
lucky break.

Alex looks at him.

ALEX
I've never been anyone's lucky charm.

Burton moves over until he's sitting next to Alex.

BURTON
I came here tonight to celebrate finishing a new script. I never think about casting when writing. That kills it. But seeing you here. You'd be perfect.

ALEX
I can only read scripts sent to me by my agent, sorry.

BURTON
Oh, you don't have to worry about all of that. I'm not a kook. I'm covered if someone lifts my idea, though maybe you'll agree that only a low-life no-talent would steal someone else's ideas.

Pulls the script from his bag before Alex can protest further. The script sits between them on the bar.

BURTON (CONT'D)
Even if you aren't interested, I'd love your opinion.

An awkward beat passes between them.

ALEX
Okay.

BURTON
(beaming)
Terrific. This is me.

Scribbles his phone number on the cover of the script.

BURTON (CONT'D)
Who knows? Maybe a great movie was made because two guys met in a bar.

Gathers hurriedly to go in case Alex changes his mind.

ALEX
(shrugs)
Anything's possible.

Picks up the script and waves it at Burton.

BURTON
Today I'm a believer.

Waves as he leaves.

BARTENDER
Everything ok?

Alex nods and fans the script without reading any of it.

EXT. MAXWELL JAY'S - LATER

Alex exits, depositing the script in the nearest trash can.

INT. BENICIO DEL TORO'S APARTMENT - NIGHT

Alex lies on the couch, asleep, one of Vernon Downs's novels open on his chest.

EXT. 425 MADISON AVENUE - DAY

Alex BUZZES an apartment. No answer. He BUZZES again, and as he does, a WOMAN IN HER THIRTIES exits.

ALEX
Hold the door?

The Woman is about to object, but a look of recognition

comes over her face.

WOMAN
You're here to see my father.

Alex nods.

WOMAN (CONT'D)
Vivian Downs. I'm a fan.

ALEX
Nice of you.

VIVIAN
I'm so glad my father changed his mind. He never does
that.

ALEX
(flirting)
Did you have a hand in that?

VIVIAN
(matter-of-factly)
My father has never been under anyone's influence, family
included.

Alex looks up, taking in the building.

VIVIAN (CONT'D)
He used to live in a nicer building. But, you know, the
thing with the doorman.

Alex nods as if he understands.

VIVIAN (CONT'D)
He's on the top floor.

Steps aside so Alex can pass.

ALEX
Thank you. I'll see you again, hopefully.

VIVIAN
That depends on what happens in the next hour or so,
guessing.

She smiles and waves good-bye.

INT. 425 MADISON AVENUE - CONTINUOUS

Alex enters the foyer and mounts the stairs.

INT. 425 MADISON AVENUE - MOMENTS LATER

Alex KNOCKS on Downs's door.

VOICE (O.S.)
Yes, come in.

Alex enters the apartment, a cluttered warren. From an
unseen hallway, VERNON DOWNS appears and gives a
cautious look. He and Alex stand looking at each other for
a moment, as if they're both staring in the mirror, save for
the fact that Downs wears glasses.

ALEX
(nervously)
It's an honor, sir.

DOWNS
Let's skip all of that. Would you like some tea?

INT. VERNON DOWNS'S APARTMENT - MOMENTS
LATER

Alex and Downs are sitting in the living room, facing each
other in high-backed chairs, drinking tea.

ALEX
I just met your daughter.

DOWNS
She checks on me more often than she need.

ALEX
Nice of her.

DOWNS
It's a source of sadness for me, actually. Somewhere along
the line she bought into the myth about me being a lonely
recluse.

Sips his tea.

DOWNS (CONT'D)
But I get along as well as anyone else. More or less.

ALEX
It's said that people don't recognize you when you go out.

DOWNS
You'd be surprised by what people don't see.

ALEX
If they're not looking, you mean.

DOWNS
A low profile is better than no profile. Salinger made a
mistake when he disappeared. It made everyone hunt him.

Alex nods.

DOWNS (CONT'D)
I imagine the same is true for actors. A little curiosity is
fine, but you have to be careful not to create a mystery that
people wish to solve.

ALEX
That's it, yes.

DOWNS
I agreed to see you to impress upon you just that point. If I
could stop this movie from being made, I would. My
contempt for Hollywood is immeasurable. But I'm advised
otherwise. So if it's going to go forward, my request is that
it doesn't make my life harder than need be.

ALEX
Absolutely.

DOWNS
I hate the movies. It's your profession, I know, but I want
to be up front about my feelings.

ALEX
I appreciate that.

DOWNS
Films are needless purveyors of phoniness. There are very
few truths to be found in the movies.

ALEX
Some people just like to escape.

DOWNS
(amused)
Ah, yes. Not everything is in service of the truth, as I'm

constantly reminded.
(beat)
I didn't appreciate your representative reaching out to me through my friend. I purposely left his letter unanswered.

ALEX
I'm sorry about that.

DOWNS
Why is this meeting necessary? I'm being made an accomplice in my own debasing.

ALEX
(forgetting himself for a moment)
I'm sure they just want to be as accurate as possible.

DOWNS
I was under the impression you wanted this meeting.

ALEX
(remembering his role)
Oh, yes. It's just—. Well, it's an enormous responsibility to portray a real person. Especially someone like yourself.

DOWNS
It's an impersonation, not a portrayal.

Alex lets the comment pass.

DOWNS (CONT'D)
I was surprised that you were interested in this role.

ALEX
Oh?

DOWNS
I know you're a serious actor, not one of those new actors

who are hired to stand and project their looks into the camera.

ALEX
I'm a fan of your work and wanted to do you justice.

DOWNS
I'm not sure I deserve justice, or want it.

ALEX
I'd think anyone would.

DOWNS
Would it offend you if I used your alleged appreciation for my books against you and ask you not to make this movie?

ALEX
Is that why you agreed to see me?

Downs tilts his head.

ALEX (CONT'D)
They'll just get someone else. There's always someone else.

DOWNS
I suppose you're right.

ALEX
Is there anything that would make you feel better about my taking the role?

DOWNS
I'm under the impression that my consent isn't necessary.

ALEX
For me, then.

Downs considers.

DOWNS
Part of the phoniness of the movies is that they give the appearance of sustained storytelling, but in truth they're filmed seconds and minutes at a time over the course of months.

Alex nods.

DOWNS (CONT'D)
That reduces your...impression...of me to a series of bits, as if I were some kind of nightclub act.

ALEX
The medium dictates that, yes.

DOWNS
What if you had to become me for not seconds or minutes but hours and days? I've heard some actors inhabit their characters in this way.

ALEX
Yes.

DOWNS
You have a reputation for such a method.

ALEX
(smiling)
I abhor all manner of flattery.

Downs likes this response.

DOWNS
This is what I propose: I'm traveling to Florida to avoid the press surrounding the publication of my new book. The

last go-round was a nightmare. While I'm gone, you'll be my doppelganger here in the city. I'll give you the details of my upcoming social obligations, and we'll see if you can fool everyone into believing that you are me. If you can do that, I'll give my blessing to the film by not causing a legal ruckus over it.

Alex is blown away by this offer.

ALEX
What happens if I'm found out?

DOWNS
My lawyer has already drafted a cease-and-desist letter for the film's producers.

Alex considers this.

ALEX
Will I be able to reach you if I need to?

DOWNS
Where I'm going, no one can reach me.

Alex gets a confident look on his face.

DOWNS (CONT'D)
What do you say? Want to put your acting skills to the challenge?

INT. BENICIO DEL TORO'S APARTMENT – LATER

Alex presses the button on the answering machine and listens to the messages as he takes off his jacket and kicks off his shoes.

AUTOMATED VOICE
Message one.

EMILY BLUNT (O.S.)
Benicio, it's Emily again. Hoping to catch you before you
leave. John's not returning my calls. It might be up to you.

AUTOMATED VOICE
Message two.

CLIVE OWEN (O.S.)
Yeah, it's Clive. I'll be in New York at the end of the
month. Would love to see you.

AUTOMATED VOICE
Message three.

SEAN PENN (O.S.)
Bennie? Pick up. It's Sean.
(beat)
I guess you're not home. It's John, man. He won't listen to
anyone but you. Give me a call.

As the last message ends, a WOMAN IN HER THIRTIES
enters, a look of surprise on her face. Alex also gives a
startled look.

WOMAN
I didn't know you'd still be here.

Alex remains startled, unsure if he's caught.

WOMAN (CONT'D)
What happened?

ALEX
What do you mean?

WOMAN
Your plans. Weren't you supposed to fly out yesterday?

ALEX
Changed my mind.

WOMAN
(cautiously hopeful)
About everything?

Alex shrugs. He doesn't really know what she's talking about and wants to change the subject.

WOMAN (CONT'D)
Should I come back later?

Alex hesitates. Wants the company.

ALEX
Stay for a drink?

WOMAN
I could do with a glass of wine.

Alex moves to the kitchen and the Woman follows. He removes two wineglasses from the cupboard, reaches for a bottle of red, and pours a glass each. Woman looks at him askance.

WOMAN (CONT'D)
White for me, please.

Alex pretends to remember.

ALEX
Oh, right. Sorry.

He finds a bottle of white in the fridge and pours it under the Woman's watchful eye. Alex holds up his glass and they CLINK them together and drink.

WOMAN
You're in a better mood. What are we toasting?

ALEX
You'll never guess who I just met with.

WOMAN
You're right.

ALEX
Vernon Downs.

Woman raises her eyebrows.

WOMAN
Wow.

ALEX
I'm such a fan of his work.

Woman gives him a look.

WOMAN
Is that for the audience?

ALEX
What?

WOMAN
You said his books were trash when they offered you the part.

Sensing something, Alex backs off.

ALEX
(mildly)
He has a couple of good books.

Woman eyes him a little more.

WOMAN
Did he mention the resemblance?

ALEX
No. But I think he likes the casting.

WOMAN
Did he say that?

Alex takes his wine and moves into the front room. She
follows.

ALEX
He wants me to impersonate him with his friends and
colleagues while he's away, to see if I can fool them. Like
an audition.

Woman is intrigued.

WOMAN
Is he crazy?

ALEX
Who knows. Maybe.

WOMAN
What did you tell him?

Alex smiles.

WOMAN (CONT'D)
You might be crazy too.

ALEX
It is a good test.

WOMAN
A movie is one thing. This is this guy's life. Why doesn't
he just invite a friend over and have you answer the door if
he wants to test you?

ALEX
I'm up to the challenge.

Sips his wine.

WOMAN
(playfully)
You who have nothing left to prove.

She gets up and disappears into the bathroom. Alex waits
to hear the DOOR CLICK and sets his wineglass down. He
reaches for her purse and pulls out her wallet, searching for
her driver's license to learn her name: Jessica Oliver.

INT. BENICIO DEL TORO'S APARTMENT -
HALLWAY - CONTINUOUS

Jessica is watching Alex look at her license from the
bathroom door. She COUGHS and Alex scrambles to put
the license back.

INT. BENICIO DEL TORO'S APARTMENT –
CONTINUOUS

Alex takes up his wineglass and Jessica re-enters.

ALEX
You can't say anything.

JESSICA
Who am I going to tell?

ALEX
A girlfriend, co-worker, whatever. Anyone knows and it'll
end up in the papers.

Jessica sits down next to him on the couch, close. She
stares into his face with a searching look. Smiles.

JESSICA
Speaking of co-workers, don't forget the fund-raiser
tomorrow night.

ALEX
Fund-raiser?

JESSICA
Not even funny. You're the main attraction. You promised.

INT. RESTAURANT - NIGHT

Crowded restaurant. Well-dressed people are mingling.
Poster on an easel by the door announces fund-raiser for
the cure for breast cancer, with an appearance by Benicio
del Toro. A KNOT OF PEOPLE surrounds Alex, with
Jessica at his side. Alex autographs a program for the
evening's festivities, smiling. He takes pictures with
people who have cameras.

INT. RESTAURANT - MEN'S ROOM - A LITTLE
LATER

Alex is washing his hands and studying himself in the

mirror.

FEMALE VOICE #1 (O.S.)
She said he changed his mind.

FEMALE VOICE #2 (O.S.)
Wonder how she got him to change it.

FEMALE VOICE #1 (O.S.)
Maybe she brought his dog back.

Alex gives a final look in the mirror, as if readying himself to rejoin the fray.

FEMALE VOICE #2 (O.S.)
Do you think she really took the dog?

FEMALE VOICE #1 (O.S.)
She admitted it to her assistant.

FEMALE VOICE #2 (O.S.)
The flyers are still up around the neighborhood.

Alex walks out of the men's room and finds Jessica waiting for him.

JESSICA
You okay?

ALEX
Ready for more.

Jessica smiles.

A WOMAN IN HER SIXTIES approaches with a wide smile.

JESSICA
(to Alex)
Benicio, this is my boss, Emily St. Cloud.

Alex extends a hand.

ALEX
It's a pleasure.

EMILY ST. CLOUD
(beaming)
I'm such a fan.

ALEX
(shyly)
That's very kind of you.

EMILY ST. CLOUD
I just wanted to personally thank you for this wonderful
evening.

ALEX
Always happy to help a good cause.

VOICE (O.S.)
Benicio, can I take a picture with you?

ALEX
Excuse me.

Turns away from Emily and Jessica.

EMILY ST. CLOUD
(to Jessica, coldly)
Congratulations. You get to keep your job.

INT. CAB - THAT NIGHT

Alex and Jessica are in the backseat as the cab moves through traffic.

JESSICA
Thank you for doing that.

Alex gives her a look that says he's a little intoxicated by the rush from so much adoration. He reaches over and puts his hand on hers. She gives him a look he doesn't see, realizing a problem she didn't think through.

INT. BENICIO DEL TORO'S APARTMENT - THAT NIGHT

Alex and Jessica enter. As Alex takes off his jacket and unwinds, Jessica walks straight to the guest room.

JESSICA
Good night.

ALEX
Good night?

JESSICA
Early start tomorrow.

Alex furrows his brow.

JESSICA (CONT'D)
And I think I'm coming down with something. I'm gonna crash in the guest room.

Alex gives her a long look.

ALEX
Feel better.

Jessica gives a wan smile and disappears into the guest
room. Alex leans back on the couch, looking around,
satisfied, feeling self-congratulatory.

INT. PUBLISHING OFFICE - DAY

Alex saunters through the bull pen of cubicles, glasses on,
moving toward a glass corner office. ASSISTANTS glance
up from their work as he passes, and there's a MURMUR.
Vernon Downs sightings are few and far between. He
reaches the office, the name Barbara West stenciled on the
door.

BARBARA, an impeccably dressed elegant woman in her
60s, moves from around the desk to greet him at the door.

INT. BARBARA'S OFFICE - CONTINUOUS

Barbara extends her hand and Alex shakes it.

BARBARA
I'm so glad to see you again. It's been too long.

Alex winces as he imagines Vernon would.

BARBARA (CONT'D)
Please.

She indicates the chair in front of the desk. Alex sits
down. Barbara closes the door and retakes her seat behind
her desk. She reaches next to her and produces a copy of
Downs's new book. She hands it to Alex.

BARBARA (CONT'D)
It arrived from the printer this morning.

Alex takes the book and turns it over in his hands. He's struggling to contain his enthusiasm at being among the first to have a copy of Downs's new book, but also maintaining his indifference to being impressed, as Downs would.

BARBARA (CONT'D)
Your cover came out beautifully. As I knew it would.

Alex sets the book down on the desk.

ALEX
Yes.

BARBARA
And I know you don't care to know anything about reviews, but you'll be on the cover of the Sunday Times Book Review, naturally.

Alex nods.

BARBARA (CONT'D)
Before I tell you why I asked you to come in, let me preface this by saying that those above me are behind the maneuver. I explained to them your resistance to requests like these and even tried to turn it down on your behalf, as I always do. If Barry knew how many requests I don't pass along, he'd have no choice but to make me your co-agent and give me a percentage.

Alex tries to hide his anxiety. He picks up the book, looks at it, and sets it back down.

ALEX
Okay.

BARBARA
It's so outlandish a proposition that I can't believe I'm
repeating it, but I'm being asked to ask you if you would
make an appearance on the Charlie Austin show.

A silence falls between them and Barbara shifts in her seat.

ALEX
I can't remember the last time I was on television.

BARBARA
(gives a look)
You've never been on television.

Alex squirms uncomfortably.

ALEX
Exactly.

BARBARA
I know it's ridiculous, and the book certainly doesn't need
the push, but it would mean something to the owners of the
publishing house.

ALEX
Why should I care?

BARBARA
(conspiratorially)
You shouldn't.

ALEX
What will happen to you if I decline?

Barbara shrugs, though with trepidation.

BARBARA
The only reason I agreed to ask you is that I wondered if you might want the opportunity to be on the record. For posterity, I mean.

ALEX
Posterity?

BARBARA
Or for future readers of your work.

Alex gives a look that indicates he doesn't care about what Barbara is saying.

BARBARA (CONT'D)
Or maybe as some truth serum to whatever this movie is going to say about you.
(beat)
I saw they got Benicio del Toro to play you.

ALEX
I met with him the other day.

BARBARA
(surprised)
Oh?

ALEX
I agreed to see him to impress upon him my concerns about making my life more miserable than it is in terms of fans. And to tell him about my immeasurable contempt for Hollywood.

BARBARA
How did he take that?

ALEX
He didn't like it. But I think my message got through.
Films are needless purveyors of phoniness. There are very
few truths to be found in movies.

BARBARA
You were wise not to give consent. I'm sure the movie will
be inaccurate however it comes out.
(beat)
He's a fine actor, though.

ALEX
The idea of them making such a film is preposterous.

BARBARA
Agreed.
(beat)
In your last letter you mentioned a problem with your
daughter's husband. Did that get resolved?

Alex doesn't know what she's referring to.

ALEX
Yes.

BARBARA
Thank goodness. Was she more annoyed or frightened
when he disappeared like that?

ALEX
She never tells me anything. I was annoyed, though.

BARBARA
I can imagine. Publishing is full of similarly unreliable
characters.
(laughs)

Speaking of characters. The mailbags are full of the usual crazy letters for you, which we'll continue to shred unless we hear otherwise—

Alex indicates it's okay to keep shredding them.

BARBARA (CONT'D)
And as I mentioned on the phone, lately we've been getting some packages messengered over from someone making outrageous claims.

She holds up the new novel.

BARBARA (CONT'D)
He's very persistent. To the point that I've alerted building security. There's some concern that he's delivering the packages himself. Would you like to see them?

Alex shakes his head no.

BARBARA (CONT'D)
I'm sure he'll go away like all the other pests over the years. I'll dispose of whatever he sends.

ALEX
So many nuts.

Alex stands to leave. He picks up the copy of the novel. Barbara realizes it's the abrupt end of the meeting and stands too.

BARBARA
If you ever need anything from me, just ask.

ALEX
I appreciate that.

An awkward silence passes between them.

BARBARA
What shall I tell the gentlemen upstairs? They're expecting me to deliver your answer.

ALEX
I'm sure they are.

BARBARA
If I had to bet, I'd say they'll call me before you even leave the building.

ALEX
I'm sorry this is around your neck, but—

Barbara winces, bracing for the answer. Alex looks at her sympathetically.

ALEX (CONT'D)
Why not? At the very least, perhaps the movie people will see it and adjust their portrayal accordingly.

Barbara smiles, relieved.

INT. MAXWELL JAY'S - NIGHT

Alex is sitting at the bar over a Maker's Mark neat. The Bartender is nearby, washing glasses.

ALEX
Nah, we're back together.

The Bartender gives a nod. Alex takes a sip of his drink.

BARTENDER
I'll put her back on the call list.

Alex smiles.

Burton LaFarge saunters in and takes an empty stool a few stools down. Alex glances at him and there's a flicker of recognition, but he's having a hard time placing him. Burton waves and Alex nods.

BURTON
(pointing at himself)
Burton.

ALEX
(remembering)
Yes. How are you?

BURTON
Another day in the big city of small dreams.

Alex laughs.

BARTENDER
(to Burton)
What'll it be?

Burton gives the Bartender a look. He doesn't appreciate the Bartender's aggressiveness.

BURTON
You got Black Pony scotch?

Bartender gives him a skeptical look.

BARTENDER
Never heard of it.

BURTON
(to Alex)

He's never heard of Black Pony scotch.

Alex takes a long sip of his drink. Doesn't want to get involved in the conversation.

BURTON (CONT'D)
It was called Four Horses in the stage version.

BARTENDER
Stage version of what?

BURTON
(to Alex)
Believe this guy?

Alex doesn't react.

BURTON (CONT'D)
The movie Laura. One of the classics.

Looks at Alex conspiratorially. The Bartender pours a beer and sets it on the bar.

BARTENDER
This or nothing.

BURTON
Okay, okay. Jeez.

Puts some money on the bar and takes the beer. He raises his glass in Alex's direction. Alex gives a small salute in return.

BURTON (CONT'D)
Dying to know what you thought of it.

ALEX
Of what?

BURTON
(disappointed)
My screenplay.

Alex remembers Burton now.

ALEX
I get a lot of screenplays. Haven't had a chance to read it
yet.

BURTON
(crestfallen)
Oh.

Beat. Alex signals to the Bartender for another drink.

BURTON (CONT'D)
It's just...the other night when we met, it seemed like it
was destiny.

The Bartender looks at Alex, who raises his eyebrows and
sips his drink. A COUPLE comes in and sits at the other
end of the bar, and the Bartender moves over to them, out
of earshot.

ALEX
What did Shakespeare say about destiny?

BURTON
"It is not in the stars to hold our destiny but in ourselves."

ALEX
Sounds right.

BURTON
(emphatically)
Yes. Yes, exactly.

Moves closer to Alex.

BURTON (CONT'D)
This is me holding my own destiny.

Reaches into his bag and produces the stained copy of the
screenplay he wrote his phone number on. Alex realizes
Burton retrieved it from the garbage can. Burton hands it
back to Alex, finishes his beer in a long draft, and stands to
leave.

BURTON (CONT'D)
Really would love to hear what you think.

INT. DINER - DAY

Alex enters. He's wearing glasses to resemble Vernon
Downs. He catches the eye of the WAITRESS, a woman in
her 50s, who nods at a booth in the corner. Alex sits in the
booth and opens the menu. As the Waitress nears, he sees
the name badge pinned to her shirt: Deanna.

DEANNA
Facing out today. That's new.

Alex looks at her quizzically.

DEANNA (CONT'D)
Thought you liked your back to the door.

ALEX
Trying something new.

DEANNA
And I assume the open menu means you're having
something other than your usual?

Alex closes the menu too quickly.

ALEX
The usual is fine, Deanna.

Deanna gives him a second look and then turns for the
kitchen. Alex looks out the window. A GIRL IN HER
TWENTIES in a far booth catches his eye and smiles. She
holds up a copy of one of Vernon Downs's books and
points at the cover, and Alex smiles and nods, which the
Girl takes as an invitation to approach.

GIRL
This is one of the most remarkable things that has ever
happened to me.

ALEX
Well, you're young yet.

GIRL
I'm Callie. Huge fan.

Awkward beat where Callie wonders if Alex is going to
ask her to sit down.

ALEX
Would you like me to sign your book?

CALLIE
Would you?

She uses the invitation to sit across from him.

ALEX
Happy to.

Callie slides the book across the table. Alex opens to the
bookmarked page.

ALEX (CONT'D)
Page thirty-three?

CALLIE
I'm rereading it!

Alex smiles. His pen hovers over the title page as he
realizes he doesn't know how to sign Vernon Downs's
name. He draws a smiley face and writes You Just Met
Vernon Downs and makes a squiggly line. He passes the
book back to Callie as Deanna approaches the table with
black coffee and a plate of scrambled eggs and dry toast.
She furrows her brow at the sight of Callie.

DEANNA
(to Callie)
Please don't bother our customers, sweetheart.

CALLIE
I was invited.

Deanna verifies this with Alex with a look.

ALEX
It's okay.

DEANNA
Opposite day, huh?

She walks away but doesn't go far. She gives Alex a look
that spooks him.

CALLIE
Mind if I ask you a question?

ALEX
Shoot.

CALLIE
Do people tell you that you look like Benicio del Toro?

Alex shrugs.

CALLIE (CONT'D)
I wonder if people tell him that he looks like you.

ALEX
He's a great actor.

Deanna overhears this and is curious.

ALEX (CONT'D)
Know which movies he won an Oscar for?

CALLIE
Easy. Fear and Loathing.

ALEX
(smiling)
That's what everyone thinks.
(beat)
Traffic.

CALLIE
Oh he was great in that.

Alex nods, sips his coffee.

CALLIE (CONT'D)
Huh.

Deanna appears and refills Alex's coffee without asking.

DEANNA
(to Callie)
I left your check, honey.

Walks away.

CALLIE
(checks her watch)
Whoa. I'm late.

ALEX
School?

CALLIE
Job interview.

ALEX
Good luck.

CALLIE
(joking)
Can I use you as a reference?

Alex smiles as Callie stands.

CALLIE (CONT'D)
Thanks for talking to me. I won't tell anyone you eat here.

Callie walks back to her booth, leaves cash for the check, and walks out with her stuff.

Deanna comes to Alex's table.

DEANNA
Since when are you such a movie buff?

Alex looks at her a little fearfully as she makes up his
check and puts it on the table.

DEANNA (CONT'D)
Stay as long as you'd like...whoever you are.

Alex stares at the check until Deanna walks away.

EXT. BROOKLYN WAREHOUSE - NIGHT

Marquee advertises Gotham Dance Company performance:
Twilight

INT. BROOKLYN WAREHOUSE – CONTINUOUS

Alex and Jessica are sitting in the front row of some risers
set up inside the warehouse. Throughout the scene the
people behind them intermittently look over at Alex,
mistaking him for Benicio del Toro.

VOICE (O.S.)
(low)
God, I loved Way of the Gun.

JESSICA
I'm sure it was just waitress talk.

ALEX
(worried)
I think she knew.

JESSICA
There's no way she could know.

ALEX
Think about it. She probably spends more time with
Downs than his own family. And I'm supposed to go to
this dinner party with his friends. Maybe I shouldn't.

A DANCER, A WOMAN IN HER THIRTIES, walks
over. Jessica stands and hugs her.

DANCER
Thank you for coming!

JESSICA
Of course.
(to Alex)
You remember Chase.

Alex stands. Several heads turn in his direction as he does.

ALEX
Yes, hello.

CHASE
(implying a double meaning)
This makes me happy.

JESSICA
We still on for drinks after?

CHASE
Definitely.

INT. BAR - LATER THAT NIGHT

Alex and Jessica are standing at a small table near the bar.
Bar patrons glance at Alex, mistaking him for Benicio del
Toro. Chase cuts through the crowd with a COUPLE OF

OTHER WOMEN IN THEIR THIRTIES in tow. All smile
when they see Alex.

JESSICA
(to Chase)
You were terrific.

CHASE
Thanks, doll.

The two Women with Chase take positions at the table and
Jessica rushes their introductions before they can speak.

JESSICA
(to Alex)
You remember Rachel and Nina.

ALEX
Of course.

RACHEL
I was flipping through the channels the other night and
that Miami Vice you did was on.

Alex smiles but doesn't say anything.

RACHEL (CONT'D)
You were so good even back then.

Chase and Jessica have a side conversation:

CHASE
When did this happen?

JESSICA
A couple of days ago.

CHASE
I'm so glad.

While this conversation goes on in the background:

RACHEL
It's amazing to recognize so many actors who were on it, too.

NINA
That show was on for years.

RACHEL
I wish it was still on.

Alex shrugs sheepishly. He looks away, toward the bar, and glimpses Burton LaFarge, who waves. Alex pretends not to see him.

CHASE
Jessica says you're playing Vernon Downs.

ALEX
Yes.

NINA
Didn't he write that book about the serial killer?

ALEX
Among others.

RACHEL
The movie of that book was terrible.

JESSICA
I thought it was better than the book.

RACHEL
I didn't read the book.

NINA
Who do you have to blow to get a drink in this place?

Alex looks again to where Burton LaFarge was sitting, but the stool is empty.

INT. BENICIO DEL TORO'S APARTMENT - MIDDLE OF THE NIGHT

Alex is asleep. The phone RINGS and Alex answers it automatically. Alex checks the clock, which reads 12:12.

ALEX
(groggy)
Hello?

EMILY BLUNT (O.S.)
Did I wake you?

INT. BLACK RABBIT BAR - AN HOUR LATER

The low-lit bar is sparsely populated. Framed pencil drawings of famous and historical figures line the walls. The BARTENDER nods at Alex and then points toward the back room, where Alex finds Emily Blunt sitting over a glass of wine.

EMILY BLUNT
Oh, thank God.

She stands and hugs Alex. They both sit down.

EMILY BLUNT (CONT'D)
I'm sorry for dragging you out like this—

ALEX
(holds up his hand)
How can I help?

A WAITER approaches the table.

ALEX (CONT'D)
(to Waiter)
I'll have a glass of wine, too, please.

EMILY BLUNT
I'll have another as well.

The Waiter nods and retreats.

EMILY BLUNT (CONT'D)
He won't listen to me. He cannot make this movie.

ALEX
What does he say?

EMILY BLUNT
Oh, you know.

She waves her hand. She's obviously a little tipsy.

EMILY BLUNT (CONT'D)
He wants to do an edgier role.

ALEX
I thought I read that Leo had taken the part.

EMILY BLUNT
Scheduling conflict.

Swallows the last gulp of her wine as the Waiter brings
them two new glasses. He lingers, hoping to overhear

something, but they both look up at him and he takes the hint.

ALEX
Where is he now?

EMILY BLUNT
He's on one of his retreats, but I think he is just hiding out until the deal is done.

ALEX
I'll try him.

EMILY BLUNT
He'll listen to you.

ALEX
I don't know why everyone thinks so.

EMILY BLUNT
He knows Clooney trusts you.

Alex nods and sips his wine.

EMILY BLUNT (CONT'D)
Anyway, there's no one else. I've done all I can.

INT. BENICIO DEL TORO'S APARTMENT - LATER

Alex falls back into bed. The clock reads 4:15. He stares at the ceiling and smiles. He's regained the confidence momentarily shaken by his encounter with the diner waitress.

INT. UPPER EAST SIDE APARTMENT - NIGHT

THREE COUPLES mingle, holding glasses of wine. The

INDISTINCT CONVERSATION is at a LOW MURMUR.

EXT. UPPER EAST SIDE BLOCK - CONTINUOUS

Alex lingers in front of a window display, killing time. He
looks at his watch and sees that it's just after six. He has
more time to kill. He turns back to the window display.
Behind him, a GIRL passes and does a double take,
recognizing him as Benicio del Toro.

INT. UPPER EAST SIDE APARTMENT -
CONTINUOUS

Wineglasses are refilled as the CONVERSATION
GROWS A LITTLE LOUDER.

EXT. UPPER EAST SIDE APARTMENT BUILDING -
CONTINUOUS

Alex glances up the face of the imposing stone building.
He checks his watch again: 6:45. He breathes deeply,
summoning his courage.

INT. UPPER EAST SIDE APARTMENT -
CONTINUOUS

BUZZER sounds. CHRISTIANNA, the host, a sleekly
dressed woman in her 50s, casually presses the button on
the intercom that opens the door in the lobby, all while
carrying on a conversation with her friend PILAR, another
woman in her 50s.

INT. UPPER EAST SIDE APARTMENT BUILDING –
ELEVATOR - CONTINUOUS

Alex takes one last look at the list Downs gave her of those
attending the dinner, along with a quick description of

each.

INT. UPPER EAST SIDE APARTMENT -
CONTINUOUS

Across the room, two men are huddled around their drinks.
PAUL,60, a tall, thin, bespectacled man, is the husband of
Christianna. NATHANIEL, 60, the husband of Pilar, is
stout and well fed. They have had a few drinks and are
talking in hushed tones while glancing toward the couple
on the couch: DAVID, a roguish-looking English teacher
in his 50s who has aged well, and BRETT, a girl in her late
20s.

PAUL
What's her name again?

NATHANIEL
Brett.

Sips his drink.

PAUL
She's one of his students?

NATHANIEL
(shaking his head no)
Former.

PAUL
Jesus.

NATHANIEL
She's a big Downs fan, apparently.

PAUL
(rolls his eyes)

He's gonna love that.

A KNOCK on the door draws everyone's attention. Christianna sets her wineglass down and opens the door on Alex, who smiles.

CHRISTIANNA
We were beginning to wonder.

Alex steps into the apartment tentatively.

ALEX
Am I late?

CHRISTIANNA
We're just about to open a fourth bottle, if that's what you mean.

INT. UPPER EAST SIDE APARTMENT - LIVING ROOM - MOMENTS LATER

Alex is clustered together with David and Brett in a corner, each holding a drink.

DAVID
Swear to God.

Alex gives an amused laugh.

BRETT
(gently but firmly)
That's not exactly right.

DAVID
Which part?

BRETT
She wasn't trying to humiliate you. You take everything so personally.

DAVID
But she told me all this stuff was true, that it had really happened to her, and it was word-for-word from Vernon's first book.

BRETT
She must've known you two were friends.

DAVID
She had no way of knowing that.

BRETT
(teasing)
I seem to remember you name-dropping him in class.

David doesn't even look embarrassed by the accusation.

DAVID
The funny thing is she was a good writer in her own right.

ALEX
Yeah?

DAVID
Her work was her own, but when she told stories in workshop, they were clearly plagiarized from published novels. It felt like a performance piece, though no one else seemed to catch on.

BRETT
That's what happens when they let other majors take creative writing as an elective.

INT. UPPER EAST SIDE APARTMENT - DINING
ROOM - LATER

Everyone is sitting around the dinner table, enjoying the
sumptuous spread.

PAUL
Have they ever asked you to do anything like that before?

ALEX
(shakes his head)
No.

DAVID
They probably think this is your last book. You know, like
the last-day-of-camp ask.

NATHANIEL
(pointedly)
Or the last day of class.

David smiles at Brett, who rolls her eyes.

ALEX
Said I would.

A MURMUR of general disbelief goes around the room.

CHRISTIANNA
I've got a hundred dollars that says you don't.

PILAR
(cackling)
A thousand!

NATHANIEL
But if you're going to do a show, Charlie Austin is it.

PAUL
It'll be a ratings coup, no doubt.

CHRISTIANNA
(dismissively)
He's an interrupter.

PILAR
Oh God. It drives me crazy. And the questions aren't questions. Just things he wants to say.

DAVID
It's Socratic.

CHRISTIANNA
It's annoying.

Everyone laughs.

INT. UPPER EAST SIDE APARTMENT - LIVING ROOM - A LITTLE LATER

Everyone has been eating and drinking.

BRETT
(to Alex)
I overheard a woman on the subway raving about your new book.

Alex smiles.

BRETT (CONT'D)
I just got my copy from the Strand.

CHRISTIANNA
(to Alex)
When are we all getting our copies?

ALEX
(teasing)
It's been out for a couple of days. I assumed you'd all read
it by now.

Everyone laughs.

PAUL
Hey, we should have Doug get us some copies.

Pushes his chair back.

CHRISTIANNA
Doug leaves at 4. Neil is on now. Paul picks up the
receiver by the door.

PAUL
How many?

Hands around the table go up.

PAUL (CONT'D)
(into the receiver)
Hello, Neil? It's Paul in 2E. Can you do me a favor?

ALEX
(to the table)
I don't miss having a doorman.

PILAR
I still can't believe you didn't have him arrested.

ALEX
That would've just put me in the papers, where I loath to
be.

BRETT
What happened?

ALEX
I had to move, is what happened.

NATHANIEL
His doorman stole some of his letters and sold them to an autograph place.

BRETT
That's terrible.

DAVID
What did he make on that?

CHRISTIANNA
Not funny.

PILAR
He made a hundred thousand dollars before he was found out.

NATHANIEL
My doorman makes that in a year. With tips.

DAVID
Didn't the guy have some story? He needed the money for something?

ALEX
There's never a good reason for violating someone's privacy.

Paul rejoins the table.

PAUL
Neil is on it. There's a bookstore a block away.

PILAR
Did I see that Benicio del Toro is going to play you in the movie?

ALEX
Yes.

NATHANIEL
What did your lawyer say about stopping it?

ALEX
Can't.

PAUL
You can sue them after the fact, if they slander you.

PILAR
Quit being a lawyer. Maybe they'll do a good job. They wouldn't go to all the trouble of making it if they were just going to get sued.

DAVID
No telling what their motives are.

ALEX
Except to expose me in a way I don't wish to be exposed.

BRETT
Benicio del Toro is a great actor, though.

ALEX
That may be, but that still doesn't give him the right.

BRETT
Are there any movies you like?

David groans as if she's made a faux pas.

PAUL
Here we go.

PILAR
(to Brett)
Vernon has one favorite movie. And no use for any others.

BRETT
Which?

NATHANIEL
You've never heard of it.

DAVID
Hey, don't condescend.

BRETT
(wrinkles her nose in jest)
Is it really old?

They all look at Alex.

ALEX
The Lost Weekend.

Everyone is silent to gauge Brett's reaction.

BRETT
Never heard of it.

Everyone at the table erupts in laughter. Alex laughs too.

INT. UPPER EAST SIDE APARTMENT - DINING
ROOM - LATER

Alex is sitting at the head of the table with a stack of
copies of Downs's new book, while the others are clearing
the table.

PAUL
Here's your last effort, just so you don't inscribe the new
one same as the old.

Laughs and puts a copy of Downs's previous title on the
table.

Alex opens the book and studies the signature. While
others are buzzing around cleaning and talking, he
surreptitiously traces the signature and then sets to work
signing the new copies. Paul is watching him carefully and
looks to make sure no one else is around.

PAUL (CONT'D)
Glad to hear about the Charlie Austin thing. Makes what I
have to ask you easier.

ALEX
(stops signing)
Yeah?

Paul double-checks that no one can hear them.

PAUL
(lowering his voice)
I need a favor. I promised this reporter I know, Peter Kline,
that he could interview you.

ALEX
(annoyed)

I don't talk to reporters.

PAUL
You're going to talk to Charlie Austin. What's the difference?

ALEX
Charlie Austin is one thing...

PAUL
Kline really wants the interview. Just meet him for lunch, talk to him. It'll square me with Kline.
(beat)
Don't make me remind you that you owe me one.

They trade looks.

EXT. UPPER EAST SIDE APARTMENT BUILDING - LATER THAT NIGHT

Alex exits and walks briskly down the street. He turns the corner and slows down. He pulled it off.

INT. MAXWELL JAY'S - STILL LATER

Alex is at his now usual place at the bar. The bar is mostly empty, as it's late. The muted TV is on above. The Bartender pours Alex another drink.

BARTENDER
Celebrating?

ALEX
You could say that.

BARTENDER
I'll join you. Just found out my girlfriend is not pregnant.

Alex laughs as the Bartender pours himself half a beer.
Over the Bartender's shoulder, on the TV, looms the face
of Burton LaFarge, the screenwriter Alex previously met at
the bar. Some kind of news item.

ALEX
(pointing at the TV)
Isn't that the guy who comes in here?

Bartender looks at the TV.

BARTENDER
Didn't realize that the first time I saw it. Looks like him,
yeah. Wild.

ALEX
What happened?

BARTENDER
Pushed under a train.

Alex continues to watch the muted news story.

BARTENDER (CONT'D)
Grand Central. Probably some crazy. I always stand with
my back to the train.

Alex nods, half listening, still staring at the television.
Jessica enters the bar and makes her way to Alex, smiling
triumphantly at the Bartender.

BARTENDER (CONT'D)
Hello, Jessica.

JESSICA
(pointedly)
Long time no see, Jeremy.

She gives Alex a peck on the cheek.

ALEX
You made it.

JESSICA
Was working late anyway. Glad you called.

INT. MAXWELL JAY'S - AN HOUR LATER

Alex and Jessica are two of the last in the bar.

ALEX
What's after this?

JESSICA
Home, I guess.

ALEX
Come back with me.

JESSICA
Is that a command or a question?

ALEX
Come back with me?

He smiles. Jessica looks at him, considering, scrutinizing him, making up her mind.

JESSICA
Maybe.

ALEX
Maybe. Not as promising as a yes, but not as devastating as a no.

She smiles.

INT. BENICIO DEL TORO'S APARTMENT -
BEDROOM - THAT NIGHT

Jessica is in bed. Alex enters from the bathroom, and
undresses. She watches intently, comparing. Alex slips into
bed and she kisses him, soft at first and then hard. She
takes his arm and wraps it around her.

JESSICA
Hold me like this again.

Alex complies, follows her lead. They kiss some more. He
kisses her neck and she moans. She suddenly rolls him
onto his back and flips on top of him.

JESSICA (CONT'D)
(deviously)
Like last time.

ALEX
(repeating)
Like last time.

She smiles and leans in to kiss him.

INT. BENICIO DEL TORO'S APARTMENT -
BEDROOM - LATER

Alex and Jessica are in bed, asleep. There's a KNOCK at
the door. Alex startles awake.

JESSICA
What is it?

ALEX
Someone's at the door.

JESSICA
Are you sure?

Alex gets out of bed and puts on a T-shirt.

ALEX
It's probably just the doorman.

INT. BENICIO DEL TORO'S APARTMENT - LIVING
ROOM - CONTINUOUS

Another KNOCK just as Alex swings the door open to find
DETECTIVE DEGNER, a man in his 50s, and
DETECTIVE KEPHART, a woman in her 40s. Detective
Degner flashes a badge.

DETECTIVE DEGNER
I'm sorry to bother you, Mr. del Toro, especially this time
of night.

ALEX
What's this about?

DETECTIVE KEPHART
Can we come in?

INT. BENICIO DEL TORO'S APARTMENT - LIVING
ROOM - MOMENTS LATER

Alex is sitting in a chair while the two detectives are on the
couch. Alex is holding the photo of Burton LaFarge he saw
earlier on the television.

DETECTIVE DEGNER
You've never seen him?

ALEX
(thinking)
I was telling the bartender at Maxwell Jay's that it looked
like someone who drank there.

DETECTIVE KEPHART
Nice place. You a regular?

ALEX
Semi.

DETECTIVE DEGNER
And you saw this Burton LaFarge there?

ALEX
Yes.

DETECTIVE KEPHART
Did you drink with him at Maxwell Jay's?

ALEX
I saw him there once or twice.

DETECTIVE KEPHART
Recently?

ALEX
I'm not exactly sure. The bartender probably has a better
sense of that. I sometimes can't tell what day of the week it
is.

Gives a weak smile.

DETECTIVE KEPHART
We'll ask him.

Awkward pause.

ALEX
You mean you haven't already spoken with him?

DETECTIVE KEPHART
We didn't know anything about the connection with the
bar until you told us.

ALEX
(confused)
Then how did you get here?

The detectives give each other a look. Detective Degner
takes a piece of paper out of his jacket pocket and hands it
to Alex. The slip of paper reads: "Ask Benicio del Toro"
Alex stares at the paper. Has no idea how to react.

DETECTIVE DEGNER
That was on the body.

DETECTIVE KEPHART
So you can see why we're confused.

DETECTIVE DEGNER
Can you say where you were at about ten o'clock?

Alex thinks, realizing that Benicio del Toro doesn't have an
alibi, since everyone at the dinner party knew him as
Vernon Downs.

ALEX
At the movies.

DETECTIVE DEGNER
Movie stub?

Alex shakes his head.

DETECTIVE DEGNER (CONT'D)
What did you see?

ALEX
Vertigo. At the Hitchcock revival downtown.

DETECTIVE KEPHART
Love Hitchcock.

Jessica appears from the bedroom.

ALEX
This is Jessica.

JESSICA
What's wrong?

ALEX
Someone was pushed under a train.

JESSICA
Oh my God.

ALEX
Said he knows me.

Hands the note to her. She takes it and reads it.

JESSICA
Who was it?

DETECTIVE DEGNER
A screenwriter. Burton LaFarge.

JESSICA
(to the detectives)
Any idea who did it?

DETECTIVE KEPHART
The CCTV in the station caught an image of the assailant, but he or she was dressed in black and wearing a black hood.

DETECTIVE DEGNER
At the moment the victim is pushed, the assailant's wrist can be seen. Whoever it was, they have a tattoo of a star on their wrist.

Alex and Jessica absorb this information. Alex involuntarily looks at his wrists, as do the detectives.

DETECTIVE KEPHART
(to Jessica)
Mind showing me your wrists?

Jessica is taken aback but raises her arms so that her robe slides away revealing her wrists. Nothing.

DETECTIVE KEPHART (CONT'D)
Thank you.

The detectives rise, and Alex does too.

DETECTIVE DEGNER
Sorry again to have bothered you at this hour.

ALEX
I'm sorry we couldn't help.

DETECTIVE KEPHART
We may call on you again.

ALEX
Of course.

DETECTIVE KEPHART
Also, if you don't mind my saying this, I loved you in
Snatch.

ALEX
Thank you. That's a nice thing to hear.

DETECTIVE KEPHART
Good night.

The detectives nod at Jessica. Alex lets them out.

JESSICA
What a weird thing.

Alex looks at her, as if debating. But he's a little freaked
out and wants an ally, so he opens a drawer and takes out
the script given him by Burton LaFarge and tosses it on the
coffee table. Jessica sees the title page and backs away
from it as if it were explosive.

JESSICA (CONT'D)
Why didn't you say anything?

ALEX
(panicked)
I don't know. Instinct. I met the guy once.
(corrects himself)
Twice.

They both stare at the screenplay on the coffee table.

INT. BENICIO DEL TORO'S APARTMENT -
BEDROOM - LATER

Alex lies in bed staring at the ceiling, unable to sleep.
Jessica is on her side, staring at the wall, also unable to
sleep.

JESSICA
Are you going to meet that reporter for lunch?

ALEX
Seems like a bad idea.

JESSICA
Maybe he knows something more about all of this.

Alex continues to stare at the ceiling, unable to sleep. He
closes his eyes and we hear the SOUND OF A SUBWAY
IN MOTION as the scene dissolves.

EXT. SUBWAY TRAIN - DAY

Alex stands in the noisy car. Glimpses headline on the
newspaper of a seated commuter: "Man Pushed Under
Train."

INT. JACKSON'S BISTRO - A LITTLE LATER

Alex walks into the darkened restaurant, letting his
eyes adjust. PETER KLINE, in his late 40s, waves from a
table against the wall. He stands when Alex approaches.

PETER
Peter Kline.

ALEX
Vernon Downs.

They sit.

PETER
Thanks for meeting me.

ALEX
I owe Paul a favor.

PETER
(amused)
I wondered.

INT. JACKSON'S BISTRO - LATER

Lunch is being cleared by the WAITER.

ALEX
What might not be true is that people assume I wrote my
last book for reasons other than the simple fact that it was a
book that I needed to write. But other than that, people just
write what they want to write.

Peter considers this answer, which ends the interview.

PETER
Coffee?

ALEX
Sure.

Peter nods at the Waiter, who goes for the coffee.

PETER
I have to say, it's an impressive performance.

ALEX
Which?

The Waiter sets the coffee in front of them. Peter takes a sip, staring at Alex over the cup.

PETER
Don't worry. I won't say anything.

Alex looks fearful.

ALEX
To whom about what?

Peter waves to someone behind Alex, who turns and sees two people he recognizes as Detective Degner and Detective Kephart.

PETER
Colleagues. This is an old newspaper hangout.

Detective Degner and Detective Kephart take a table on the other side of the room from them.

ALEX
I don't—

PETER
Yeah, sorry about that. Years of trying to get the scoop clouds my thinking sometimes. I was hoping you'd tell them something useful. Or printable. Saw the thing about the tattoo on the news and thought it might sell it.

Reaches into his bag and produces the same note the detectives showed him that night: "Ask Benicio del Toro."

ALEX
Where did you get that?

PETER
I wrote it.

Alex gives him a look.

PETER (CONT'D)
Or transcribed it, I should say. Burton left that message on my answering machine the day before he died.

ALEX
Why?

PETER
He came to me about a month ago with an interesting story about how Vernon Downs had plagiarized him for his new book. The one that just came out.

ALEX
That's ludicrous.

PETER
It's a bit outlandish. But Burton said he had proof. He was going to show it to me, but then there was an unfortunate accident.

ALEX
What was the proof?

PETER
He didn't say. But he seemed to suggest that Benicio del Toro knows.

ALEX
Well, it's libel. Good thing you didn't run with it. My lawyers have an impressive winning streak.

PETER
You mean Vernon Downs's lawyers do.

Awkward silence as Alex realizes that Peter knows he's
not Vernon Downs.

PETER (CONT'D)
The resemblance is pretty remarkable, I have to admit. And
I didn't put it together until I was having lunch with my
old college roommate a week or so ago. He's a casting
agent. And he told me about this actor he'd seen who was
the spitting image of Benicio del Toro. Who for some
reason is impersonating Vernon Downs.

Alex eyes him coolly.

ALEX
Talk about outlandish stories.

PETER
My friend told me the actor's name, but I've forgotten it. I
could ask him again, I guess. My readers might be
interested in that story.

ALEX
What do you want?

PETER
I want the truth about Vernon Downs and his new book.

ALEX
Why do you care?

PETER
Let's just say I have a personal interest in the matter.

Alex considers this and debates telling him something.

ALEX
(reluctantly)
There's a letter.

PETER
What kind of letter?

ALEX
LaFarge mailed a letter to my—to Downs's editor,
detailing his accusations.

PETER
Have you read it?

Alex shakes his head no.

PETER (CONT'D)
If you can get me that letter, we'll forget all this other
business, as interesting as it might be to my readers.

ALEX
How am I supposed to do that?

Peter stands.

PETER
You seem like a resourceful person.

The fake detectives at the other table glance up.

ALEX
I can't—

PETER
I've got two interesting stories to choose from. And I don't
care which one I tell, but my deadline either way is the end
of the week. Lunch was on the paper, by the way.

Peter pats Alex on the back and waves to the fake detectives as he exits. Alex stares in disbelief at Peter's empty seat.

INT. BENICIO DEL TORO'S APARTMENT - LATER

Alex enters and finds Jessica lying on the couch, reading the screenplay Burton LaFarge gave him.

JESSICA
You obviously didn't read this.

ALEX
Why would I?

JESSICA
Oh, I don't know. It's just the story of an unknown writer whose work is stolen by a famous author.

ALEX
What?

JESSICA
But the writer is killed in what looks like an accident—

ALEX
(incredulous)
Pushed under a train?

JESSICA
Falls down an elevator shaft. At the famous author's publishing house.

Alex processes this information.

ALEX
Why does he go to the publishing house?

JESSICA
I think you know.

ALEX
To give the editor a letter?

JESSICA
(covers her mouth)
Oh my God.

ALEX
Then what?

Jessica flips through the pages as she recounts the plot.

JESSICA
He tips off a journalist, who is really the bitter, jilted ex-college boyfriend of the famous author's daughter.

ALEX
(thinking)
Really.

JESSICA
They were engaged, but she broke it off. Anyway, the writer is paranoid and thinks he's being followed. The famous author's book is about to be published, and the writer knows he's a liability.

Alex sits down on the couch next to her and puts his head in his hands.

ALEX
Jesus.

JESSICA
You haven't even heard the best part. He makes friends

with the actor playing the famous author in an upcoming movie before he's killed.

Alex moans.

JESSICA (CONT'D)
And the actor is sympathetic to the writer and avenges his death by helping catch the famous author.

ALEX
How does he do that?

JESSICA
He gets the letter from the editor and gives it to the journalist.

Alex is astounded by this.

ALEX
How?

JESSICA
He goes to the publishing house at night, pretending to be the famous author and tells the security guard he left something in his editor's office.

Alex takes this in, thinking.

ALEX
Does he name the security guard?

INT. VERNON DOWNS'S APARTMENT - DAY

Downs and Alex are sitting across from each other, as in their first meeting. Alex is turning over a snow globe from Florida while Downs looks on. Vivian is in the background, making coffee in the kitchen.

ALEX
Relaxing trip?

DOWNS
Yes, very.

ALEX
Get any sun?

Vivian sets down a coffee cup for each of them. Alex notices that her wrist is wrapped in a bandage.

DOWNS
I'm not really the beach type.

ALEX
(to Vivian)
What happened?

VIVIAN
It's nothing.

DOWNS
So? How did it go? Were you convincing?

ALEX
Everyone except Deanna, the diner waitress, I think.

DOWNS
She's naturally suspicious. Comes with the trade. What about Christianna's dinner party?

Alex waits a beat. Downs seems keen on the answer.

ALEX
No problems.

DOWNS
(delighted)
It's amazing how little attention people pay, is it not? I
mean outside of the attention they pay to themselves.

ALEX
There was one thing.

DOWNS
Oh?

ALEX
One of the dinner guests. Paul?

DOWNS
Saint Paul, yes.

ALEX
He said you owed him a favor and wanted it paid in the
forof lunch with a reporter, Peter Kline.

A long pause is broken by a CLATTERING in the
background. Vivian has dropped something in the kitchen.

DOWNS
And how is Peter?

ALEX
He has an interest in you.

DOWNS
It's not me he's interested in.

Looks off toward the kitchen.

ALEX
So I gathered.

DOWNS
Was he convinced?

Alex pauses, letting the question float between them. How
he answers will determine the course of action he'll take.

ALEX
Seemed to be.

This pleases Downs.

ALEX (CONT'D)
Oh, and your editor cornered me about appearing on
Charlie Austin.

DOWNS
(amused)
Nothing I can't undo.

Beat. The interview is over, and Downs puts his hands on
the armrests of his chair, as if to rise, but doesn't when
Alex shows no sign of doing the same.

ALEX
You may have missed the news while you were away. A
man was pushed under a train.

DOWNS
(resignedly)
This city.

ALEX
I actually met him a few days prior.

DOWNS
Oh?

ALEX
He was a writer, too.

Downs gives a dismissive look.

DOWNS
The world is full of writers, seems.

ALEX
He showed me some of his work.

Downs gives a surprised look.

ALEX (CONT'D)
A screenplay.

DOWNS
(relieved)
I'm guessing you get a lot of that.

ALEX
Yes.

DOWNS
As do I.

ALEX
Anything interesting?

DOWNS
I make it a practice not to read anything sent to me. The
work of others must remain behind a wall, for their
protection and for mine. I imagine the same is true for you.

ALEX
I made an exception in this case.

DOWNS
Exceptions can become precedent. Very dangerous.

ALEX
True.

DOWNS
I worry an exception would do great damage to my
reputation. When you've spent your life curating your
reputation, you're loath to have some nobody from
nowhere wreck it with carelessness.

ALEX
It must be wearying, that kind of vigilance.

DOWNS
A golden cage, don't you find?

EXT. VERNON DOWNS'S APARTMENT BUILDING -
A LITTLE LATER

Vivian exits the building. Alex is across the street and
crosses over to her as she starts to walk down the sidewalk.
She looks terrified when she sees him. She doesn't stop,
and he walks alongside her.

VIVIAN
You scared me.

ALEX
I didn't mean to.

VIVIAN
What do you want?

ALEX
I just want to talk to you.

VIVIAN
I don't have anything to say.

ALEX
Peter is out to get your father.

Vivian stops and turns to face him, a quizzical look on her face.

VIVIAN
Poor Peter.

ALEX
Why does he hate your father?

VIVIAN
It's me he hates. He wants to hurt me.

ALEX
There's something going on and it may involve your father.

Vivian gives him a strange look.

ALEX (CONT'D)
There's a letter that connects your father to the writer that was pushed under the train.

VIVIAN
(fearfully)
I'm sure he doesn't know anything about that.

ALEX
He's involved, Vivian.

VIVIAN
He could never be involved in something like that.

ALEX
I know he's your father and it's hard to hear, but I think
he's a bad person.

VIVIAN
A bad person? You don't know anything about him.
Would a bad person help Mike the way my father helped
him when he was in trouble?

ALEX
What kind of trouble?

VIVIAN
Please stay away from me and my father.

Turns to go, but Alex grabs her by her bandaged wrist.

ALEX
I had a friend who had a tattoo removed. Said it hurt like
hell.

He unravels the bandage as she tries to squirm free. He's
expecting to see the fresh scar of a removed tattoo, but it's
just a burn. She storms off.

INT. BENICIO DEL TORO'S APARTMENT - DAY

Alex enters to find Jessica with her bag packed, making
one last check of the place.

ALEX
What happened?

JESSICA
More cops. Different ones, who had never heard of the first
ones.

She nods toward a business card on the side table.
Alex reads the card: J.D. Martens, Homicide Detective.

JESSICA (CONT'D)
Asked me a bunch of questions I didn't know the answers to.

She's clearly rattled.

JESSICA (CONT'D)
Said they'd be back.

ALEX
Did they say when?

Jessica zips up her bag.

JESSICA
You should go too.

ALEX
Go where?

JESSICA
Wherever.

ALEX
Is that where you're going?

Jessica stops what she's doing and looks at him.

JESSICA
It's better if we don't know where each other is.

Alex is a little frightened by her behavior.

ALEX
Slow down. Tell me what's happened.

JESSICA
It's not what's happened. It's what is happening.

ALEX
Tell me.

JESSICA
(a little frantic)
It's partly my fault. But I had no idea—

ALEX
No idea about what?

Jessica gives him a long look.

JESSICA
That day when you found me, I was picking up my things.
Benicio wanted me to clear out my stuff while he was
gone. I begged him for a second chance, but I could see it
was over.

Alex realizes what she's saying.

JESSICA (CONT'D)
Yeah, okay, I knew. But I'd promised that Benicio would
show up for the fund-raiser at work, and I needed you to
save face. And the rest of it was... I'm a curious person,
let's just say. Which is at the root of all my problems.
Benicio understood that, until one day he didn't. But
whatever is happening now is bad and we should both
move on.

ALEX
It's going to be fine. I'll go to the police and tell them

everything. I'll give them the script and they'll see that we had nothing to do with any of this.

JESSICA
I burned the script.

ALEX
(rising panic in his voice)
Why? Why would you do that?

JESSICA
It connects us to this mess. Now we're free to go. Don't you see?

Alex sinks onto the couch.

JESSICA (CONT'D)
What?

Alex looks at her. Wants to confide in her that he's not free of the situation, but doesn't.

ALEX
Nothing. You should go.

Jessica gives him a last look and exits.

INT. MAXWELL JAY'S - NIGHT

Alex is sitting at the bar with a drink. The place is packed. CUSTOMERS keep glancing over at Alex, recognizing him as Benicio del Toro.

The late news plays on the television, and Alex reads the closed captioning: "Full CCTV Video of Victim Being Pushed Under Train Released to the Public."

Alex watches the video, which has been slowed down. In the top corner, at the far end of the platform, he sees Vernon Downs wearing the same shirt Alex wore when he first met Downs at his apartment. Downs is also not wearing his glasses, trying to look as much like Benicio del Toro as possible. In the video Downs stares straight ahead as LaFarge is pushed, not reacting like the others do as LaFarge screams out.

Startled, Alex leaves the bar, pushing his way through the crowd of customers, who recognize him as he passes.

EXT. PUBLISHING HOUSE - NIGHT

Alex approaches the building.

INT. PUBLISHING HOUSE LOBBY - CONTINUOUS

Alex approaches the security desk. The security guard, a large man, looks up. Alex notes his name tag: C. BOCK. They exchange a look.

BOCK
You here for the thing you forgot in your editor's office?

ALEX
Uh-huh.

Bock checks to see that no one else is around and opens the drawer of his desk. He takes out his metal lunch box and opens it. Under a false bottom he procures an envelope and hands it to Alex.

BOCK
The original was shredded. This is just a copy.

ALEX
Okay.

BOCK
I'm glad to have that in someone else's hands. Especially
after what happened to Burton.

ALEX
Did you know him well?

BOCK
We went to graduate school together.

ALEX
You're a writer too?

BOCK
Nah. I turned out just to be a reader. Which makes this a
pretty good job.

ALEX
The world needs readers, too.

BOCK
No one wanted it more than Burton. When I got the job
here, he would buy me lunch in the cafeteria upstairs, just
to be near the action.

Looks sadly at the envelope.

BOCK (CONT'D)
That's his last chance to be published.

Alex nods grimly.

ALEX
Can I count on you if I need to?

BOCK
(shakes his head no)
I can't get involved, sorry. I've got my own problems.

INT. VERNON DOWNS'S APARTMENT - DAY

Downs opens the door and is surprised to find Alex.

DOWNS
What is it?

ALEX
We need to talk.

DOWNS
Not today. I'm busy.

ALEX
This can't wait.

Pushes his way into the apartment.

DOWNS
My worst nightmare come true.

ALEX
Not yet.

Sits at the kitchen table. Downs sits reluctantly.

DOWNS
What do you want?

ALEX
I know about Burton LaFarge.

DOWNS
What of him?

ALEX
It's going to come out. Peter Kline is going to make sure of it.

Downs regards him.

DOWNS
I've handled Mr. Kline in the past, and could again. Besides, it's just LaFarge's word against mine. And he's no longer with us.

ALEX
Conveniently.

Downs gets up and goes to a nearby closet. He opens it and removes a small cardboard box. He places the box on the table and sits back down. Alex sees that the box is from Burton LaFarge, addressed to Downs.

ALEX (CONT'D)
What is it?

DOWNS
I'm afraid the price of knowing the answer is too high.

Alex reacts.

ALEX
When did he send it?

DOWNS
(nonchalantly)
Oh, about the same time he started sending letters accusing me of this and that.

ALEX
Why didn't you take it to the police?

DOWNS
It wouldn't have made sense to be so proactive.
Narratively, I mean.

ALEX
(thinking out loud)
Better to hold on to it and present it as a defense against
LaFarge's claims.

DOWNS
They say novels can't compete with real life. I have to say,
sometimes I agree.

Pushes the box aside.

DOWNS (CONT'D)
For instance, the fiction you've been perpetrating.

Alex starts.

ALEX
I have no idea what—

Downs picks up the box and replaces it in the closet.

DOWNS
The problem with coincidence is that most times it isn't
believable. Character A in a story needs X to happen, but
true to life X doesn't happen. But then some random act
occurs and suddenly X is realized.

ALEX
What random act?

DOWNS
My having lunch in a Midtown restaurant I don't normally
frequent.

Alex considers this.

DOWNS (CONT'D)
And who else do I see at this restaurant? An Academy
award-winning actor lunching with a companion.

INSERT: Scene where Alex and Karen are having lunch.
Jared is taking their order. Pull back to reveal Downs
sitting at another table in the far corner.

DOWNS (CONT'D)
I'm not easily starstruck, but what a coincidence.

ALEX
What coincidence?

DOWNS
I'd been expending an extraordinary amount of energy
thinking about Benicio del Toro, and here he appears at
lunch.
(beat)
Remarkable.
(beat)
But even more remarkable is that in short order Benicio del
Toro reveals himself to be but a mirage.

INSERT: Back-and-forth when Karen tells Jared that Alex
isn't Benicio del Toro.

DOWNS (CONT'D)
What a strange curse, to so closely resemble someone so
well known in your own chosen field.

Alex is stunned into muteness.

DOWNS (CONT'D)
My own resemblance to del Toro is a bit of a debate. I
don't see it, but others do. But for you it must be a constant
irritation. Or worse.
(beat)
I suppose it was simple curiosity that made me follow you
from the restaurant.

ALEX
Rather a dull way to spend the day.

DOWNS
Perhaps. But it was addicting to see how your curse
affected your day-to-day life.

INSERT: Scene where Alex signs autograph for the
tourists. Reveal that Downs is watching from nearby.

DOWNS (CONT'D)
But then, of course, your path was altered.

INSERT: Scene in front of Benicio del Toro's building
where the Doorman mistakes Alex for del Toro.

DOWNS (CONT'D)
My disappointment was only momentary. I suddenly
realized the wonderful opportunity I'd been given.

INSERT: Phone conversation between Downs and Alex.
Reveal that Downs is calling from a pay phone on the
street below.

ALEX
You want me to believe that you dreamed up all of this
stuff on the spot?

Downs shrugs.

DOWNS
When your life revolves around narrative, plots are not
hard to come by.
(beat)
Here's another plausible plot: A not-very-good actor who
looks like another, more talented and more famous actor
uses that resemblance as an excuse for his inability to
realize his aspirations.

Alex is stunned.

DOWNS (CONT'D)
And let's not forget our latest plot: poor Benicio del Toro.
Dreamed of being an actor, put in the work, only to have a
talentless nobody steal his reputation and all that he's
achieved.

Alex looks like he wants to disagree but can't.

DOWNS (CONT'D)
And for what? So you could know what it's like to be
famous? So you could feel like a real actor, even if you're
not?

ALEX
Everyone believed—

Downs waves him off.

DOWNS
That's less about your acting skills and more about
people's inattention.

There's a KNOCK at the door, and Downs's son-in-law

MIKE enters. He gives a cowed look, as if he's embarrassed at interrupting.

DOWNS (CONT'D)
Mike. You know...
(looks at Alex)
What is your name?

ALEX
Alex.

DOWNS
Huh.

Mike gives a halfhearted wave, and Alex notices the star tattoo on the inside of his wrist.

MIKE
Vivian said you wanted to see me.

DOWNS
Yes, Alex was just leaving.

Alex gets up and goes to the door, keeping his eye on Mike. Downs trails him.

DOWNS (CONT'D)
I expect our paths won't meet again.

Alex gives him a questioning look as Downs closes the door.

INT. BENICIO DEL TORO'S APARTMENT - THAT AFTERNOON

The Doorman opens the door and sets down a couple of suitcases, then goes out again, closing the door.

INT. SUBWAY STATION - THAT AFTERNOON

Peter Kline is standing on the platform with a crowd of other straphangers, waiting for the train. Lost in the crowd, many people deep, is Mike, who is staring at Kline. The train ROARS into the station.

INT. BENICIO DEL TORO'S APARTMENT BUILDING - LOBBY – THAT AFTERNOON

Alex enters and the Doorman waves.

DOORMAN
All taken care of, sir.

Alex nods as if he knows what the Doorman means, though he doesn't.

INT. BENICIO DEL TORO'S APARTMENT - MOMENTS LATER

Alex enters and is startled to see the suitcases. In a panic, he begins packing up his meager belongings. The door opens and Benicio del Toro walks in with Emily Blunt, who GASPS.

ALEX
I can explain.

SUPER: A MONTH LATER

INT. VERNON DOWNS'S APARTMENT – LATE AFTERNOON

Downs is seated, watching an entertainment news program on television.

TV ANCHOR (O.S.)
Production of the film based on the life of celebrated
novelist Vernon Downs, starring Academy award-winning
actor Benicio del Toro, has been moved up to capitalize on
the recent news involving charges of plagiarism by another
writer, who was subsequently pushed under a Midtown
subway train. Peter Kline, the reporter who broke the story,
has been hired as a consultant.

INSERT: Scene where Kline and Mike are on the platform.
Mike approaches Kline and gives him an envelope, the
letter.

INSERT: Scene where Alex approaches Mike coming out
of Downs's apartment building. They sit in the window of
the coffee shop. Alex is doing all the talking. Mike is
listening, his head down, nodding. Alex passes him the
letter.

Downs gets up and goes to the closet where he keeps the
box from LaFarge.

TV ANCHOR (O.S.) (CONT'D)
Producers have also announced plans to include the bizarre
true-life story of Alex North, the out-of-work actor bearing
a resemblance to Benicio del Toro who impersonated both
del Toro and Downs for a number of weeks before the
deception was uncovered.

INSERT: Footage from entertainment news channel:

JARED
He pretended to be Benicio and gave me his autograph.

JEREMY
Had no idea. The guy must be a good actor.

DEANNA
You could tell something was off. It makes sense now.

KAREN
He's not a bad person, not the person you're making him
out to be. If you're watching, Alex, please let me or
someone know if you're okay.

Downs sits down again and puts the box on the coffee table
in front of him. He picks up a remote and switches off the
TV. He sits with the box in front of him for a long
moment. He stares at the box, then out the window. He's
ready.

EXT. VERNON DOWNS'S APARTMENT BUILDING -
CONTINUOUS

TWO DETECTIVES flash their badges at the building's
SUPERINTENDENT. The Super points up the stairs.

INT. VERNON DOWNS'S APARTMENT -
CONTINUOUS

Downs takes out a pocketknife and slices off the return
address from Burton LaFarge and burns it in an ashtray. He
watches the embers die out. He cuts open the box,
carefully folds the knife and sets it on the table. There's a
KNOCK at the door, but it doesn't startle him. He's been
expecting it. He reaches for the box to open it.

EXT. DESERT - DAY

An old pickup truck pulls into an unpaved parking lot in
front of a diner, kicking up a tornado of dust.

INT. DINER - CONTINUOUS

The DRIVER takes a seat at the counter. The WAITRESS smiles at him as a BELL DINGS.

WAITRESS
Be there in a minute, darling.

She saunters to the corner booth, where Alex is seated, alone, looking at the paper. The headline says: "Celebrated Novelist Victim of Anthrax." The article has a picture of Vernon Downs. Alex turns the paper over when the Waitress sets down the food.

WAITRESS (CONT'D)
Can I get you anything else, sweetheart?

ALEX
I'm good, thanks.

Waitress writes out his check and sets it on the table. Goes to take the Driver's order.

Alex leaves cash for the bill and leaves.

DRIVER
Who was that?

WAITRESS
He's the one interested in buying Old Man Fuller's place.

DRIVER
He looks like that actor, the one in the news.

WAITRESS
Told him the same thing. Says he doesn't watch the movies.

They both look out the window as Alex gets into his car and drives away.

DRIVER
What's good today?

THE END

WORLD GONE WATER

EXT. BILL AND ALLISON'S HOUSE - NIGHT

A middle-to-upper class home in a suburban neighborhood. All of the lights are on. BILL, a man in his forties, stares out one of the upper windows.

INT. BILL AND ALLISON'S HOUSE - BEDROOM - CONTINUOUS

Bill stares at his reflection in the window. Bill's wife, ALLISON, a woman in her early to mid-thirties, enters the room. Bill sees her reflection behind him and turns around.

ALLISON
All packed?

BILL
It never gets any easier. I always forget something.

Allison walks over to Bill and puts her arms around him.

ALLISON
I wish you didn't have to go.

BILL
Me neither.

ALLISON
Maybe it won't take a week. Maybe you'll be home by the weekend.

(leans in and kisses him)
And we can go to the beach again.
(kisses him again)
And maybe dinner at that place down by the water.

Bill looks at Allison wistfully. The DOORBELL RINGS.

BILL
That's probably Steve.

ALLISON
I don't know why you won't let me drive you to the
airport. I said I would.

BILL
Steve owes me for the last time I took him. Guy code.

ALLISON
(smiles)
One more kiss.

The DOORBELL RINGS again.

INT. BILL AND ALLISON'S HOUSE - CONTINUOUS

Allison comes down the stairs. Bill follows a few steps
behind, lugging his suitcase. Allison opens the door, and
STEVE, a man in his forties, stands in the doorway.

STEVE
Hey, Allison.

Steve kisses Allison on the cheek.

ALLISON
Come in.

STEVE
(to Bill)
Ready, handsome?

BILL
All packed.

STEVE
Need help?

BILL
Just the one bag.

STEVE
You must have it down to a science by now.

ALLISON
Bill was never very good at science.

Steve laughs. Bill smiles sheepishly.

STEVE
We should move. Heard on the radio there's an accident on
the Ninety-Five, so we're gonna have to improvise.

BILL
An auspicious start.

He adjusts his grip on his suitcase and heads for the door,
Steve and Allison trailing. Bill gets to the door and stops,
turning around. Steve senses something.

STEVE
I'll go start the car.
(kisses Allison on the cheek again)
Good night.

ALLISON
Good night, Steve. And thanks.

Steve exits.

FRONT PORCH - CONTINUOUS

Bill and Allison walk out under the porch light and
embrace.

BILL
I'll miss you.

ALLISON
I'll miss you, too.

She looks awkwardly at Steve's car. Bill continues to look
her in the eyes.

BILL
I love you.

Allison gives a surprised look.

BILL (CONT'D)
I love you as much today as I did when I met you.

ALLISON
(blushing)
Bill.

BILL
I never say it enough.

ALLISON
You don't have to say it.

INT. STEVE'S CAR – NIGHT

Steve watches as Bill and Allison kiss and hug goodbye.
He HONKS the horn. Bill and Allison kiss quickly, and
Bill reluctantly moves away, finally heading for the car.
Allison watches him go. Bill gets in the car.

STEVE
(joking)
Thought maybe you'd changed your mind.

Steve backs out of the driveway.

INT. STEVE'S CAR - MOMENTS LATER

Steve and Bill sit silently as the car navigates traffic.

STEVE
This case has really been dragging on.

BILL
Yeah. I thought it was a slam dunk.

STEVE
What is this, your tenth trip to Minneapolis?

BILL
I quit counting.

STEVE
How's Allison holding up?

BILL
You know. Okay.

They ride in silence for a moment.

BILL (CONT'D)
Hey, do you remember Charlie Martens? From the sixth grade?

STEVE
Who?

BILL
C'mon. Martens. His mother came over and chewed out your old man when you beat Charlie up after school for looking at your girlfriend.

STEVE
(thinks)
Martens...Martens...

BILL
Tall, skinny kid. Always wore a Yankees cap.

STEVE
(remembering)
Charlie Martens. Sure. Jesus, what made you think of him?

BILL
(slowly)
Just popped into my mind.

STEVE
Man, we gave it to Martens pretty good.

BILL
You gave it to him good. He transferred out, remember?

STEVE
Jesus, I forgot. I wonder what ever happened to him.

BILL
He killed himself.

STEVE
(looks at Bill in horror)
What?

BILL
(laughs)
Not because of you. He was a depressive.

STEVE
How do you know all of this?

BILL
My mother sees Mrs. Martens at the grocery store.

STEVE
Didn't Martens have a little sister?

BILL
Brother.

STEVE
Right. What was his name?

BILL
Can't remember. B something.

STEVE
Ah, the old days.

They ride in silence.

MOMENTS LATER:

Steve pulls up to the curb at the airport.

BILL
Okay.

STEVE
Have a good trip, buddy.

BILL
Yeah, thanks.

He gives Steve a long look and then gets out. He pulls his suitcase from the backseat. He slams both doors shut and waves as Steve pulls away. Steve HONKS goodbye.

INT. STEVE'S CAR - CONTINUOUS

Steve glances in the rearview mirror as he pulls away.

EXT. AIRPORT TERMINAL - CONTINUOUS

Bill enters the terminal through sliding glass doors.

INT. STEVE'S CAR - CONTINUOUS

Steve watches Bill in the rearview mirror until Bill is inside and then pulls into traffic.

EXT. AIRPORT TERMINAL - CONTINUOUS

Bill reappears through the sliding glass doors. He walks quickly to the parking lot.

PARKING LOT:

Bill pulls out the keys to a rental car and gets in.

EXT. STREET – CONTINUOUS

Steve is driving back on the highway. Bill follows about two minutes behind on the same route. He doesn't need to tail Steve. He knows where he's going.

EXT. BILL AND ALLISON'S HOUSE - MOMENTS LATER

The house is dark except for the front porch light. Steve pulls into the driveway and turns off his car.

EXT. STREET - CONTINUOUS

Bill turns onto his street and kills the lights. He stays out of sight and watches his house.

EXT. BILL AND ALLISON'S HOUSE - CONTINUOUS

Steve walks to the front door and RINGS the doorbell. Allison answers in her nightgown, and Steve and Allison embrace and kiss.

INT. BILL'S CAR - CONTINUOUS

Bill's expression reveals that he is not surprised. Rather than angry, he's sad and disappointed.

EXT. BILL AND ALLISON'S HOUSE - CONTINUOUS

Steve and Allison go inside and shut the front door. The front porch light goes out.

EXT. STREET - CONTINUOUS

Bill drives away, remembering to flick on his headlights.

FADE OUT.

FADE IN:

EXT. BILL AND ALLISON'S HOUSE - VERY EARLY
MORNING

The house and street are quiet except for the SQUEAKY
WHEEL of the bicycle of the newspaper boy, who tosses
the Boston Globe onto the porch.

INT. BILL AND ALLISON'S HOUSE - CONTINUOUS

Steve and Allison are cuddled together in bed, sleeping.
The clock shows "5:00." The phone RINGS. Steve reaches
for it instinctively, groggy, but Allison starts awake and
grabs the receiver from him.

ALLISON
(tentatively)
Hello?

INT. AIRPORT HOTEL ROOM - A LITTLE LATER

Bill's body is on the unmade bed, a hole in his head and
the gun nearby. The room is a frenzy of Police Officers
and EMTs. An Officer picks up Bill's suitcase and tags it
as evidence.

EXT. CEMETERY - DAY

Mourners are gathered in the rain. Allison is standing with
Bill's parents, MR. AND MRS. MEADE, a couple in their
late sixties. Steve is across the coffin from Allison. He
glances up as she weeps uncontrollably. He wants to
comfort her but can't.

The Minister finishes his sermon and Mourners place
flowers on the coffin and give Allison their condolences.

TRINY, a man in his thirties, watches from the back of the crowd. Triny waits for the crowd to thin then makes his way toward Allison.

TRINY
(to Allison)
Mrs. Meade?

Allison looks in his direction.

TRINY (CONT'D)
I'm Triny Scott. I was a friend of Bill's.

Allison clearly doesn't recognize him. Steve is watching from a distance.

ALLISON
How did you know my husband?

TRINY
We were business associates.

ALLISON
Do you work for the firm?

TRINY
(smiles)
I'm not a lawyer, Mrs. Meade.

Allison is confused. Steve approaches.

STEVE
(to Allison)
Bill's parents are waiting in the car.

ALLISON
(in a bit of a daze)

Okay.

TRINY
(eagerly, to Steve)
Triny Scott.

STEVE
Nice to meet you.

They shake hands.

TRINY
Likewise. I recognized you. You're Bill's best friend,
right?

STEVE
Yes. How did you know Bill?

TRINY
We met recently.

STEVE
Oh?

ALLISON
(obviously out of it)
I need to get Bill's parents...we should--

STEVE
Yeah.

He takes Allison's elbow, but she subtly shakes him off.
Steve and Allison turn to walk away.

TRINY
(calling after them)

Nice to finally meet you both. And I'm sorry. Bill was a great guy.

ALLISON
(stops and turns)
I didn't mean to be rude. Why don't you come by the house?

TRINY
Thank you. I'd like that.

STEVE
(eyeing Triny cautiously)
You can follow me.

EXT. BILL AND ALLISON'S HOUSE - A LITTLE LATER

The driveway and street are jammed with cars.

INT. BILL AND ALLISON'S HOUSE - CONTINUOUS

The house is filled with Mourners. Food covers every available surface. Allison sits on the couch in a trance. Some Mourners are gathered around her. Steve keeps his distance but clearly wants to comfort her. Triny is in the far corner, and Steve watches Triny watching Allison. He finally crosses the room.

STEVE
It's Triny, right?

TRINY
(mocking him a little)
Good memory.

STEVE
Steve.

TRINY
(coolly)
Yeah, I remember.

STEVE
So, did you know Bill well?

TRINY
I think so. We didn't know each other for long. But I had a
pretty good sense of him.

STEVE
It's just funny, because I'm his best friend and he never
mentioned you.

TRINY
(smirks)
You're Bill's best friend?

STEVE
(cocky)
That's right.

TRINY
(leans in and whispers)
What kind of best friend fucks his friend's wife?

Steve shoves Triny, and Triny falls into a table of food,
knocking it over. Someone SHRIEKS. Triny staggers,
acting a little.

ALLISON
Jesus, Steve!

Steve starts toward Triny, but a Mourner holds him back.

ALLISON (CONT'D)
(angrily)
What are you doing?

TRINY
It's okay. A little clumsy, is all.
(laughs)
Well, I should go.
(to Allison)
Again, you have my condolences.

Steve's eyes narrow and his gaze follows Triny as Triny leaves.

INT. BILL AND ALLISON'S HOUSE - KITCHEN - LATER

Steve and Allison are cleaning up.

STEVE
Let me do these.

ALLISON
(agitated)
It helps me to do something.

STEVE
But you should--

He tries to take some dirty dishes from her, but Allison jerks away.

ALLISON
Stop telling me what to do!

Steve is taken aback, and Allison sets the dishes down and turns away, weeping. He reaches for her, and she sobs into his chest.

ALLISON (CONT'D)
(pulling back)
On top of everything else, it's the guilt.

STEVE
(softly)
I know.

Allison breaks free of the embrace and wipes her eyes.

ALLISON
Do you think Bill knew?

STEVE
(shakes his head too quickly)
There's no way.

ALLISON
God, what kind of people are we? What have we done?

STEVE
(trying to convince her)
He didn't know.

ALLISON
(gives a lost look)
Then why?

STEVE
(tenderly)
I don't know. There must've been something else...

He reaches for her arm, but she pushes him away.

ALLISON
Let's not invent things to make ourselves feel better.

STEVE
(raising his voice)
Don't you think if he knew, he would've done something about it?

ALLISON
The very fact that we're having this conversation is sickening.

Bill's parents enter.

MRS. MEADE
(to Allison)
We're going, dear.

She gives Allison a hug. Mr. Meade stands mute.

MRS. MEADE (CONT'D)
Be strong, dear.
(to Steve)
You're such a help, Steve. Are you going to stay over?

Steve looks like he's going to say yes, but Allison cuts in.

ALLISON
Steve was just going.

Steve hesitates, wants to argue, but not in front of Bill's parents.

STEVE
I'll call tomorrow.

He kisses Allison on the cheek. then does the same with Mrs. Meade. He pats Mr. Meade on the shoulder but Mr. Meade only grimaces.

EXT. BILL AND ALLISON'S HOUSE - CONTINUOUS

The street has cleared out. Steve exits the front door and gets into his car. Down the street, Triny sits in his car with the lights out. He watches Steve back out and drive away. Triny follows.

STREETS OF PROVIDENCE:

Triny follows Steve at a distance. Steve pulls into an apartment complex, and Triny slows down.

APARTMENT COMPLEX PARKING LOT:

Steve parks and enters his apartment. Triny notes the apartment number.

EXT. BILL AND ALLISON'S HOUSE - NEXT MORNING

Steve tries to pull into the driveway but it's blocked by Triny's car.

INT. BILL AND ALLISON'S HOUSE - CONTINUOUS

Steve rushes in, without knocking, and finds Triny sitting next to Allison on the couch in the living room. Mr. and Mrs. Meade sit opposite. It's clear Steve has interrupted them mid-conversation. Triny stands up.

TRINY
We can talk more later.

(to Mr. and Mrs. Meade)
I think you're doing what's right.

Allison gets up and walks Triny to the door.

ALLISON
(to Triny)
Call me later.

TRINY
Okay.
(to Steve)
Good morning.

Triny extends his hand to Allison, but she hugs him
instead. He returns the hug and leaves. Steve nods as Triny
passes.

STEVE
What's going on?

Allison sits back down on the couch.

ALLISON
Bill told Triny about a charity he wanted to start.

STEVE
First I've heard of it.

ALLISON
(curtly)
You don't know everything.

MRS. MEADE
It was Bill's last wish. And Triny is going to help us fulfill
it.

Steve gives a pained look.

MRS. MEADE (CONT'D)
Unless you know some reason why we shouldn't?

STEVE
Just seems a little...rash. How much does he want?

ALLISON
(sharply)
That's really none of your business.

MRS. MEADE
(to Allison)
Honey.

Allison buries her face in her hands and then runs her fingers through her hair.

ALLISON
(to Steve)
Sorry.

Steve sits next to her on the couch, but not too close.

STEVE
It's okay. I just hate for you to jump into something.

ALLISON
But Bill wanted it.

STEVE
(delicately)
I just find it hard to believe that he never mentioned this guy Triny to me. Or that he wanted this...thing.

MRS. MEADE
He mentioned it to me.

STEVE
(shocked)
Really? When?

MRS. MEADE
A couple of months ago. He called us and said he wanted
to do something good.

STEVE
Did he mention Triny?

MRS. MEADE
No, not by name.
(looks at Allison)
He wanted it to be a surprise.

Mr. Meade gets up without saying a word and goes into the
kitchen.

STEVE
(a bit defeated)
So. What's the first step?

ALLISON
Triny's going to call tomorrow.

STEVE
Where is he staying?

ALLISON
He said he was at the Hilton on River Street for a few days.

EXT. HILTON HOTEL PARKING LOT – DAY

Triny walks to his car and unlocks the door. Steve pulls in behind Triny's car. Triny regards Steve cautiously. Steve gets out of his car and approaches Triny.

STEVE
Can I talk to you for a minute?

Triny leans casually against his car.

TRINY
Sure.

STEVE
Listen, I think things got off on the wrong foot.

TRINY
(raises his eyebrows)
Yeah?

STEVE
How did you know about me and Allison?

TRINY
Hey, don't try to involve me in that.

STEVE
Did Bill tell you?

TRINY
I'm just trying to carry out Bill's last wish. Once I wrap that up, I'm out of here, back to Minneapolis.

STEVE
Is that where you met Bill? Minneapolis?

Triny opens his car door. Steve catches the door and pushes it back, blocking Triny.

STEVE (CONT'D)
I just hope you won't let on to Allison that Bill knew. She's been through enough.

TRINY
(smiles)
Like I said. That's none of my business. Can I go?

STEVE
As long as we're agreed.

Triny stares at Steve like he might say something, but doesn't. Steve removes his hand from the car, and Triny gets in, slamming the door.

INT. STEVE'S APARTMENT - NIGHT

Steve is lying on the couch with his eyes closed. His phone RINGS, startling him.

STEVE
(picks up receiver)
Hello?

INT. BAR - NIGHT

Steve walks in. He sees Triny at the bar, drinking a beer. Steve stares for a moment, then walks over.

TRINY
You made it.

The Bartender comes over.

STEVE
(to Bartender)
Beer is fine.

He takes the stool next to Triny.

TRINY
I'm glad you came out. I felt badly about what I said at the
house the other day about you and Allison. It really isn't
any of my business.

The Bartender sets a beer down in front of Steve. Steve
reaches for his wallet, but Triny slides some money off the
pile in front of him.

STEVE
Thanks.

Triny nods. They both drink in silence for a moment.

TRINY
So, how long did you know Bill?

STEVE
Since we were kids. He was like a brother to me. I know
how stupid that sounds. I hate myself for what happened.

TRINY
You're not the first person it's happened to.

STEVE
I suppose. Ever happened to you?

TRINY
(shaking his head)
I don't sleep with married women.

He takes a long swallow of his beer.

TRINY (CONT'D)
Did you know that there are eighty-two million single
people in the world? If half of them are women, that makes
forty- one million women out there who are single, and a
good many of them are looking.

STEVE
(demurs)
But that's not exactly the same thing.

TRINY
But it illustrates a point.

STEVE
(reluctantly)
It does.

TRINY
How is Allison feeling about it?

STEVE
I don't know. Her house is full of relatives. I can't seem to
reach her.

TRINY
You should try to talk to her.

STEVE
(gives a look that says he's tried)
What about you? Are you married?

TRINY
Yeah, wife and kids.

STEVE
How long have you been married?

TRINY
Ten years.

STEVE
Well, congratulations.

TRINY
Ever plan on getting married? Or are you planning to
marry Allison?

STEVE
(winces, then quickly:)
Don't know.

TRINY
Tell you something I know.

STEVE
What's that?

TRINY
When you're married, whether it's to Allison or someone
else, you'll feel worse about what you've done than you do
now, because you'll mistrust every man she knows, every
trip she takes without you, every place she goes on her
own.

Steve sips his beer, waiting for Triny to say more, but
Triny is finished. Triny stands and pushes the pile of
money toward the Bartender.

TRINY (CONT'D)
Anyway, no hard feelings.

He walks out.

INT. COFFEE SHOP - DAY

Steve is waiting at a booth. Allison walks in and sits down.

STEVE
How are you?

Allison exhales, can't answer.

STEVE (CONT'D)
I just wanted a chance to--

ALLISON
I only agreed to meet you to tell you that it's over between us. I don't want to see you again. For any reason.

STEVE
You're just upset--

ALLISON
(yelling)
Of course I'm upset!

Waitress nearby and other Patrons glance in their direction. Allison settles down, looks at Steve blankly.

STEVE
(softly)
I'm sorry.

ALLISON
(whispering)
How could we...

She looks out the window and starts muttering.

ALLISON (CONT'D)
He knew, he knew, he knew, he knew.

Steve reaches for her hand, but she snaps out of it and pulls
her hand back.

STEVE
I just want to be there for you. Don't you think I feel
terrible too?

ALLISON
(to herself)
I can't believe I let this happen.

STEVE
I'm as much to blame as you are. Maybe more. I love you,
Allison. Nothing has changed that.

Allison stands abruptly.

ALLISON
Don't say that. Don't ever let me hear you say that again.
Not ever.

She walks out.

EXT./INT. STEVE'S APARTMENT - DAY

Steve unlocks the front door of his apartment and goes
through it, then shuts it behind him. A roach scurries
across his path, and he chases it, trying to stomp on it. The
roach leads him into the kitchen, which is infested with
hundreds of roaches.

FADE OUT.

FADE IN:

SUPER: "Boston - One Year Later"

INT. STEVE'S OFFICE - DAY

Steve is smartly dressed in a suit, sitting at a desk. A mid-level associate's office. He's cradling the phone on his shoulder while he shuffles some papers, talking to his girlfriend, LISSA.

STEVE
What about that place we went to last month, that Italian place down by the harbor?

LISSA (V.O.)
That place was filthy.

STEVE
(playfully)
You said you liked the food.

LISSA (V.O.)
I liked the food, but the place was dirty. Remember the rat?

STEVE
Alleged rat.

The door to Steve's office opens and JOHN, another associate, 40s, walks in. Steve motions that he'll just be a minute.

STEVE (CONT'D)
I have to go, honey. Call me later if you think of a place.

LISSA (V.O.)
Is someone there?

STEVE
Yeah, uh-huh.

LISSA (V.O.)
Is it John?

STEVE
Yes, gotta go.

LISSA (V.O.)
Tell him to quit looking at my tits.

STEVE
Yup. Love you. Bye.

He hangs up the phone.

JOHN
(concerned)
Did McDermott find you?

STEVE
No, why?

JOHN
Some of the files from the Rector case are missing.
McDermott needed them for a meeting last night.

STEVE
(under his breath)
Shit.
(thinking)
What does the file log say?

JOHN
Nothing. According to the log, the files should be in the

cabinet.

STEVE
What about Ginny?

JOHN
She says no one has asked to see anything.

STEVE
Shit.

JOHN
I just wanted to alert you. McDermott is on the warpath.
Says Rector is threatening to quit us.

STEVE
Okay. Thanks.

INT. RESTAURANT - NIGHT

The restaurant is filled with couples hunched over candlelit
tables. Steve and Lissa, late 30s, are at a table, eating.

LISSA
What did you say?

STEVE
No one asked. But I have no idea where they are.

LISSA
They'll turn up.

STEVE
They better.

Lissa takes a gulp of wine.

STEVE (CONT'D)
Hey, go easy.

LISSA
It makes me feel good.

STEVE
Just don't start feeling too good.

LISSA
What is that supposed to mean?

STEVE
The other night?

LISSA
(waves him off)
That was nothing. Plus, that guy had it coming. You saw how he was eyeing me.

STEVE
Yeah, well. Please just pace yourself.

LISSA
(leans in and strokes his hand)
Baby, you need to relax. You're too uptight.

Steve smiles at her. Lissa takes another gulp of wine.

INT. STEVE'S CONDO - NIGHT

Steve and Lissa lie on the couch, one at each end, their legs entwined. Lissa has an open shoebox in her lap and is rolling a joint. She is obviously drunk.

LISSA
This ought to relax you a little.

She licks the joint paper and rolls it.

STEVE
Make mine a double. You want to hear something funny?

LISSA
What?

STEVE
I never smoked pot before I met you.

LISSA
Really? When Margo set us up, she warned me you were a drug-addled businessman.

STEVE
Ha! Never touched an illegal drug in my life.

LISSA
The word "illegal" is offensive.

She puts the box on the floor and lights the joint. She inhales and holds, then exhales slowly through her nose. She passes the joint to Steve, who takes a hit.

LISSA (CONT'D)
Drugs are great.

STEVE
(opens his mouth and lets the smoke waft out)
Margo broke up with Ty.

LISSA
Yeah, I know. He was an ass anyway.

STEVE
She needs a rebound. She calls at least once a day, bored.

LISSA
I've been asking around, but nada. I got the last good one.

STEVE
I've been called a lot of things, but never that.

Lissa climbs over his legs to give him a kiss.

INT. STEVE'S OFFICE - DAY

Steve is at his desk when his secretary, GINNY, 50s, hurries in with a plastic cup in her hand. She puts the cup on the desk.

STEVE
What's this?

GINNY
(a little breathless)
Drug test. Everyone has to pee in a cup.

Steve stares at the cup.

GINNY (CONT'D)
And Mr. McDermott wants you in his office.

STEVE
Everyone? It's not random?

GINNY
(unfazed)
Everyone. We're switching insurance companies.

Steve stares again at the cup, mildly panicked.

GINNY (CONT'D)
Did you hear me about Mr. McDermott?

STEVE
(without looking away from the cup)
Yeah, I heard you.

GINNY
(timidly)
Not to press, but Mr. McDermott wanted you fifteen
minutes ago.

Steve stands. Ginny gets a look on her face.

GINNY (CONT'D)
But the thing is, the man from the insurance company is
here now, collecting the...samples.

STEVE
(annoyed)
What are you telling me, Ginny? I have to piss in a cup
right this minute?

Ginny is flustered and Steve backs off, runs his fingers
through his hair.

STEVE (CONT'D)
Okay, listen, sorry. Give me a minute, okay? Tell
McDermott I'm on a conference call and that I'll be in
after the call...

He picks up the plastic cup and lets it fall onto the desk.

STEVE (CONT'D)
...and after the drug test.

GINNY
Yes, sir.

Ginny exits, closing the door behind her. Steve waits until

she's gone and then picks up the phone, dialing furiously.

LISSA (V.O.)
Hello?

STEVE
(desperately)
It's me.

LISSA (V.O.)
What's wrong?

STEVE
(whispering loudly)
They want me to take a fucking drug test!

LISSA (V.O.)
Who?

STEVE
(impatiently)
Work. They just brought in the cup! Jesus.

LISSA
It's legal now.

STEVE
But you can still get fired for it!

LISSA (V.O.)
Calm down. Okay. Let's think.

Beat.

STEVE
Can you please think a little louder, and faster?

LISSA (V.O.)
Jesus, you need to slow down. There's something you can take to mask it.

STEVE
(relieved)
Okay, good. Good. What is it?

LISSA (V.O.)
You'll have to run out and get it at a specialty store.

STEVE
Any chance you can bring it? I don't think I can get out.

LISSA (V.O.)
I'm out in the suburbs.

STEVE
Please!

LISSA (V.O.)
Okay. Stall.

STEVE
The insurance guy is in the building.

LISSA (V.O.)
My advice is to avoid him. Get lost for an hour or so.

STEVE
(worriedly)
I'll try.

He hangs up. Ginny pokes her head in again.

GINNY
Um, well, Mr. McDermott--

STEVE
Fuck McDermott! Tell him--

The door swings open and MR. MCDERMOTT, a well-dressed man in his sixties, stands behind Ginny.

MCDERMOTT
Tell him what?

STEVE
(surprised)
Mr. McDermott! I was just on my way to see you.

MCDERMOTT
Damn it, Steve. I wanted you in my office right when you arrived. Now I have to come down the hall and get you? It looks bad, Steve. I don't mind telling you, it looks bad.

Steve notices an Older Man loitering behind McDermott. This is the insurance representative.

GINNY
(guessing the questions)
That's the man from the insurance company. He's waiting for the...cup.

MCDERMOTT
Christ, Steve. Piss in the cup and get in my office.

McDermott walks back down the hall. Steve gives a defeated look and picks up the cup.

INT. MCDERMOTT'S OFFICE - DAY

Steve enters. McDermott is seated at his desk. John is standing in the corner with a helpless look on his face.

MCDERMOTT
Have a seat.

Steve sits. McDermott is having a hard time finding the
words.

STEVE
What is it, Martin?

MCDERMOTT
(pained)
There's no other way to say it than to just say it.

STEVE
(looking at John)
Say what?

MCDERMOTT
(frankly)
We found the Rector files.

STEVE
Terrific.

MCDERMOTT
We found them stuffed behind the credenza in your office.

STEVE
(taken aback)
Impossible.

MCDERMOTT
The night janitor found them.

STEVE
But I haven't been in the Rector files for weeks.

MCDERMOTT
(holds up his hand to silence Steve)
I'm very disappointed, Steve.

His attention drifts. He looks out the window. Nobody says anything.

MCDERMOTT (CONT'D)
Why don't you take the rest of the day and meet me for breakfast at Gerardi's. Seven o'clock.

STEVE
Yes, sir. Seven.

Steve stands and looks at John, who stands with his arms crossed. John glances away.

EXT./INT. STEVE'S CAR - A LITTLE LATER

Steve pulls out into traffic. He looks at himself in the rearview mirror, deciding.

EXT. STREETS OF BOSTON - CONTINUOUS

Steve navigates traffic, heading for the highway.

HIGHWAY - CONTINUOUS

Steve drives with the flow of traffic toward Providence. Passes a sign that reads: "Welcome to Rhode Island." Steve exits the highway and follows the streets to a sign that reads: "Evergreen Cemetery." He drives through the gates and slowly winds his way through the cemetery. He pulls behind another car he recognizes. He gets out and shields his eyes, spotting someone in the distance. As he draws near, he sees it is Mrs. Meade, standing over Bill's grave. She turns as Steve approaches and gives a wan smile.

MRS. MEADE
What a terrific surprise.

She hugs Steve.

STEVE
It's nice to see you again, Mrs. Meade. I've been meaning to call on you...

MRS. MEADE
Oh, that's quite all right. Boston must be keeping you busy.

Steve looks sadly at the grave. Mrs. Meade's eyes follow. They stand in silence for a moment.

STEVE
I miss him all the time.

MRS. MEADE
Me too. One minute you think you're doing fine, and then some small thing...

She breaks down a little. Steve hugs her until she can compose herself.

STEVE
How is Mr. Meade?

MRS. MEADE
(shaking her head)
Not well. He's gone downhill dramatically this last year.

STEVE
(nods)
I'm curious about something.

MRS. MEADE
Yes?

STEVE
What ever happened with the charity? Did it get going?
I never really heard what kind of charity it was.

MRS. MEADE
(a little ashamed)
No, it never did. After the funeral we didn't have the
money to go through with it. Bill's insurance company
wouldn't pay because of how he...because of the
circumstances. And he was just getting started at the firm,
really, so there wasn't a lot of savings. Allison was entitled
to what was there.

STEVE
Have you seen her?

MRS. MEADE
(gives a concerned look and shakes her head)
I think she was the most disappointed about the charity.
She put all her energy into it. Was something for
underprivileged children. You know they tried to have
children.

STEVE
It's the thought, really. It's important to have generous
thoughts.

MRS. MEADE
Still, I think it would've made a difference if we could've
pulled it off.

STEVE
(off-handedly)
And what ever happened to Triny?

MRS. MEADE
(wrinkling her nose)
He disappeared early on. Allison was annoyed, but I think
he realized there was nothing he could do.

They both glance down at the grave.

EXT. CEMETERY - LATER

Steve pulls out of the cemetery and into traffic.

EXT. STREETS OF BOSTON - DUSK

Steve switches on his headlights as the sun disappears. He
comes to an intersection and starts to turn left when a car
screams out of nowhere and broadsides him. Pedestrians
on the street scatter as Steve's car strikes a telephone pole,
and the other car speeds away.

INT. STEVE'S CAR - CONTINUOUS

Steve is unconscious in the driver's seat while the horn
BLARES.

PEDESTRIAN #1 (O.S.)
Someone call 9-1-1.

INT. HOSPITAL ROOM - NIGHT

Steve is sedated. He is unconscious and his breathing is
labored. Lissa stands over him, looking worried and
concerned. A NURSE enters.

NURSE
Are you his wife?

LISSA
Girlfriend. Is he going to be okay?

NURSE
He's pretty banged up. Lucky he was wearing his seatbelt.

LISSA
Where are the police? Did they find out who did this?

NURSE
I'm sorry, honey. I don't know anything about that.
Visiting hours are over in a few minutes. You'll have to
leave then.

Lissa nods. She reaches down and touches Steve's hand.
The Nurse leaves, and Lissa studies her own reflection in
the window.

INT. BAR BATHROOM - NIGHT

Triny is staring in a mirror at a bruise on the side of his
head. He examines it closely, touching it and wincing.
Someone POUNDS on the locked door, but Triny ignores
it.

INT. HOSPITAL ROOM - DAY

Steve is conscious. The DOCTOR, a woman in her forties,
and a Male Nurse are tending to Steve. The Doctor is
making notes in Steve's chart while the nurse checks
Steve's vitals. Lissa enters and Steve smiles.

LISSA
(to Doctor)

How's the patient?

DOCTOR
He'll be a little sore, but he can go home.

LISSA
(flatly)
Sure you don't want to keep him?

STEVE
Hey.

The Male Nurse smiles and leaves.

DOCTOR
Your cuts are superficial, but you've got some deep bone
bruises that are gonna take a while to heal. So pain
management with these...

She shakes a pill bottle.

DOCTOR (CONT'D)
...and I can prescribe more if need be.

STEVE
I'm sure there'll be a need.

LISSA
Man up.

DOCTOR
(smiles)
They'll have some paperwork for you when you checkout.
Keep wearing a seatbelt.

Steve gives a half-smile. The Doctor exits.

LISSA
Lucky me, I get to play chauffeur.

STEVE
It's an easy gig. I can't go far.

LISSA
This was at the front counter.

She hands Steve his cell phone. Steve turns the phone on
and checks his messages.

STEVE
(groaning)
Oh man.

LISSA
What?

STEVE
I missed my breakfast with McDermott.

LISSA
He'll understand.

Steve gives her a look that says he doubts it. A HOSPITAL
ADMINISTRATOR, a woman in her fifties, enters with a
worried look.

LISSA (CONT'D)
Let me guess. You're keeping him?

HOSPITAL ADMINISTRATOR
(forces a smile)
There's a problem with the patient's insurance.

INT. LISSA'S CAR - LATER

Lissa is driving as Steve leans back in the passenger seat gingerly.

STEVE
(moaning)
Nine-thousand dollars. That's all my savings.

LISSA
I'm sure it can be straightened out with the insurance company. You'll get your money back.

STEVE
I better.

LISSA
First thing in the morning. You just need to rest.

INT. STEVE'S CONDO - LATER

Steve is splayed out on the couch while the TV PLAYS SOFTLY in the background. Lissa is in a chair opposite, alternately looking at Steve, the TV, and her cell phone. Her phone BUZZES, and when she sees the number, she frowns and declines the call. Steve MOANS.

LISSA
What is it?

STEVE
Pain shooting through my leg.

Lissa reaches for the bottle of pain pills. She opens the bottle and shakes out two.

LISSA
Here. You need these.

Steve swallows the pills and takes a sip of water from a
glass on the coffee table.

LISSA (CONT'D)
That should hold you for a few hours. I have to go pick up
Carol. Her car is in the shop.

STEVE
(sighs)
How long will you be gone?

LISSA
I don't know. A couple of hours. I need to use your
computer to print the directions.

STEVE
Why don't you use the GPS on your phone?

LISSA
I can't stand that thing. It always tells you to turn a second
too late.

Steve laughs. Lissa goes to Steve's laptop and begins
typing.

LISSA (CONT'D)
How do you make this thing print?

STEVE
(matter-of-factly)
Click the Print icon.

LISSA
I did.

She clicks it again.

STEVE
Is the printer on? It's been shutting itself off lately.

LISSA
Nope.

She presses a button on the printer and it WHIRS to life and begins printing. The directions print out twice.

STEVE
Sounds like you're wasting paper again.

Lissa takes one of the sheets of paper and folds a paper airplane. She throws it at Steve, but it sails around the room and disappears.

LISSA
Nope.

She gets up from the computer.

STEVE
Don't be gone long. I may need you.

LISSA
(absently)
Do you want me to roll you a couple of joints?

STEVE
When you get back.

Lissa kisses him on the forehead, then on the lips. She gathers her purse and leaves.

INT. STEVE'S CONDO - LATER THAT NIGHT

Steve is on the couch, asleep. He is sweating profusely. He tosses and turns, startling himself awake. His eyes adjust to the darkened condo. The only light visible is the screen saver on his computer. He gets up slowly and limps gingerly over to the kitchen sink for a glass of water, which he gulps down, wiping the sweat from his forehead. A SWOOSHING SOUND indicates that he has a new e-mail, and Steve makes his way to the desk and sits. He opens his inbox and sees an e-mail from Lissa. He wrinkles his nose, wondering. He clicks on the e-mail, and the screen goes black except for the words "Click here." Steve clicks and Triny's smiling face fills the screen, startling Steve.

TRINY (O.S.)
That's right, old buddy.

The video pulls back a little to reveal Triny sitting in a chair in the middle of a hotel room.

TRINY (O.S.) (CONT'D)
Bet you thought you wouldn't see old Triny again, eh? Bet you thought that chapter was over. Well, here we are.

Steve flinches.

TRINY (O.S.) (CONT'D)
I thought it was over between me and you. And then I remembered something Bill said to me that first night, when he came to me about arranging a hit on his best friend for sleeping with his wife.

Steve reacts.

TRINY (O.S.) (CONT'D)
That's right. (grins) Bill was so mad he wanted to put you
down. How does that feel? Not good, I'm guessing.

Triny lights a cigarette and exhales smoke.

TRINY (O.S.) (CONT'D)
Lucky for you, Bill was too decent. Couldn't go through
with it. But I remember what he said that night: He said he
wished that you could feel the sort of loss he felt when he
found out about you and Allison.

He points to his head with cigarette in hand.

TRINY (O.S.) (CONT'D)
So that got me thinking. How could I help Bill with his last
wish? How could Steve learn about loss?

He draws on the cigarette again, exhales.

TRINY (O.S.) (CONT'D)
I'll admit I lost my nerve a little when I met you. I can see
why Bill backed off. I actually felt sorry for you and for
Allison. I changed my mind, like Bill. But old Triny
doesn't give up easy. So I decided to go for the money.

He draws on the cigarette again, exhales.

TRINY (O.S.) (CONT'D)
I hear what you're thinking. "What money?" Those
insurance assholes fucked the whole thing into a cocked
hat. It was a real bummer. But I always know how to make
myself feel better.

The video pulls back and we see Lissa on her knees, giving
Triny head. Steve's eyes widen in disbelief.

TRINY (O.S.) (CONT'D)
Surprise! Now you know how Bill felt, at least a little.
(to Lissa)
Say hi to Steve, baby.

Lissa looks up with a goofy grin and different hairstyle, her chin shiny with spit. She is clearly high.

LISSA (O.S.)
Who's Steve?

TRINY
Nobody, baby. He's nobody.

Steve looks at the date in the corner of the video, which reads "January." The date in the corner of the computer says "September."

The video goes black and the "Click here" screen reappears. Steve clicks it again, and a picture of a hot-air balloon sailing through a blue sky filled with daisies appears.

INT. STEVE'S CONDO - DAY

Steve is dressed for work, his shoulder in a sling. There's a KNOCK on the door, and he moves slowly to answer it. He opens the door and finds MARGO, a woman in her thirties, on the step.

MARGO
Taxi's here.

STEVE
(smiles weakly)
Sorry to have to ask.

MARGO
It's on my way. You sure you should be going back to
work?

STEVE
I'm on thin ice as it is.

INT. MARGO'S CAR - MOMENTS LATER

Margo and Steve ride down the street.

MARGO
Sounds like you're lucky to be alive.

STEVE
Shit. Realized I left my wallet at the hospital. Mind?

MARGO
Downtown?

STEVE
No, the outpatient place, in Waltham.

MARGO
(kidding)
Great, now I'll be late and we'll both be on thin ice.

EXT. LARGE OFFICE BUILDING - MINUTES LATER

Margo slows the car in front of an abandoned storefront.

MARGO
This can't be it.

Steve looks around, confused.

MARGO (CONT'D)
Maybe this is an old address.

She checks her phone, while Steve continues to stare out the window.

MARGO (CONT'D)
Hmm.

STEVE
We got fries there right after.

He points out the window at the McDonald's down the block from the empty storefront.

MARGO
I'll call Lissa.

Steve watches Margo as she dials and puts the phone to her ear. She screws up her face when she hears the out-of-service message.

MARGO (CONT'D)
She get a new number?

STEVE
(staring at the empty storefront)
What made you hook us up?

MARGO
(gives a look)
Are you in a fight? Is that why she changed her number?

Steve doesn't laugh, and Margo realizes he's really asking.

MARGO (CONT'D)
You seemed to hit it off that night you met, at the Middle

East.

Steve nods.

MARGO (CONT'D)
Plus, I didn't hook you up. She asked me to put in a good word. What happened?

STEVE
Nothing. Just all confused from the accident. And now I'm late to work.

INT. MARGO'S CAR - MOMENTS LATER

Margo drives while Steve talks on the phone.

STEVE
(into the phone)
I just need to cancel the check. (beat) Already?

EXT. STEVE'S OFFICE BUILDING - MOMENTS LATER

Steve exits Margo's car gingerly.

MARGO
Need a ride home?

STEVE
I can get someone to drop me, thanks.

MARGO
Call if you need me. Make up with Lissa and you won't.

She smiles as she pulls away.

INT. STEVE'S OFFICE BUILDING - ELEVATOR - CONTINUOUS

Steve presses the button for his floor and then notices that the plastic sign with his company's name is missing. He touches the sticky part where the sign was.

HALLWAY - CONTINUOUS

Steve walks down the hall and slows as he reaches the door, which is scraped up where the company sign was. He pushes open the door.

RECEPTION AREA - CONTINUOUS

All the furniture is there, but the office is deserted. He walks zombie-like through the office. He opens a file cabinet and pulls out a random file, noticing that the tab is blank. So are the pages in the file. In all the files. He pulls at a leaf on the plant atop the file cabinet, and the plant bends toward him. Plastic.

STEVE'S OFFICE - CONTINUOUS

He sits in his chair and takes in the empty office. He looks through his desk drawers. Empty. He picks up the phone. No dial tone. He replaces the receiver slowly and sits back, stunned.

INT. STEVE'S CONDO - NIGHT

Steve sits across from Margo at the kitchen table.

MARGO
How many pain pills did you pop?

STEVE
Knew you wouldn't believe me.

He rattles the pill bottle.

STEVE (CONT'D)
These are shit. Which is why I switched to this.

He lifts his glass of whiskey.

MARGO
You shouldn't mix. That's how Jim Morrison died.

Steve rolls the pill bottle across the table to Margo.

STEVE
They're yours.

Margo scoops up the pill bottle and rolls it in her palms.

MARGO
(flatly)
So your job wasn't real and the hospital was staged and now Lissa is missing. Who do we call first? The cops or the news?

STEVE
Neither will believe me.

MARGO
Yeah.

STEVE
What about my office? The place was cleaned out.

MARGO
We'll probably read about the bankruptcy in the Globe.

STEVE
Even if true, why disappear everything?

MARGO
Before a bankruptcy judge changes the locks, is why.

Steve gives a skeptical look.

MARGO (CONT'D)
No hint of anything from anyone else who worked there?

STEVE
Nada. We were getting a new insurance policy one day and after a long weekend the entire enterprise folds.

MARGO
Call your boss?

STEVE
Voicemail.

MARGO
Your secretary?

STEVE
Same. Everyone goes right to voicemail. Except the mailroom guy. His phone is disconnected.

MARGO
Did you try Lissa again?

Steve takes a sip of his whiskey, squinting at Margo.

MARGO (CONT'D)
What?

STEVE
Nothing.

MARGO
What?

STEVE
Someone e-mailed me a video.

MARGO
Yeah?

STEVE
Of Lissa.

MARGO
Porn?

STEVE
(surprised)
Why do you ask that?

MARGO
She once mentioned that she'd done some things she
wasn't proud of. Assumed it was porn.

STEVE
This wasn't that. Not exactly.

MARGO
What, then?

STEVE
You're gonna need a drink.

INT. STEVE'S CONDO - KITCHEN - LATER

Steve and Margo are sitting in silence, wasted.

STEVE
You don't believe me?

MARGO
I think I do. It's a lot to ask, though.

STEVE
I know.

MARGO
Can I crash on your couch? I shouldn't drive.

STEVE
I'll take the couch.

INT. STEVE'S CONDO - FRONT ROOM - LATER

Steve is on the couch, eyes closed in restless sleep.

BEGIN FLASHBACK:

STEVE (V.O.)
(matter-of-factly)
Click the Print icon.

LISSA (V.O.)
I did.

STEVE (V.O.)
Is the printer on? It's been shutting itself off lately.

LISSA (V.O.)
Nope.

STEVE (V.O.)
Sounds like you're wasting paper again.

END FLASHBACK.

Steve startles awake and lifts himself off the couch. He
turns on a light and searches for the paper airplane. After a
moment he finds it wedged between the wall and his stereo
console. He unfolds the paper airplane and sees the
directions Lissa printed. Steve rummages through Margo's
purse and lifts her keys.

INT. MARGO'S CAR - NIGHT

Steve programs the address from the directions into the
GPS.

EXT. STREETS OF BOSTON - CONTINUOUS

Steve drives Margo's car in the direction of the address,
following the prompts from the GPS.

EXT. BEACON HILL BROWNSTONE – CONTINUOUS

Steve pulls up in front of the brownstone and looks it over.
He shuts off the car. He gets out and knocks on the door of
the stately brownstone. Nothing. He knocks again, and this
time the door opens slightly to reveal a woman in her
thirties, CAROL.

STEVE
I'm very sorry to disturb you, but I'm looking for Lissa.

CAROL
(shielding herself behind the door)
You've got the wrong address.

She begins to shut the door, but Steve blocks it with his foot, startling her.

CAROL (CONT'D)
I have an alarm button that summons the police.

STEVE
No, wait! If I step back, will you hear me out?

Carol nods and Steve retreats. He fishes out his phone and scrolls through his pictures. He shows Carol a photo of him and Lissa. Carol's eyes betray that she knows Lissa.

STEVE (CONT'D)
Maybe you know her real name.

Carol gives him a look.

STEVE (CONT'D)
Please.

EXT. SUBURBAN HOME - EARLY MORNING

Steve and Margo sit in a parked car down the street from the house and its manicured lawn. Both are drinking coffee.

MARGO
Can I assume this is rock bottom?

Steve concentrates on the house, his eyes searching.

MARGO (CONT'D)
If you knocked on my door in the middle of the night, I would've said anything to get you to leave too.

The street is eerily quiet. The garage door of the house

they're parked in front of opens silently and a shiny new car backs out slowly. The Driver gives a neighborhood-watch stare at Margo and Steve as he drives away.

MARGO (CONT'D)
Maybe we should move to another--

STEVE
Look.

The front door of the house they've been watching opens, and two small children spill out, Lissa in tow. She locks the front door and loads the kids into the SUV parked in the driveway.

MARGO
No way.

The SUV backs out and Margo follows at a distance. Steve is stunned into silence, wearing a mask of anger.

SCHOOL - CONTINUOUS

Lissa pulls into the circle in front and lets her kids out. They disappear into the sea of children waiting for school to start.

COFFEE-HOUSE - CONTINUOUS

Lissa parks and runs inside.

STEVE
(angrily)
Bitch!

He throws open his car door and it smacks the car next to him, startling the WOMAN in the driver's seat, who is nursing a baby.

WOMAN
Hey!

The baby starts CRYING.

STEVE
Oh, I'm really sorry. I--

WOMAN
Did you scratch my door?

STEVE
It looks okay. I'm sorry.

The Woman rolls up her window. Steve turns his attention
to the coffee-house. Through the glass, he sees Lissa
waiting for her coffee.

MARGO
You wait here.

STEVE
I'm coming in.

MARGO
If you go in, you'll just start shouting. You want to find out
what's going on? Wait here.

Steve knows she's right but doesn't like it.

Margo exits the car, and Steve watches as she enters the
coffee-house. Lissa sees her and gets a panicked look.
Steve watches the exchange between Margo and Lissa. The
conversation is strained, and at some point Margo points
angrily at Steve and they both turn in his direction. Lissa

looks fearful but then sorry as she grabs her coffee from the counter and flees.

Margo exits the coffee-house, shaking her head. She gets back into the car.

MARGO (CONT'D)
Jesus.

STEVE
What?

MARGO
She's terrified.

STEVE
Of me?

MARGO
(shaking her head)
Triny. He put her up to it.

STEVE
Up to what? Ruining my life?

Margo gives him a long look.

STEVE (CONT'D)
But why?

MARGO
I asked the same question. She said she didn't know.

STEVE
Wait, wait, wait. Back up. She was just pretending to date me?

MARGO
She said it started that way, but then she actually had
feelings.

STEVE
Oh, Christ.

MARGO
She tried to walk away, but Triny has something on her.
Said he'd tell her husband.

Steve is overwhelmed and just stares out the window.
Margo starts the car.

EXT./INT. - STEVE'S RENTAL CAR - DAY

Steve zooms along I-95 South. He exits at Providence and
navigates the streets.

EXT. MEADE RESIDENCE - CONTINUOUS

Mrs. Meade opens the door and is surprised to find Steve.

STEVE
I should've called.

MRS. MEADE
What's wrong, dear?

INT. MEADE RESIDENCE - A LITTLE LATER

Steve is sitting at the kitchen table with Mr. and Mrs.
Meade, drinking coffee.

MRS. MEADE
You're lucky you weren't killed.

STEVE
I keep looking at it that way.

MR. MEADE
Crazy Boston drivers.

STEVE
Have you seen Allison?

MRS. MEADE
Not much. I saw her once at the farmers' market. I don't
want her to feel like she has to worry about us.

Mr. Meade reaches for the coffee-pot and tries to pour
himself more, but his hand shakes too badly. Mrs. Meade
takes it and pours.

MRS. MEADE (CONT'D)
(to Steve)
Another?

STEVE
Sure, thanks.

Mrs. Meade pours him another cup.

STEVE (CONT'D)
I saw Triny in Boston.

MRS. MEADE
Oh?

STEVE
Just in passing.

MRS. MEADE
If you see him again, please give him our regards.

MR. MEADE
(bluntly)
He never went to school with Bill.

STEVE
What's that?

MRS. MEADE
(gently)
He didn't, dear. He said so.

Mr. Meade stares in the middle distance. He's already forgotten.

STEVE
Why was he talking about Bill in school? Law school?

MRS. MEADE
(dismissively)
Oh, once when Triny was here, I had to take a phone call, and when I came back to the table, Henry thought Triny said he went to high school with Bill.

She gives Steve a private look that says Mr. Meade was just confused.

STEVE
I remember Triny said he knew Bill from work.

MRS. MEADE
I'm sure that's right.

STEVE
(sips his coffee, remembering something)

Bill did say he ran into someone from the old days. Charlie something?

MRS. MEADE
Martens, I think. He told me, but I couldn't place him.

STEVE
That's it. Charlie Martens.

EXT. MEADE RESIDENCE - LATER

Mrs. Meade watches Steve drive away.

EXT. BILL AND ALLISON'S HOUSE - A LITTLE LATER

Steve watches from down the street. Allison eventually pulls into the driveway. She gets out and retrieves her groceries from the trunk, before disappearing inside the house.

INT. BAR AZTECA - NIGHT

Steve is at the bar. JASON, 30s, pours him another beer.

JASON
That's a helluva tale.

He passes the beer to Steve.

STEVE
Wish it were only that.

JASON
Chicks.

Steve takes a drink of the beer.

JASON (CONT'D)
Speaking of. You still friends with Margo?

Steve nods.

JASON (CONT'D)
Did you tell her I thought she was a babe?

STEVE
No, but I told you she was a lesbian.

JASON
Doesn't mean she's not a babe. What's her thing again?

STEVE
Girls.

JASON
No, her work.

STEVE
Real estate. She sold me my condo.

JASON
Right, right. And where's she from?

STEVE
Florida.

He takes another drink.

STEVE (CONT'D)
You remember a guy from school, Charlie Martens?

Jason thinks.

JASON
Don't think so.

STEVE
Bill knew him.

JASON
(wistfully)
I heard about Bill too late to pay my respects. Too sad,
man.

STEVE
Yeah. (beat) He mentioned this kid Martens to me last time
I saw him. Said there was a little brother, too.

JASON
Why was he bringing up those days?

Steve shrugs.

JASON (CONT'D)
(SNAPS his fingers)
That luscious single mom over on Lowell Avenue had a
kid named Charlie. No other kids, though. But her last
name was Dale, I think. Natalie Dale.

Steve gives him a quizzical look.

JASON (CONT'D)
(sheepishly)
Some things you never forget.

INT. STEVE'S CONDO - NIGHT

Steve is resting on the couch, while Margo is at the kitchen
table on a laptop.

STEVE
Toss my pills, will you?

Margo reaches for the pill bottle, but the cap isn't on tight and they spill across the table. She corrals the pills back into the bottle.

MARGO
These pills are blank.

STEVE
Useless, more like.

MARGO
No, I mean they're not stamped with the identifying code that tells what they are. These look like aspirin.

Steve gets up awkwardly and ambles to the kitchen table.

STEVE
(sarcastically)
Why not? Makes sense that a fake doctor couldn't prescribe real painkillers.

Margo gives him a look.

STEVE (CONT'D)
(motioning at the laptop)
Anything?

MARGO
The county assessor's database says Natalie Dale still lives on Lowell Avenue. (typing) And Google says Charlie Martens committed suicide after serving a tour in Iraq.

STEVE
Is there a picture?

MARGO
(typing)
Here.

She shows Steve the screen, a picture of a soldier in full
military dress.

MARGO (CONT'D)
Recognize him?

STEVE
(studying the photo)
No.

Margo flips the laptop back to her and types.

MARGO
No obituary.

STEVE
Wonder why.

MARGO
Suicides sometimes don't.

She continues to type.

MARGO (CONT'D)
Okay, here. His military bio.
(reading)
"Mother: Natalie. Brother...Jeffrey."

STEVE
(under his breath)
Jeffrey Martens.

MARGO
Or Jeffrey Dale.

STEVE
Is there an address for either name in Providence?

Margo types.

MARGO
Nothing.
(types)
Or Boston. Let me try the MLS database.
(types)
There's a Geoffrey Dale in Milton. But "Geoff" is with a
G.
(types)
And there's a J.M. Dale in Allston.

STEVE
Could be.

MARGO
Condo. But it's been repossessed.

STEVE
Can you get the key?

INT. J.M. DALE'S CONDO - NIGHT

Steve and Margo enter the darkened condo. Margo flips
the light switch, but nothing. They both take out their cell
phones and turn on flashlights. The condo still has some
furniture but looks like someone is half moved in, or out.

MARGO
I'll check the kitchen for any photos on the fridge.

STEVE
Done this before?

Margo moves into the kitchen. Steve shines his light over
the leather couch, then the wires on the wall where the TV
used to hang. Margo filters back into the living room.

MARGO
Nada.

STEVE
Dead end maybe.

MARGO
With repos they usually surprise the owner so they can't
steal the stove. But this place looks a little dismantled.

They both turn in the direction of the front door at the
SOUND OF SOMEONE PICKING THE LOCK. Margo
kills her flashlight and Steve does too. They stand in the
pitch dark. The door opens and a figure quietly enters. The
figure moves like he knows the layout. Margo shines her
light on Triny, who is startled.

MARGO (CONT'D)
Surprise.

Triny turns to bolt, but Steve blocks the door and flashes
on his light.

STEVE
Gotcha, asshole.

TRINY
(smirking)
It's Nancy Drew.

STEVE
Real funny. Let's call the cops and see if they laugh too.

TRINY
You don't want to do that.

Steve lunges at Triny and they both hit the floor, but because Steve's arm is still in a sling, it's not much of a fight.

MARGO
Enough!

STEVE
I want my money!

Triny stands and dusts himself off. Steve uses the furniture to stand.

TRINY
I don't know anything about any money.

STEVE
Oh? What about my job? And Lissa? I enjoyed your little video.

TRINY
Hey, that was just for personal use.

Steve grabs up a small lamp and throws it at Triny's head, but he misses.

MARGO
Jesus! Can we get calm for a minute?
(to Triny)
Tell us what's going on.

TRINY
Why should I?

MARGO
Breaking and entering, for starters. And I'll bet you've done more interesting things than that.

TRINY
This is my place. You're the one trespassing.

MARGO
(pointedly)
Is it?

TRINY
(considers)
Yeah, okay. Whatever. I told you...
(looks at Steve)
...that Bill came to me. Wanted to whack you for sleeping with his wife. But then he backed out. Didn't come up with the money.

MARGO
How did he know to come to you?

TRINY
Friend of a friend of a friend.

STEVE
He mentioned Charlie to me the day he died.

TRINY
(angrily)
Don't fucking say his name like you were friends. I know what you two pussies did to him when you were kids.

MARGO
(to Steve)
What did you do?

STEVE
Nothing.

TRINY
Nothing? Nothing?! How about throwing a cup of warm
piss on him? And that's the only example I can give you in
mixed company. It was because of you and people like you
that he dropped out and joined the service.

MARGO
Okay, calm down. That was a long time ago.

TRINY
(gives a calm, creepy grin)
Bill didn't remember Charlie either, but I brought it up. Ma
sent me to private school rather than to you public school
animals. Think it spooked him, hearing Charlie's name.
Might be why he backed off. You should thank me for
saving your life.

STEVE
(sarcastic)
Thanks.

MARGO
Why did you show up at the funeral?

TRINY
(cocky)
Decided to make a play for the money with the bogus
charity angle. Fucking insurance company ruined that. This
country, am I right?

STEVE
But you knew Lissa.

TRINY
A real sweetheart. Could suck a golf ball through a--

MARGO
Charming. She said you forced her to do that. Said you
hired her to play Steve's girlfriend, but then it turned into
something else.

STEVE
Sounds like we got a pimp here.

MARGO
Or a white slaver.

TRINY
Oh, no, no, no. Not me. You've got the wrong man.

STEVE
Then who?

TRINY
I can't tell you that.

MARGO
You can. And will.

TRINY
No, I mean I literally don't know his name. After the
funeral a guy called me up and offered me a pot of money
to help get Sheila, I mean Lissa, close to you.

STEVE
Why?

TRINY
Didn't say, didn't ask. Money is money, right?

MARGO
How much money?

TRINY
I'm too modest to say.

Steve dials a number on his cell phone.

911 OPERATOR (O.S.)
9-1-1. What's your emergency?

STEVE
(into phone)
I think I heard shots fired at 15 Melvin Avenue.

He hangs up.

MARGO
What the…

Triny tries to flee, but Steve moves in front of him.

STEVE
Who hired you?

SIRENS sound in the distance. Triny knows he has to act fast.

TRINY
Meet me at Newtonville Books tomorrow at noon, and I'll take you to him.

MARGO
You don't strike me as much of a reader.

TRINY
My therapist is in the same building.

Sirens GET LOUDER. Steve steps aside and Triny bolts.

MARGO
I'll handle the cops.

INT. NEWTONVILLE BOOKS - DAY

Steve and Margo idly browse the store. A BOOKSELLER
approaches.

BOOKSELLER
Can I help you find anything?

MARGO
We're just looking, thanks.

The Bookseller walks away.

STEVE
He's late.

MARGO
He said his therapist was in the building.

INT. BUILDING FOYER - A MOMENT LATER

Steve and Margo scan the directory, but it's all doctors and
they don't find a clue.

MARGO
Start knocking on doors?

Steve stares angrily at the directory.

INT. TRINY'S CONDO - LATER

Margo opens the door and enters, Steve following. Triny appears to be asleep in the chair.

MARGO
What the...

STEVE
(yelling)
Hey!

He gives Margo a look when Triny doesn't respond. Margo approaches slowly, and they both notice the blood oozing from Triny's temple, the gun in his lap.

MARGO
My God.

Steve sees a soft glow under the couch. He gets on his knees and fishes out a cell phone.

MARGO (CONT'D)
Check the last call he made.

STEVE
(looking at phone)
Fifteen minutes ago.

MARGO
Call it.

Steve does, and as it rings, a cell phone RING TONE SOUNDS. Steve and Margo sweep the darkness for the sound, and as they do, a MAN IN HIS THIRTIES steps out of the shadows. Margo SHRIEKS and Steve backs away cautiously. The Man puts up his hands.

MAN
I'm unarmed.

MARGO
Jesus. What are you doing here?

STEVE
He killed Triny.

MAN
(shaking his head)
I got here a few minutes before you. Found him like that.

STEVE
But you knew him.

MAN
I did.

MARGO
And you know what he's been up to.

MAN
Yes.

STEVE
You're a part of it.

MAN
In a way.

MARGO
In what way?

The Man smiles. He can't say.

STEVE
Why me?

MAN
(shrugs)
Dunno.

MARGO
Know why he's got a bullet in his head?

MAN
(looks at Triny)
Looks like suicide.

MARGO
Looks that way, but if it's not, whoever you're working
with or for might have you in mind. Two loose ends at
once.

MAN
Nice try.

MARGO
That confident about your employer?

The Man grins.

STEVE
Tell us who hired you.

MAN
I'm not going to do that, no.

STEVE
That's okay. Triny gave us all we needed to go to the cops.
That's why you killed him.

MAN
(laughs)
Again, I didn't kill him. And if Triny had given up my
employer, you'd know the cops would be of little use.

MARGO
Maybe Triny was gonna roll over on you.

MAN
We can't know that for sure.

MARGO
But you were his handler.

MAN
(sighs, glances around)
I've got to move on.

He takes out a gun, but it's not threatening.

MARGO
Thought you were unarmed.

MAN
Surprise! Wait a minute or two after I leave, please.

STEVE
We'll see you again.

MAN
Maybe.

The Man exits.

MARGO
Maybe there's a clue to what Triny was going to tell us in
his phone.

Steve hands her Triny's phone.

MARGO (CONT'D)
It's dead. I'll charge it at home and see what I can find.

INT. STEVE'S CONDO - NIGHT

Steve is on the couch, staring mindlessly at the muted TV.
His cell phone RINGS and he sees it's Margo.

STEVE
Anything?

MARGO
(breathlessly)
I got him! You have to meet me now.

STEVE
(jolts upright)
Who is it?

MARGO
I'm on my way. We can't let him slip away. Meet me at 25
Rosewood Street. Found the address in Triny's phone.

STEVE
Wait! Slow down.

MARGO
It all makes sense now. Lissa said something in the coffee
shop that day I couldn't figure out, but now I get it.

STEVE
What? What?

MARGO
Just meet me!

Hangs up.

STEVE
Hello? Margo? Damn it!

EXT. 25 ROSEWOOD STREET - LATER

A yellow cab rolls up to a darkened warehouse, and Steve gets out. He looks around tentatively as the cab drives away. He turns in the direction of a LOUD, GRINDING NOISE as the front door slides open and Margo saunters out.

MARGO
He's on his way.

STEVE
Who?

MARGO
I don't want to ruin the surprise. Follow me.

INT. WAREHOUSE - CONTINUOUS

Steve follows Margo through the warehouse, piled high with boxes, and emerges in a showroom outfitted with hundreds of hanging light fixtures. Margo begins pulling the string on each fixture, illuminating the space. The various fixtures cast shadows everywhere.

There's a KNOCK on the showroom door.

MARGO
(yelling)
Yeah.

CHAD, 30s, steps through the door wearing a confused

look.

MARGO (CONT'D)
You Chad?

CHAD
Yeah.

STEVE
Who is Chad?

CHAD
My boss said you found my phone.

MARGO
Yup.

She takes out Triny's phone and holds it up.

CHAD
(relieved)
That's so cool. I set it down for a second and it was gone.

MARGO
What's the reward?

Chad gives a look.

MARGO (CONT'D)
Just kidding. Here you go.

She tosses the phone to Chad, who catches it with two hands.

STEVE
Can you tell me--

CHAD
This isn't my phone.

Margo whips out a pistol and aims it at Chad. Chad raises
his hands reflexively, dropping the phone.

CHAD (CONT'D)
Whoa!

MARGO
Down! Down! Get down!

She motions with the gun for him to get on his knees. Chad
falls slowly to the floor.

STEVE
(panicked)
What's going on?

MARGO
This guy killed Bill. Good as did it.

CHAD
Who is Bill? I don't know who that is!

MARGO
Fucking liar!

She kicks an empty box at Chad, and it bounces off his
chest.

MARGO (CONT'D)
(to Steve)
This guy fucked up your life!

STEVE
(confused)

What did Lissa say in the coffee shop?

MARGO
(not listening)
He crashed into your car and took your money...

STEVE
I thought that was Triny!

MARGO
(still not listening)
Thinks he can get away with destroying people's lives...

CHAD
Not me! No!

MARGO
(to Steve)
Guys like this need extinction.

She tries to hand the gun to Steve, but he won't take it, backs away.

MARGO (CONT'D)
Shoot this fucker!

STEVE
Can we just slow down a second?

MARGO
If you won't shoot him, I will.
(to Chad)
You're done.

She clasps the gun with both hands and gets in a stance. She PULLS THE TRIGGER. Chad YELLS OUT, then realizes Margo missed. Chad gets to his feet and tries to run away.

Margo fires again and a LOUD CLANK is heard, then HISSING. The three of them look in the direction of the noise just as the building EXPLODES.

Super: "Three Weeks Later"

INT. BOSTON GENERAL HOSPITAL - DAY

Steve opens his eyes to find a DOCTOR, 50s, staring down at him.

DOCTOR
There he is.

Steve is slowly aware of his surroundings, hears the rhythmic beeping of machines.

DOCTOR (CONT'D)
Breathe easily. That's it. You've been in a medically induced coma for a few weeks. We're still in the weeds a bit, but you're strong enough now to assist us in getting you back to a hundred percent.

Steve nods through the fog.

INT. BOSTON GENERAL HOSPITAL - NEXT DAY

Steve is sitting up in bed sucking on ice chips when DETECTIVE HATCH, an extremely tanned man in his fifties, enters.

HATCH
You don't look too bad, considering.

Steve gives a confused look.

HATCH (CONT'D)
I'm Detective Hatch. Phoenix homicide.

STEVE
Phoenix, Arizona?

HATCH
Yessir. My wife told me not to pack the cowboy hat, so I didn't.

STEVE
Do you mind if I ask for ID?

HATCH
Not at all.

He reaches into his jacket pocket and produces his ID, which he carefully places in Steve's lap. Steve reaches for it tentatively and inspects it while Hatch talks.

HATCH (CONT'D)
Doc tell you you're lucky to be alive?

Steve nods.

HATCH (CONT'D)
You shoot a gas main like that and nothing good happens. Steve passes back the ID, and Hatch slips it into his jacket pocket.

STEVE
Why are you here?

HATCH
Fair question. You want the short answer or the long answer?

Steve shrugs.

HATCH (CONT'D)
Your friend, Margo? We know her in Phoenix as Holly.

STEVE
She said she was from Boca Raton.

HATCH
She is. Was. Grew up there. And all of this is about her
childhood friend who knew the only body ID'd so far from
this little dance at the warehouse.

STEVE
(remembering)
Chad?

HATCH
Chad. He was a bartender in Boca Raton. Had one of those
apartment-above-the-bar arrangements. You know. Handy.

He gives a look.

HATCH (CONT'D)
Anyway, our man Chad and Holly's childhood friend have
a few drinks and go upstairs, and then who knows what
happens. You know: He said, she said. Like that. The
childhood friend goes to the police, but then she
disappears. No charges. The police tell Chad maybe he
should move along, so he does. Goes back home to
Phoenix.

He points at himself.

HATCH (CONT'D)
But Holly follows him and starts harassing him in public
and at his work. Ugly stuff, but nothing exactly illegal. We

can't really touch her but have to warn her not to go too far. That's when it comes out that the childhood friend ended her life and Holly is on a revenge trip.

A NURSE, 30s, enters and smiles at Hatch. She checks Steve's vitals.

NURSE
(to Hatch)
You working him up?

HATCH
No, ma'am.

Nurse smiles and leaves.

HATCH (CONT'D)
Where was I? Right. We relay what we know to Chad, and he says he's got a friend in Boston who can give him a job. We say go, and everything quiets down until my phone rings about a John Doe in a warehouse explosion. And so.

Steve takes a spoonful of ice chips, rapt.

HATCH (CONT'D)
Sorry. I guess there was no short answer.

STEVE
Did they find her?

HATCH
Not yet.

STEVE
I don't know anything about any of this.

HATCH
She didn't mention the childhood friend?

Steve shakes his head.

HATCH (CONT'D)
How did you know her?

STEVE
She sold me my condo.

HATCH
(interested)
So she was a real estate agent?

He takes out his notebook and writes.

STEVE
I don't understand how that's of interest.

HATCH
Oh. Well, truth is I'm retired. But this case…

He gets a wild look in his eyes.

HATCH (CONT'D)
It's so fascinating. Don't you think? Imagine what it would
take to keep that kind of hate alive. The bitterness. The toll
it would exact.

They both sit in silence.

HATCH (CONT'D)
I'm thinking about writing a book and hoped you might be
able to fill in her time in Boston. You know, before you
talk to the cops. Officially.

INT. BOSTON GENERAL HOSPITAL - A FEW DAYS
LATER

Steve is dressed and sitting on the bed. The Nurse enters
with a clutch of paperwork.

STEVE
Kicking me out?

NURSE
Otherwise you're gonna have to start paying rent.

STEVE
Not sure I can even pay what I owe so far.

NURSE
All taken care of. These are your discharge papers.

STEVE
(confused)
But my insurance--

NURSE
You must have a guardian angel.

She hands him the paperwork, which includes a card with
his name on it.

NURSE (CONT'D)
An angel with nice taste in perfume, too.

She smiles and leaves.

Steve sniffs the envelope and opens it.

INSERT: A card that reads: "Not over by a long shot."

INT. BANK - DAY

Steve is sitting across the desk from a Bank Manager, who is shaking his head.

INT. CAR DEALERSHIP - DAY

Steve sits at a table in the showroom while a Salesman points with a pen at a document between them, his face grim.

INT. COFFEE SHOP - DAY

Steve is scrolling through jobs on his laptop, sipping a cup of coffee. A Girl walks by and adds the magazine she was browsing to the pile of complimentary magazines. Steve doesn't notice, but after the Girl walks away, he sniffs the air, following his nose back to the pile of magazines. He turns the pages of the magazine until he finds a full-page ad for a new perfume from Buckley Cosmetics. He sniffs the page and his eyes widen. He rips the page from the magazine and pockets it.

INT. OLIVER & DANIELS - DAY

Steve sits at an expensive desk in a tidy office, across from CALVIN MERCHANT, a man in his early forties.

CALVIN
We're all still shocked about Bill.

STEVE
(nodding)
I wanted to find out if he worked on the Buckley Cosmetics account.

CALVIN
(gets a look)
Did he tell you Buckley was a client?

Steve smiles.

CALVIN (CONT'D)
Oh.
(affecting a serious tone)
Of course, we never divulge who are clients are.

STEVE
Of course.

CALVIN
(leans and says quietly)
Is it something to do with what happened?

STEVE
Maybe.

Calvin considers, then resumes the company line.

CALVIN
Wish I could help.

He stands, and Steve does too.

RECEPTION AREA - CONTINUOUS

On his way out, Steve notices a Buckley Cosmetics tote
bag slung on the back of the RECEPTIONIST'S chair.

STEVE
Can you tell me where I can catch the downtown bus?

RECEPTIONIST
A left out of the building and cross the side street and
you'll see it. That's my bus too.

STEVE
Thanks. Like the tote bag.

RECEPTIONIST
Oh, thanks.

STEVE
Was it free with a purchase? My girlfriend's birthday is
coming up.

RECEPTIONIST
We got these at one of their parties.

STEVE
Cool perk.

RECEPTIONIST
(sighs)
Yeah, the last, though.

STEVE
Oh?

They exchange looks.

RECEPTIONIST
Too bad, too. Those parties were the best. Free everything.
And tons of celebrities.

STEVE
Yeah?

RECEPTIONIST
Totally. Check this out.

She grabs her phone and scrolls through her pictures.

RECEPTIONIST (CONT'D)
You a Sox fan?

STEVE
Since I was seven.

RECEPTIONIST
Here it is. Me with you-know-who.

She shows Steve the picture. In the background is the man from Triny's condo.

STEVE
(pointing)
Who is that?

RECEPTIONIST
Dunno. He was always around, though. First one to arrive, last to leave. Real cut-up.

STEVE
Do you have a color printer?

INT. BUCKLEY COSMETICS - DAY

Steve is at the concierge desk, manned by a large GUARD, 30s.

GUARD
I told you, you have to have an appointment.

Steve gives a defeated look. He produces the color photo

and shows it to the Guard.

STEVE
I'm trying to find out who that is. He works here. Know
him?

The Guard eyes the photo, then eyes Steve.

GUARD
Don't know him.

Steve starts to fold up the picture and sees the Guard give
him a look. He unfolds the picture and takes a twenty from
his wallet, clamping the bill and the picture together.

STEVE
Maybe another look?

The Guard casually slips the twenty into his pocket.

GUARD
He doesn't work here and I don't know his name. But I've
seen him.

STEVE
Where?

GUARD
I do security for Buckley parties. Dude works for the
catering company.

STEVE
Know the name of the caterer?

GUARD
Not for twenty dollars.

Steve reaches for his wallet.

INT. HOTEL - DAY

Steve approaches the front desk and the WOMAN, 20s, behind it looks up and smiles.

STEVE
I'm here for the luncheon.

WOMAN
Bandes Room. Second floor.

STEVE
Thank you.

BANDES ROOM - CONTINUOUS

The room is filled with People sitting at tables, enjoying their catered lunch. A sign on an easel reads, "Laprade Institute Fund-raiser." There's a MURMUR as people chat. Steve saunters through the crowd toward the kitchen doors. The doors suddenly swing open, and the Man from Triny's condo exits holding a pitcher of water. He's startled to see Steve, who is equally startled.

MAN
Not here.

Steve nods toward the kitchen.

MAN (CONT'D)
No.

A Catering Assistant exits the kitchen.

MAN (CONT'D)
(to Catering Assistant)
Can you do refills? I'm going on break.

The Catering Assistant gives an annoyed look but takes the pitcher.

EXT. HOTEL - ALLEY - MOMENTS LATER

The Man exits and Steve follows. The door SLAMS behind them.

MAN
(smiling)
Pretty clever.

STEVE
Yeah, thanks. Before I call the cops, want to tell me what I don't know?

The Man lights a cigarette.

MAN
You're not gonna call the cops.

STEVE
Yeah? Why not?

MAN
Because you're this close to knowing and I can take you the rest of the way.

STEVE
Bullshit. It's you. Admit it. All I don't know is why.

MAN
It's not me. I don't even know you.

STEVE
(considers)
You're saying it's someone I know?

MAN
Not saying that, no. Someone who knows you, though.
Steve grabs the Man and throws him to the ground and
stands on his chest. He pulls out his phone to call the
police.

STEVE
I'm done with you.

MAN
Okay, okay!

STEVE
Okay what?

MAN
I'll tell you.

Steve lets him up. The Man dusts himself off.

MAN (CONT'D)
He's a lawyer.

STEVE
(skeptical)
What's this alleged lawyer's name?

MAN
I can't tell you his name. He'll know it's me.

STEVE
What's your name, then?

MAN
My name won't do you any good. I'm just the guy in the
middle between the guy you know and the guy you don't.
Steve starts dialing the police.

STEVE
Life is full of choices.

MAN
He works for Buckley Cosmetics. He's one of their in-
house lawyers.

Steve eyes him.

MAN (CONT'D)
Guy throws these legendary parties at his house in
Newport ever since his divorce.
(beat)
I can get you in.

EXT. NEWPORT HOUSE - NIGHT

A large stone mansion is lit up against the dark night sky.
Expensive cars line the driveway and the lawn, too, parked
haphazardly. Revelers loiter everywhere. LOUD MUSIC
filters out the open windows. In the distance, at the far end
of the lawn, as long as a runway, the sea crashes against a
breaker wall.

INT. NEWPORT HOUSE - CONTINUOUS

Steve steps into the warm glow of the foyer. No one
notices. He sidesteps a Woman, who rushes out, chased by
a Man holding a champagne bottle and two glasses, both
laughing hysterically.

Steve takes in the surroundings, a once expensively

decorated house that has suffered obvious recent abuse. He takes the drink offered him on a silver tray by a Server, who smiles.

STEVE
I'm looking for the host.

The Server shrugs and wanders on.

Steve sees a Woman, 20s, in a sheer blue dress standing by herself, drink in hand, and he migrates toward her.

STEVE (CONT'D)
I'm Steve.

The Woman smiles.

WOMAN
Kelli.

STEVE
You a regular at these parties?

KELLI
Semi.

STEVE
My first one.

Kelli is not interested in this conversation, and her bored face shows it.

STEVE (CONT'D)
Have you seen the host?

KELLI
He's not here.

STEVE
He's not at his own party?

KELLI
I overheard someone say he wasn't here.

STEVE
Know what he looks like?

Kelli shrugs, wanders into the crowd.

Steve pokes around the house, interrupting Partygoers
involved in various play in the upstairs rooms. He tries a
door at the end of the hall, and it's locked. He puts his ear
to the door and hears MURMURING on the other side. He
hears a LOW MOAN and traces it to the bathroom. He
pushes open the door and sees the Receptionist in the tub,
fully-clothed. She looks up when he opens the door.

STEVE (CONT'D)
Hey.

RECEPTIONIST
Hey yourself.

She giggles.

STEVE
Remember me?

The Receptionist squints at Steve and shakes her head.

RECEPTIONIST
Nope.

STEVE
We met at your office. We ride the same bus.

RECEPTIONIST
You can't take the bus here.

STEVE
Right, you can't.

RECEPTIONIST
I'm getting pancakes.

STEVE
Yeah?

RECEPTIONIST
Room service pancakes are the best.

Steve sits down on the closed toilet.

STEVE
Are you okay?

RECEPTIONIST
I'm fine. Are you okay?

STEVE
Sort of. I'm supposed to give something to the host of this party.

RECEPTIONIST
Jay? I just saw him.

She points aimlessly.

RECEPTIONIST (CONT'D)
He's supposed to be getting the pancakes.

STEVE
What's Jay's last name?

RECEPTIONIST
He's not gonna have a last name if he doesn't hurry up
with those pancakes.

She leans her head back and closes her eyes. In a brief
moment, she's SNORING. Steve leaves but locks the
bathroom door before he does.

EXT. NEWPORT HOUSE - MOMENTS LATER

Steve traipses slowly over the green lawn to the cliff walk
behind the house. He leans against the railing and looks
down at the breaker wall below. Ocean spray reaches near
where he's standing.

A PARTYGOER in his fifties, appears, startling Steve.

PARTYGOER
Breath of fresh air, eh?

Steve nods.

PARTYGOER (CONT'D)
Gets a little crazy.

STEVE
You a regular?

PARTYGOER
Neighbor. I drift in and out, depending.

STEVE
So you know the guy who throws the parties?

PARTYGOER
Enough to say hello to. And to be invited.

STEVE
What's his name?

PARTYGOER
Jay Stanton.

STEVE
Heard he's a lawyer.

PARTYGOER
Heard the same thing. He's a funny guy.

STEVE
How?

PARTYGOER
He caught me in front of my house once, trading some mis-delivered mail, and we got to talking. He'd just come back from a funeral up in Providence.

STEVE
(startled)
Did he say who the funeral was for?

PARTYGOER
Guy who was sleeping with his wife.

He sips his drink. Steve looks on, stunned.

PARTYGOER (CONT'D)
Said he'd gone to the wake at the guy's house, and two lightweights got into a fight. Right in the middle of the wake.

Steve stares out at the black ocean.

PARTYGOER (CONT'D)
Turns out his wife wasn't the only one being unfaithful.
The dead guy's wife was sleeping with his best friend.

Waves CRASH violently below them.

PARTYGOER (CONT'D)
I'll give it to Stanton. For a lawyer, he has a morality
streak a mile wide. That kept him from killing the guy who
fucked his wife--or even killing his wife, for that matter--
but he's a creative type. For a lawyer.

Steve finishes his drink in a long pull and throws the glass,
which SPLINTERS on the rocks below.

STEVE
This is all because of your wife?

PARTYGOER
Not my wife. Stanton's.

STEVE
(drunkenly)
Stop bullshitting me. I know it's you.

PARTYGOER
(ignoring Steve)
This whole area was settled by those kicked out of
Massachusetts by the Puritans. So maybe it's not a
surprise, the on-going legacy of debauchery.

STEVE
You killed Triny.

PARTYGOER
(ignoring Steve)
Stanton is a huge fan of the Puritans. Their way of life,

their code of conduct. Morality was their second nature. Never a question about what was or wasn't right.

The wind kicks up, as does the ocean spray. The SOUND OF THE SEA CRASHING against the breaker wall gets louder.

STEVE
(repeating)
You killed Triny.

PARTYGOER
Triny killed Triny.

STEVE
You fucked up my life!

STANTON
(expression changes to menace)
You fucked up your own life. No one made you sleep with your best friend's wife. You did that. You did that.

He throws a glass at Steve's feet and turns to walk away. He stops abruptly. Allison appears from the darkness, shaking, a gun in her hand.

STEVE
Allison!

Allison advances slowly and Stanton takes a step back.

STANTON
Well, this is a nice reunion.

STEVE
It's not worth it. Don't.

ALLISON
I can't live like this.

STANTON
(quips)
Imagine how Bill felt.

This enrages Allison, who takes two quick steps toward Stanton, who freezes.

The wind whips around them. The cliff walk is soaked.

ALLISON
I've paid a hundred times over.

STANTON
It's the debt that can't be satisfied, I'm afraid.
(to Steve)
Am I right?

STEVE
(to Allison)
Let's go to the police. They can sort it out.

ALLISON
(shaking her head no)
The police can't do anything with people like him.

STANTON
(cocky)
She's right, you know. Who gets punished and what goes unpunished isn't up to the police. Sometimes it requires someone righteous to punish the adulterers and the selfish, otherwise--

Allison PULLS THE TRIGGER and a bullet strikes Stanton. He falls against the railing and she SHOOTS

AGAIN. Stanton flips over the rail, landing on the breaker wall below. Ocean waves rage around him, and the water teases Stanton's body out to sea.

ALLISON
It was the only way to get out from under it.

Steve reaches for Allison to console her, but she shrugs him off.

EXT. NEWPORT HOUSE - LATER

Dawn is breaking over the house. The air is painted blue and red from the police cars parked all over the lawn. Most of the Partygoers have left, though a few remain in an effort to sober up. Allison sits in the back of one police car; Steve in the back of another. Steve glances out the window at Allison, who glances away. TWO OFFICERS, 30s, stand nearby, surveying the scene.

OFFICER #1
They find the body?

OFFICER #2
Might be weeks before it surfaces, and then who knows?

OFFICER #1
Which one shot him?

OFFICER #2
They're both claiming they did. Captain wants them kept separate until we can figure it out.

OFFICER #1
Might not matter, if there's no gun and no body.

OFFICER #2
Not with the kind of money this guy has. Someone will be made to pay.

OFFICER #1
Hey, what do you call a dead lawyer at the bottom of the ocean?

OFFICER #2
Yeah, I heard that one.

THE END

GARDEN LAKES

EXT. SUNSET MERIDIAN HOUSING
DEVELOPMENT - DUSK

DELLA ANDERSON, 30s, a journalist for the Phoenix
Gazette pulls up to a street cordoned off with police tape.
Blue and red lights paint the air. Della parks and spots
DETECTIVE ERIN BERRY, 30s, and nods.

DETECTIVE BERRY
That was quick. How'd you find out?

DELLA
Social Media.

DETECTIVE BERRY
I miss the days when people had police scanners.

DELLA
What happened?

Nods toward area still marked with blood and evidence
markers.

DETECTIVE BERRY
Girl out riding her bike.

DELLA
Who did it?

DETECTIVE BERRY
Witnesses say a Mexican.

Della surveys the housing development, pink and beige

stucco houses built around a golf course.

DELLA
Worker you think?

DETECTIVE BERRY
Definitely not a resident. Not here anyway.

DELLA
(mock innocence)
Just 'cause McCloud doesn't let blacks live in his
developments doesn't mean Mexicans can't, does it?

Detective Berry smirks along.

DETECTIVE BERRY
How's Collins doing?

DELLA
Not good.

DETECTIVE BERRY
I'm sorry. Always liked him.

DELLA
He's an asshole, victim of a bigger asshole.

DETECTIVE BERRY
You sure McCloud did it?

DELLA
Had it done, guessing. McCloud isn't clever enough to
wire up a car bomb. That takes skill.

DETECTIVE BERRY
Was Collins close to nailing him?

DELLA
Relentlessness usually pays off. If anyone knows that, it's McCloud.

DETECTIVE BERRY
Speaking of. Got a tip in a cold case from 87, a woman we found buried in a shallow grave in the desert off the 10.

DELLA
I remember. Young girl?

DETECTIVE BERRY
Right. We did a fresh round of posters and canvassed some of the local farmers. A migrant worker swears one of the kids from Garden Lakes came into a camp he was living in and the kid and the girl left together.

DELLA
The girl lived at the camp?

DETECTIVE BERRY
Apparently.

DELLA
Did he know her name?

DETECTIVE BERRY
He knows little English now, less back then. You covered that mess about Garden Lakes and Randolph Prep. Anything ever come up about a girl being there?

DELLA
Nothing. Doesn't mean it didn't happen, though.

INT. RANDOLPH COLLEGE PREP - PRESIDENT MATTHEWS'S OFFICE – DAY

Detective Berry is seated across from PRESIDENT
MATTHEWS, late 60s. Sunlight blasts through the ornate
windows, casting colorful shadows across the room. Mr.
Matthews is grimacing, his primary expression.

DETECTIVE BERRY
I was just a street cop then, but I remember the story was
everywhere. A bunch of kids stranded in the desert without
adult supervision--

MATTHEWS
Which was the result of an administrative mix-up. And
was quickly resolved once discovered.

DETECTIVE BERRY
And I seem to recall all the press muted that fact. The spin
was the students and their heroic acts in the face of
abandonment. They seemed to enjoy all the press. One of
them made the half-court shot before a Suns game.

MATTHEWS
I found the tone of the coverage hostile, to say the least.
And terrifically aided by facts known only to the police.

Detective Berry stifles a smirk. Matthews gives her a long
stare, considering.

MATTHEWS (CONT'D)
What brings you to me?

DETECTIVE BERRY
I'm working a cold case, a girl found dead in the desert. A
new witness believes the girl passed through Garden Lakes
at the time of Randolph's fellowship program there.

She puts a poster with the girl's picture on his desk. He
examines it without picking it up.

MATTHEWS
What witness?

DETECTIVE BERRY
A credible one.

MATTHEWS
Nothing was ever said about this girl during our
investigation into the matter. This so-called witness must
be mistaken.

DETECTIVE BERRY
There's an easy way to discredit the information.

MATTHEWS
Oh?

DETECTIVE BERRY
If you'll open your alumni directory, I'll ask those who
were there and that'll be that.

MATTHEWS
Providing up-to-date information is elective for our alum.
I'm not sure we'll have what you seek.

DETECTIVE BERRY
Whatever you have then. And I'd like to speak to the
faculty who were administering the fellowship.

MATTHEWS
I'm afraid Mr. Hancock has passed on.

DETECTIVE BERRY
I'm sorry for your loss. What about the other one?

MATTHEWS
Mr. Malagon teaches somewhere in California. Last I

heard.

DETECTIVE BERRY
Any reason. Officially, I mean.

MATTHEWS
He has family in California and wanted to be closer to
them.

DETECTIVE BERRY
I see. Could you arrange for me to speak to someone at
your sister school about whether or not she was a student?

Matthews glances again at the poster.

MATTHEWS
I'd be surprised. Maybe across the canal.

Detective Berry shoots him a look.

EXT. RANDOLPH COLLEGE PREP - DRIVEWAY -
MOMENTS LATER

Detective Berry pulls up, signals, and enters the flow of
traffic. She travels a few feet, over an irrigation canal, and
turns into the parking lot for Central High School, the
public school next door to Randolph.

EXT. CENTRAL HIGH SCHOOL - PARKING LOT -
CONTINUOUS

Detective Berry pulls through two spots and parks facing
the entrance. She fiddles with the radio as the BELL
RINGS. Students filter out, including her son, NATE, 16,
who spots the car and heads her way.

INT. DETECTIVE BERRY'S CAR - CONTINUOUS

Nate slips into the passenger seat, rearranging his bag at his feet. He immediately turns the radio station to something else.

DETECTIVE BERRY
Hey. I might've been listening to that.

NATE
No one listens to that.

DETECTIVE BERRY
Rebecca catch a different ride home?

NATE
Absent.

DETECTIVE BERRY
She sick?

Nate shrugs.

DETECTIVE BERRY (CONT'D)
Know how a cop can tell when someone is hiding something?

NATE
No, how?

DETECTIVE BERRY
They look like you look right now.

NATE
It's not a big deal.

DETECTIVE BERRY
Then you can tell me.

NATE
It's personal.

DETECTIVE BERRY
For you, or for her?

NATE
Not for me.

DETECTIVE BERRY
Spill.

NATE
This guy asked her to the Winter Formal and she told him no. Happy?

DETECTIVE BERRY
And for that she's missing school?

NATE
She's just laying low a bit.

A pearl-colored Trans Am blows through the parking lot and they both look.

NATE (CONT'D)
That's him. Keith.

DETECTIVE BERRY
And what, he's hassling her?

NATE
Sort of.

DETECTIVE BERRY
Sort of how?

NATE
Why do you have to know every last detail about
everything?

DETECTIVE BERRY
Professional curiosity.

NATE
He printed up these stupid little cards that say He-Man
Becky Haters Club on them and is passing them out to
people.

DETECTIVE BERRY
Christ. Principal Sprung know?

NATE
You're not going to tell Principal Sprung.

DETECTIVE BERRY
He should know.

NATE
It'll blow over. Can we go?

EXT./INT. DETECTIVE BERRY'S CAR -
CONTINUOUS

Detective Berry pulls into traffic. As the car sails down
Central Avenue, she spots the pearl Trans Am parked
across a number of parking spots in front of a coffee shop.
Nate continues to tune the radio.

NATE
Have you given any thought to what we talked about?

DETECTIVE BERRY
I have given thought to what we talked about.

She smiles at him.

NATE
And?

DETECTIVE BERRY
I think I'd miss you too much.

NATE
It's just for the summer.

DETECTIVE BERRY
Summer is a fourth of the year.

NATE
California's not that far. You could visit. And I'll rustle up
a summer job. Anything is better than another summer at
the fish and chips.

DETECTIVE BERRY
I'm sure your father would love that. Also, you might get
that summer fellowship.

NATE
I'm not getting that fellowship.

DETECTIVE BERRY
Not with that attitude, no.

NATE
You're old enough to know who gets picked for those
kinds of scholarships and why, Mom.

The comment cuts her and she swallows whatever she was
going to say.

NATE (CONT'D)
It's too hot here in the summer, anyway.

EXT. OLIVE INN AND SPA – DAY

Della is standing in the hotel parking lot, shielding her
eyes. She tracks the path from the underground parking to
where she's standing. Looks down and sees the charred
pavement. A maroon Ford Escort circles and parks near
her. She recognizes her fellow journalist, JOSEPHINE,
30s, and walks to the car. Josephine rolls down the
window.

JOSEPHINE
First visit?

DELLA
Yeah.

JOSEPHINE
I keep circling back.

DELLA
How is he?

JOSEPHINE
(shrugs)
His wife is with him, so thought I'd scoot.

DELLA
(smiles)
Guess the divorce hasn't gone through, eh?

JOSEPHINE
I didn't believe him when he said he'd filed.

DELLA
Smart.

JOSEPHINE
Doesn't matter now, I guess.

She reaches under her sunglasses to touch away a tear.

JOSEPHINE (CONT'D)
What are you thinking?

DELLA
McCloud did this.

JOSEPHINE
There's no proof.

DELLA
But if you woke up and looked out the window and saw
snow, you'd think it was winter, right?

JOSEPHINE
If I looked out my window and saw snow, I'd know hell
had finally frozen over.

Della smirks.

DELLA
Why was he here?

Looks up at the hotel sign.

JOSEPHINE
For a different story. Something about the piece he was
writing about Greyhound Park.

DELLA
Illegal shit going on at the track?

JOSEPHINE
He thought so. Didn't say what though. Ever been?

DELLA
Dog racing. Nah.

JOSEPHINE
If you see it, you can't watch horse racing anymore either.

DELLA
He ever mention a connection between the track and
McCloud?

JOSEPHINE
No. Maybe there isn't one.

DELLA
(giving a look)
Collins was hammering McCloud pretty hard. Got his
liquor license revoked. Those restaurants around the new
stadium were gonna be his cash machine. Not to mention
all the labor violations Collins uncovered. All those fancy
real estate developments built by illegal aliens.

JOSEPHINE
He's never done anything like this.

DELLA
Perhaps he's expanding his resume.

EXT. TEMPE DIABLO STADIUM - DAY

Detective Berry and Della hang on the fence while the
Double-A Sidewinders baseball team take batting practice.

DUANE HANDLEY, 23, is in the batter's box. They
watch as he takes the last of his pitches and then steps out
of the box, heading toward the dugout.

DETECTIVE BERRY
Duane Handley?

Handley glances up casually, expecting fans, but she
flashes him her badge. He cautiously trudges over.

HANDLEY
Am I in trouble?

DETECTIVE BERRY
Everyone is in some kind of trouble. I'm Detective Berry
and this is Della from the Phoenix Gazette.

DELLA
Do you remember me, Hands?

HANDLEY
I see a lot of faces...

DELLA
I interviewed you about Garden Lakes. For the paper.

HANDLEY
Okay.

DELLA
You really know how to hurt a girl's feelings.

DETECTIVE BERRY
What about this face?

She shows him the poster. He stares at it, possibly in
disbelief, possibly trying to place the face.

HANDLEY
There was a team trainer when I started who--

DELLA
She's not a team trainer.

HANDLEY
Ok, I give. Who is she?

DETECTIVE BERRY
A corpse we found in the desert about five years ago.

Handley flinches.

DELLA
Near Garden Lakes.

A teammate CALLS OUT to Handley and he flashes the guy the peace sign.

DETECTIVE BERRY
We found a witness that says she was at Garden Lakes when you and the others were there.

The suggestion catches Handley off-guard and he stands mute.

DELLA
That horseshit story you all sold that summer makes a little more sense if you had someone to keep you on the straight and narrow. Or to try to impress.

HANDLEY
If I remember correctly, that horseshit story won you an award.

DELLA
Won you and the others more than that. Scholarships, the matching cars from that dealership. And that potato chip commercial everyone thought was so clever.

Handley doesn't respond.

DETECTIVE BERRY
I was just chatting with President Matthews—
Handley flinches.

DETECTIVE BERRY (CONT'D)
--and I was saying how neat it was the school was able to spin the story so you sort of forget why the teachers disappeared. In fact, I can't even remember.

DELLA
One took a family leave and was due to be replaced, but there was a mix-up with the school and they didn't send anyone. The other teacher had some kind of emergency and left thinking the other was on his way back.

DETECTIVE BERRY
Whoa. How long were they on their own?

DELLA
Couple of weeks, right?

Handley nods.

DETECTIVE BERRY
Amazing. And what were you doing all that time?

HANDLEY
Fulfilling the obligations of the fellowship.

DETECTIVE BERRY
Such as?

HANDLEY
(nodding at Della)
Read her articles.

DELLA
There was a daily schedule. Some classroom work, some manual labor.

DETECTIVE BERRY
Randolph kids doing manual labor? Do tell.

DELLA
Under supervision of a construction company, a Randolph donor. Some dry-walling and some other light work.

HANDLEY
Maybe light to you. Was a bitch, especially in the heat.

EXT. GARDEN LAKES HOUSING DEVELOPMENT – DAY (FLASHBACK)

HIGH SCHOOL JUNIORS are performing various tasks inside and outside the frame of a new house on a street in the abandoned development under the blazing sun. The juniors are being directed by MR. BAKER, 30s, who is standing near a pickup truck emblazoned with the name Statewide Construction. A YOUNG DUANE HANDLEY (17) opens a ladder in the middle of all the activity and wipes his arm across his sweaty brow.

EXT. TEMPE DIABLO STADIUM - CONTINUOUS

DETECTIVE BERRY
(holds up poster again)

And she wasn't out there with all you Lords of the Flies?

HANDLEY
Think I would've known.

DELLA
We'll ask the others just to be sure.

DETECTIVE BERRY
(mocking)
Think you'll make the team this year?

HANDLEY
Not if I don't practice.

Detective Berry and Della turn and walk away and
Handley watches them go.

DETECTIVE BERRY
He recognized her.

DELLA
Yeah. Hard to imagine any of them killing someone,
though. The kids at that school are--

DETECTIVE BERRY
Bunch of pussies?

DELLA
(laughs)
Generally, yeah. Still amazed that they were able to get
through that summer, though. Hands was one of the
leaders.

DETECTIVE BERRY
Can't wait to meet the others.

EXT./INT. VILLA DE PAZ GOLF COURSE - DAY

DAVE FIGUEROA, 23, walks off the course with OTHER
GOLFERS after a round and heads for the clubhouse.

Figueroa enters the clubhouse and spies Handley at a table
with an empty beer glass in front of him. Figueroa
separates from the group and motions to the bartender for
two more beers. He leans his clubs against the wall and
takes the other seat at Handley's table.

FIGUEROA
This can't be good.

HANDLEY
It's not.

The bartender sets the beer down and nods at Figueroa,
who nods in return. The bartender starts cleaning the other
tables in the room.

HANDLEY (CONT'D)
That journalist from before showed up at the ballpark with
a cop.

FIGUEROA
(sips his beer)
And?

HANDLEY
They had a picture of what's-her-name from Garden
Lakes.

FIGUEROA
What do they want with her?

HANDLEY
They found her body. Near Garden Lakes.

FIGUEROA
(leans back in his chair, stunned)
But I thought--

HANDLEY
Yeah, me too.

FIGUEROA
Have you talked to any of the others?

HANDLEY
Came to you first. I don't even know where half of them
are.

FIGUEROA
I'll bet the cop does.

HANDLEY
How?

FIGUEROA
She found you.

HANDLEY
Maybe she's a fan.

FIGUEROA
Didn't know minor leaguers had fans.

HANDLEY
Fuck you. (beat) Better think about what you're gonna say.

Gets up and walks out. Figueroa stares off into the
distance.

INT. PHOENIX GENERAL HOSPITAL - ROOM - DAY

JIM COLLINS, 40s, is unconscious. Machines do his
breathing for him. A leg and arm have been amputated. His
estranged wife, JENNIFER, 40s, sits on one side of the
hospital bed, Della on the other.

JENNIFER
He told me he wanted to be re-assigned from the
investigative unit.

DELLA
Did he say why?

JENNIFER
Because of this.

DELLA
Was he getting death threats?

JENNIFER
How would I know. We were barely speaking. You know
he's fucking that reporter you work with.

Della grimaces. A beat passes between them.

DELLA
I have a suspicion about who did it.

JENNIFER
Who?

DELLA
Evan McCloud.

Jennifer gives a hard stare and then glances at Collins with
pity.

JENNIFER
Rather it be anyone else.

DELLA
Why?

JENNIFER
Because guys like McCloud are untouchable. No one ever gets to them.

DELLA
Jim clearly got to him.

JENNIFER
(dismissive)
Jim said he was just a fly buzzing around McCloud's head. That's part of why he wanted to be transferred. Said he was just harassing McCloud rather than doing any good.

DELLA
But he got the liquor license pulled. That's motive.

JENNIFER
Jim said McCloud would get the liquor license back and we'd never hear about it. He'd use a dummy company or get it in someone else's name. There's too much money at stake.

DELLA
(animated)
Jim wouldn't have let him get away with it. He would've found out.

JENNIFER
He said you have a thing against McCloud.

DELLA
(bitterly)
He's been getting away with too much for too long.

EXT. CENTRAL AVENUE - DAY

Detective Berry is parked down the street from Central
High School. Students are milling up and down the
sidewalk. The pearl Trans Am appears and everyone looks
when KEITH, 17, PEELS OUT of the school driveway.
Detective Berry hits the lights and SIREN on her
unmarked police car and pulls him over. She approaches
the driver's side. Keith has his arm out the window,
listening to music.

DETECTIVE BERRY
Turn the music off.

Keith reaches for the radio and turns it down but not off.

KEITH
Are you a cop? Or did you buy one of those old cop cars at
a police auction?

Detective Berry flashes her badge.

DETECTIVE BERRY
Let's see your license and registration.

KEITH
What's the charge?

DETECTIVE BERRY
If you don't hand over your license and registration it'll be
resisting and obstructing. And I get to put you in handcuffs
and lean you against your pretty car for your friends to see.

KEITH
Yeah, ok. Here.

Hands over his license and registration.

DETECTIVE BERRY
Right back, slick. Keep your hands where I can see them.

She walks back to her car and gets in. She checks both license and registration to make sure address matches. She pulls out a pad and copies down Keith's address. She turns on the radio and listens to the SONG PLAYING until it ends while Students pass by, HOOTING AND LAUGHING at Keith. When the song ends, she gets out of the car and approaches the Trans Am again.

KEITH
Am I good?

Detective Berry hands back his license and registration.

DETECTIVE BERRY
Sort of a girly color for a car.

KEITH
(annoyed)
Am I good. Can I go?

DETECTIVE BERRY
Yup.

KEITH
(flippantly)
Great, thanks.

He pulls away, BLASTING HIS MUSIC.

STUDENT #1
You shoulda put him in prison!

Detective Berry smiles at the student as he walks by, but is also smiling to herself. She turns her car around and pulls into the school parking lot.

MOMENTS LATER:

Nate gets in the car and hands her a sheet of paper and the envelope it was ripped from.

NATE
Told you.

The smile on Detective Berry's face drops as she reads the letter.

NATE (CONT'D)
California here I come.

INT. THE FIGUEROA COMPANIES OFFICE -
RECEPTION - DAY

The elevator DINGS and Detective Berry and Della exit. The Receptionist looks up.

INT. THE FIGUEROA COMPANIES OFFICE -
CONFERENCE ROOM - MOMENTS LATER

Detective Berry, Della, and Dave Figueroa are seated around the conference table. The poster of the dead girl is on the table and Figueroa keeps glancing at it.

DETECTIVE BERRY
So the whole time all of you were out there on your own you didn't see her or anyone else?

FIGUEROA
I remember once while we were playing soccer a car drove
in. A couple who was lost.

DELLA
Did they think it was strange to find a bunch of high school
kids on their own?

EXT. GARDEN LAKES HOUSING DEVELOPMENT –
DRY LAKEBED – DAY – (FLASHBACK)

A scrum of juniors kicks up dust as they play soccer in the
dry lakebed while HIGH SCHOOL SOPHOMORES (16)
watch on the sideline. The midafternoon sun casts the
players' shadows across the arid landscape. A YOUNG
JASON FIGUEROA (17) passes the ball but it's
intercepted by Young Duane Handley, who drives and
scores. Young Jason Figueroa puts his hands on his knees
for a moment and when he looks up, he sees two
sophomores pushing each other on the sideline. He and
Young Duane Handley sprint to the sideline to break up
the fight just as it starts. All heads turn at the SOUND OF
A CAR HORN. A silver Ford LTD floats along, the
DRIVER, 50s, blowing the horn. The car stops and Young
Duane Handley and Young Jason Figueroa exchange
glances before Young Jason Figueroa steps towards the car
and the driver, who is leaning out the window.

DRIVER
Excuse me, boys. Can you tell me how to get back to the
freeway? I'm turned around.

YOUNG JASON FIGUEROA
Through the gate and turn right. Go about fifteen minutes.

DRIVER
Appreciate it. (looks around, takes in the scene for the first

time.) What're you fellas up to out here anyway?

YOUNG JASON FIGUEROA
Just a friendly game of soccer.

DRIVER
(squinting)
Where's the field?

YOUNG JASON FIGUEROA
(smiles)
We make do. (beat where the Driver seems like he might ask another question.) This is a pretty sharp car. Is it new?

DRIVER
Hell, no. I wish. They quit making these things years ago.

YOUNG JASON FIGUEROA
Man, coulda fooled me. This is a beaut.

DRIVER
Thanks for saying so. I take good care of it.

YOUNG JASON FIGUEROA
I can tell. (flashes a grin.) Well, we better get back to it. Big stakes!

DRIVER
Good luck! Thanks again.

Young Jason Figueroa backs away as the car begins to reverse.

INT. THE FIGUEROA COMPANIES OFFICE –
CONFERENCE ROOM – CONTINUOUS

DETECTIVE BERRY
Why didn't you ask them to go for help?

FIGUEROA
We wanted to prove we could do it. We all agreed.

DELLA
Lucky nothing happened.

Figueroa glances at the poster again and then looks away.

DETECTIVE BERRY
Wasn't there something about someone sneaking their
girlfriend in?

DELLA
Casey Murfin. The one they call Smurf.

DETECTIVE BERRY
Clever.

DELLA
Smurf got kicked out for it, but he was somehow there
when it all ended.

FIGUEROA
He came back and we let him stay. It was only fair.

DETECTIVE BERRY
(nods at the poster)
Maybe she was a friend of the girlfriend.

FIGUEROA
You'd have to ask him. His girlfriend went to public
school.

This rankles Detective Berry.

DETECTIVE BERRY
He couldn't pull any of that private school sweetness, eh?

Figueroa is flummoxed and a little horrified. He looks again at the poster and there's a long quiet moment where it seems like he might say something. Detective Berry and Della glance at each other, waiting.

FIGUEROA
I'm sorry I don't know anything.

INT. THE FIGUEROA COMPANIES OFFICE - ELEVATOR - MOMENTS LATER

Detective Berry and Della ride down.

DELLA
I could never sort out what really happened the last day out there. Was impossible to know who arrived on the scene first: the head of security for Randolph or the police. And it was fishy that one was the brother of the other.

DETECTIVE BERRY
Who was the officer?

DELLA
Simpson. Killed later that year during a traffic stop.

DETECTIVE BERRY
I remember.

DELLA
The brother is still security for Randolph, though.

Elevator DINGS and the doors open and a Woman gets on. The doors close and reopen two floors later and the

Woman exits.

DELLA (CONT'D)
By the time the crush descended on Garden Lakes, they all
had their stories straight. And Baker recanted his about
being assaulted.

DETECTIVE BERRY
Who did what?

DELLA
The guy from Statewide Construction who was monitoring
the kids while they worked on the house out there. He
called 911 and said he'd been kidnapped, which is what
brought the police. But later when I interviewed him, the
story was that a kid pranked 911 from his car phone.

DETECTIVE BERRY
Sounds like bullshit.

DELLA
Especially since he retired right after. At 39. Lives in a
house on Camelback Mountain now with an infinity pool.

DETECTIVE BERRY
Oh that's not suspicious at all.

INT. PHOENIX POLICE DEPARTMENT - HALL

Della leans against the soundproof window and watches as
DETECTIVE KENNARD, 50s, sits calmly across the table
from a portly MAN, 30s. Detective Kennard stands and
saunters out of the interrogation room.

DETECTIVE KENNARD
Terrific, the press. You supposed to be here?

DELLA
That him?

DETECTIVE KENNARD
That him who?

DELLA
The guy who did Collins.

DETECTIVE KENNARD
I should fire whoever let you back here.

DELLA
Please.

DETECTIVE KENNARD
(sighs)
Yeah, it's him. Admits it.

DELLA
Who is he?

DETECTIVE KENNARD
A nobody. No priors. Some nut. Walked in and just confessed.

DELLA
He say why?

DETECTIVE KENNARD
Probably wants you to put his name in the paper.

DELLA
(peering through the glass again)
He didn't mention McCloud?

DETECTIVE KENNARD
Actually he did.

Della starts.

DETECTIVE KENNARD (CONT'D)
Said he thought the press was giving McCloud a raw deal.
Said you all were hounding him.

DELLA
And what, he makes a play that throws suspicion on
McCloud. That doesn't make sense.

DETECTIVE KENNARD
He said he wanted to do McCloud a favor. Like I said, a
nut.

Della glances again at the man in the interrogation room,
who has his head down on the table.

DELLA
Anything new on the hit and run. The little girl?

DETECTIVE KENNARD
We're in all the barrios. We'll come up with someone.

INT. KUKQ RADIO STATION - DAY

Detective Berry is in the lobby, scanning the wall covered
in posters and the head shots of radio personnel. She spies
the one for Vince Glassburn whose DJ name is Assburn.

VOICE (O.S.)
Yeah?

She turns and sees ASSBURN, 23, in person.

DETECTIVE BERRY
I'm Detective Berry with Phoenix PD.

ASSBURN
Is my show that bad?

DETECTIVE BERRY
Oh good, you're funny.

Assburn looks deflated.

DETECTIVE BERRY (CONT'D)
This isn't about your show. This is about Garden Lakes.
Assburn is startled to hear the name again.

ASSBURN
Garden Lakes?

DETECTIVE BERRY
(sarcastic)
Heard of it?

ASSBURN
Oh good, you're funny.

DETECTIVE BERRY
(cracks a half-smile)
Was reading through all the press coverage and didn't pick
up in real time that you and another kid, Roger, were
actually expelled. Must've been a good reason.

ASSBURN
I hated that fucking school.

DETECTIVE BERRY
That's not the question.

ASSBURN
(gives a look)
I wasn't expelled. I transferred.

DETECTIVE BERRY
So the papers got it wrong?

Assburn shrugs.

DETECTIVE BERRY (CONT'D)
What about Roger. He transfer too?

ASSBURN
Dunno.

DETECTIVE BERRY
Maybe I'll ask him.

ASSBURN
He's deployed somewhere overseas.

DETECTIVE BERRY
Oh, are you in touch with him?

ASSBURN
(bitterly)
Saw it in the newsletter, which for some reason they keep
sending me. Look I'm on in a bit. Is that all?

DETECTIVE BERRY
No, that's not all. We found out there was a girl out at
Garden Lakes.

ASSBURN
(brightens)
That bastard Malagon finally gonna get his due?

DETECTIVE BERRY
(nodding)
Mm-hmm. Once we learn her name.

ASSBURN
Katie Sullivan.

Detective Berry shows him the poster.

DETECTIVE BERRY
This her?

ASSBURN
(scrutinizing the poster)
Could be. Never really saw her.

DETECTIVE BERRY
What do you mean?

EXT. GARDEN LAKES HOUSING DEVELOPMENT –
MALAGON'S HOUSE – NIGHT – (FLASHBACK)

Young Duane Handley and Young Jason Figueroa peer
through the lit window of a finished home and see
MR. MALAGON, 30s, kissing a TEENAGE GIRL, whom
they can only see from the back, her long hair obscuring
her face.

ASSBURN (V.O.)
Malagon kept her in his house at Garden Lakes. We didn't
even know she was there. Hands and Figs sniffed it out.

INT. KUKQ RADIO STATION – DAY – CONTINUOUS

DETECTIVE BERRY
Know where she is now?

ASSBURN
Never saw or heard about her again once Malagon ran off
with her, leaving us all to die in the desert.

LOUD MUSIC plays overhead.

ASSBURN (CONT'D)
That's my intro, gotta run.

DETECTIVE BERRY
Let's talk again.

She hands him her card. He gives her a half-salute as he
heads down the hall to the studio.

INT. PHOENIX GAZETTE - NEWSROOM - DAY

Della is at her desk, a chaotic mess, typing on her laptop.
INCESSANT PHONE RINGING is all around her. Her
editor, BRENNAN, 50s, appears at her desk in his
trademark breathless fashion, as if he'd just eluded capture.

BRENNAN
That the piece on the hit-and-run?

DELLA
Something else.

She stops typing and half closes her screen.

BRENNAN
Heard you were down at police headquarters.

DELLA
I'm always down at police headquarters.

VOICE (O.S.)
Brennan. Need you!

BRENNAN
In a minute! (to Della) Whatever else you're up to, Collins
would want journalistic principles to prevail.

Della winces.

BRENNAN (CONT'D)
Ok?

Della nods and Brennan rushes off. Della closes her laptop
and taps her fingers on it, staring after Brennan. Detective
Berry appears in his wake. Della screws up her face in
surprise.

DELLA
Hey.

DETECTIVE BERRY
One of them, the radio DJ, ID'd the girl. Katie Sullivan.
Know the name?

DELLA
(thinking)
No. Who is she?

DETECTIVE BERRY
The teacher, Malagon, ran off with her that summer.

Della gives a start.

DELLA
Randolph said he had some kind of family emergency.
You think he ran off with this girl and it went bad and he

killed her and left her in the desert?

DETECTIVE BERRY
Or maybe abandoned her in the desert and someone else
did it.

DELLA
She a student?

DETECTIVE BERRY
We've been through all the missing persons reports for that
time. Nothing.

DELLA
Maybe it wasn't reported.

DETECTIVE BERRY
(nods, considering)
Bet the security guard knows.

DELLA
I've dealt with him. He'll never talk if he does. That little
shit Assburn could've told all of this much sooner.

DETECTIVE BERRY
Have to say it took very little prodding. Seems bitter.

DELLA
They booted him. And the ROTC kid.

DETECTIVE BERRY
Roger. Assburn said he's in Iraq.

DELLA
Think if you lean on Assburn he'll tell more?

DETECTIVE BERRY
Maybe.

DELLA
There's one kid...

She flips open her laptop and searches for a moment.

DELLA (CONT'D)
...Charlie Martens. He was an orphan or some such and emancipated after that summer at Garden Lakes. Never got to interview him. He was the one kid who didn't participate in all the press circus that summer.

DETECTIVE BERRY
What happened to him?

DELLA
(shrugs)
Vamoosed. But his benefactor is Jay Stanton Buckley.

Detective Berry gives a surprised look.

DETECTIVE BERRY
Buckley Cosmetics?

DELLA
I like their lipstick.

EXT./INT. ARROWHEAD RANCH - DAY

Detective Berry and Della idle in the driveway as the gate slowly retracts. Detective Berry pulls forward, and they take in the manicured lawn running up to the gleaming mansion. The estate has impeccable landscaping but is ghostly quiet. Detective Berry shields her eyes and spots JAY STANTON BUCKLEY, 70s, looking out a floor-to-ceiling window.

MOMENTS LATER:

Buckley is arranged neatly in a leather armchair in a sitting room that overlooks the pool. Detective Berry and Della are similarly comfortable.

BUCKLEY
I'm sorry I wasn't at the office. I'm mostly retired from the company, I'm afraid. I hope it wasn't an inconvenience.

DETECTIVE BERRY
None at all.

BUCKLEY
My secretary didn't reveal the purpose of your visit.

DELLA
I never had a chance to interview Charlie Martens for my articles on Garden Lakes and I was hoping to follow up with him.

BUCKLEY
That was a while ago. Is there still interest in the subject?

DELLA
It's more background material for another matter.

BUCKLEY
The bombing of the reporter?

DETECTIVE BERRY
You think there's a connection between Garden Lakes and the bombing?

BUCKLEY
A birdie told me that they have the person who did it in
custody, and that he said it was a favor for McCloud. And
if I recall, the press coverage about Garden Lakes revived
the government's complaint about McCloud donating the
land to Randolph before filing for bankruptcy.

DETECTIVE BERRY
That's a coincidence, not a connection.

BUCKLEY
And yet, here you are.

DELLA
Where is Charlie now?

BUCKLEY
He's resting.

DELLA
In the house?

BUCKLEY
(chuckling)
No. He's recuperating at Sonoran Behavioral Center.

DETECTIVE BERRY
Is he ill?

Buckley glances at her but doesn't answer.

DELLA
Does he receive visitors there?

BUCKLEY
Only those on the approved list.

DETECTIVE BERRY
We'll need to be added to that list.

BUCKLEY
Oh, I'm afraid not.

Detective Berry produces the poster of the dead girl and
holds it out for Buckley to see.

DETECTIVE BERRY
Know this girl?

BUCKLEY
I do not.

DETECTIVE BERRY
We'd like to ask Charlie if he does.

BUCKLEY
Who is she?

DELLA
She was found buried near Garden Lakes the same summer
of the Randolph fellowship.

BUCKLEY
So many bodies turning up on McCloud properties.

DETECTIVE BERRY
What do you mean?

BUCKLEY
The hit-and-run the other day, and now this poor
unfortunate.

DELLA
So you can see why it's imperative that we speak with

Charlie. We're asking everyone who was there that summer.

BUCKLEY
What did the others say?

DELLA
Nothing useful as of yet.

BUCKLEY
I'm sure Charlie will be as useless on the topic.

DETECTIVE BERRY
No offense, but we'd like to hear that from him.

Buckley gives her a pitying look, knowing she's powerless to compel Charlie's testimony on the subject.

BUCKLEY
If you'd like to leave the photo, I'll try to show it to him the next time we speak.

A GIRL, 20s, appears in a bikini and towel, fresh from the pool. She shivers when the air conditioning blasts her.

BUCKLEY (CONT'D)
How was the water, my sweet?

GIRL
It's freezing in here.

She strides down the hallway, out of sight. Detective Berry and Della exchange looks while Buckley stares after the girl.

INT. KUKQ RADIO STATION - DAY

Detective Berry is at the front desk. A RECEPTIONIST, 20s, looks up at her with a bored expression. LOUD MUSIC plays overhead.

DETECTIVE BERRY
How long will he be out?

RECEPTIONIST
Didn't say.

DETECTIVE BERRY
Is he sick?

RECEPTIONIST
Don't think so.

DETECTIVE BERRY
Terrific.

INT. EL FUEGO CANTINA - NIGHT

Della sits across the table from her date, TOM, 30s. El Fuego is a tastefully decorated Mexican restaurant with low lighting and discreet servers. The shadows from the candles on the table alternately light and cast their faces in shadow.

TOM
I'm glad Susan suggested we meet. You're lovely.

DELLA
Your mother teach you that word?

TOM
Sorry, I'm nervous.

DELLA
Kidding. Sort of.

TOM
Eaten here before?

DELLA
(looks around)
Never.

TOM
It's a special occasion place.

DELLA
Is this a special occasion?

TOM
We'll have to see.

Della flinches inadvertently.

DELLA
Go on many blind dates?

TOM
Some. You?

DELLA
My first. How do they usually start?

TOM
Getting-to-know you stuff, typically. Ask a lot of
questions, listen to the answers. You know.

DELLA
(laughs)

I do that for a living, so this should be easy.

TOM
Yeah, Susan says you're a reporter.

DELLA
Journalist.

TOM
Right. The difference being...

DELLA
Same as the police not wanting to be called cops.

TOM
Got it. I'm an engineer with the city.

DELLA
Susan said.

TOM
I see you're taking the night off from your journalistic instincts.

DELLA
Sorry.

TOM
That's okay. There's nothing to say about being an engineer. It's interesting work, but not to anyone who isn't an engineer. Always wanted to be a journalist?

DELLA
I studied fashion in college. Wanted to be a designer.

TOM
Sounds cool. What happened with that?

DELLA
Impractical. (beat) So I switched majors to photography.

Tom laughs. She smiles, a little.

TOM
My college girlfriend wanted to be a photographer.

Della doesn't take the bait.

DELLA
I actually started at the Gazette as a freelance
photographer.

TOM
And worked your way up?

DELLA
Someone quit.

A SERVER, 20s, brings their food and they sit in silence
for a moment.

TOM
Working on anything interesting?

Della looks like she doesn't want to go into it, is already
checked out of the date, but also doesn't want to be rude.

DELLA
One of my colleagues was the target of a car bomb.

TOM
Oh, I saw that on the news. They caught the guy, right?

DELLA
They caught a guy, yeah.

TOM
But you don't think he did it?

DELLA
I'm looking into whether or not someone put him up to it.

TOM
Wow. You're like a cop, er, police officer.

They each take bites of their food.

TOM (CONT'D)
Why did the guy say he did it?

DELLA
He thought the journalist was picking on a public figure and says he took it upon himself.

TOM
But you don't believe him?

Della shrugs.

TOM (CONT'D)
So either the guy is telling the truth, or he's lying and someone put it up to him.

DELLA
Basically.

TOM
And all because of the articles in the paper.

Della eyes him.

TOM (CONT'D)
A lot of the news is bullshit anyway. Guessing your guy

wishes he'd thought twice, eh?

He smirks.

SERVER
Can I get you anything else?

Della leans back in her chair, offended.

INT. ST. AGNES HIGH SCHOOL - LIBRARY - DAY

Detective Berry walks the shelves while Students are busy studying. She locates the yearbooks section and traces her finger along until she finds the one she's looking for. She pulls it down and flips to the index, scanning for the last name Sullivan. She sees the page reference for Katie Sullivan and turns to it:

INSERT: Yearbook page. Katie Sullivan is only one NOT PICTURED.

Detective Berry replaces the yearbook and selects the one on the shelf for the previous year and repeats the search. But there is no Katie Sullivan.

EXT. ST. AGNES HIGH SCHOOL - COURTYARD - MOMENTS LATER

Detective Berry exits the library and catches a glimpse of Keith chatting up some girls near the fountain. She saunters over.

DETECTIVE BERRY
Thought this was an all-girl's school. Don't you belong on the other side?

Some of the girls titter.

KEITH
Oh, it's you.
(cocky)
My British Lit class is here.

DETECTIVE BERRY
Who's your favorite?

KEITH
Favorite?

DETECTIVE BERRY
British author.

The girls giggle.

KEITH
(annoyed)
All of them, I guess. Why are you hassling me? What are you even doing here?

DETECTIVE BERRY
Homework. Have fun in class.

She puts on her sunglasses and walks away.

EXT. GLENROSA LANE – NIGHT

Detective Berry drives down the residential street, killing her lights when she spots Keith's pearl Trans Am in the driveway of a brick and stucco Tuscan mansion. The gate is open and a fountain featuring two bronze stallions GURGLES near the entrance of the lighted home. She pulls to a stop a few houses away and gets out.

EXT. KEITH'S HOUSE - NEXT MORNING

Keith jogs to his car, clearly late. He hops in and starts the car and then YELPS. He jumps out, making a face. He searches the interior of the Trans Am and sees an empty vinegar bottle on its side in the backseat.

INT. WARREN'S APARTMENT - MORNING

WARREN, 23, is on the couch in his University of Arizona Law School T-shirt, reading the newspaper. The TV is on low and a black cat stalks into the room and nestles into a sunbeam. Warren sees the article by Della:

INSERT: headline "Cold Case Victim May Be Tied to Garden Lakes."

Warren's girlfriend, SARAH, 20s, pads into the room, just awake.

SARAH
What's wrong?

WARREN
What? Why?

SARAH
You have that look.

WARREN
(smiles)
I'm glad you're the only one who knows about the look, or my law career will be short-lived.

Sarah pours herself a cup of coffee and flops down in the easy chair across from Warren.

SARAH
So?

WARREN
Nothing. Just a thing in the paper.

He hands her the paper and she quickly reads it. Warren
watches her reaction.

SARAH
They love the Garden Lakes story still, I see.

WARREN
Yeah.

SARAH
Maybe every local mystery will eventually be tied back to
it. It'll become a thing.

She tosses the paper on the coffee table.

SARAH (CONT'D)
It's like the moon landing and the Kennedy assassination.
Everyone wants to believe in the conspiracy.

WARREN
Wait, you think the moon landing was real?

SARAH
(rolling her eyes)
Oh right, you think the CIA and the mob killed Kennedy, I
forgot.

Warren laughs. He picks up the paper again, banging it
against his knee.

WARREN
In this case, the official story had a few elisions.

Sarah screws up her face.

INT. GARDEN LAKES HOUSING DEVELOPMENT –
CAFETERIA HALLWAY – DAY – (FLASHBACK)

YOUNG WARREN JAMES, 17, Young Duane Handley,
and Young Jason Figueroa are huddled together.

YOUNG DUANE HANDLEY
She can't stay.

YOUNG WARREN JAMES
Who says?

YOUNG JASON FIGUEROA
I'm sorry, man. But you know the rules. We've got work
to do.

YOUNG WARREN JAMES
We could use her help, right?

YOUNG DUANE HANDLEY
No way. She stays and Smurf will want to bring his
girlfriend back and this whole thing will blow up on us.
C'mon.

YOUNG JASON FIGUEROA
Hands is right, Warren. We gotta finish this thing on our
own if we want credit.

YOUNG DUANE HANDLEY
Not to mention becoming legends.

Warren knows what they're saying is true and doesn't
persist.

INT. WARREN'S APARTMENT – MORNING –
CONTINUOUS

SARAH
Hey. Yoo-hoo. You gonna tell me?

WARREN
Yeah. After breakfast, though.

INT. TIBURON BAR - LATE AFTERNOON

Detective Berry and Della enter the barely lit bar. A
smattering of patrons drink at tables here and there. The
bar has no decorations save for a mural of a giant shark
and Christmas lights hanging from the ceiling.

DETECTIVE BERRY
This isn't depressing.

DELLA
Speak for yourself. This is the kind of place I lived in back
in college.

DETECTIVE BERRY
Really. Figured you for a Fat Tuesday's kind of girl.

They spot GEORGE SIMPSON, 50s, drinking at the end
of the bar.

DELLA
How do you want to play this guy?

DETECTIVE BERRY
Well, seems like our choices are either the promise of sex
with one or both of us, or I flash my badge.

DELLA
Stark choices.

DETECTIVE BERRY
Guy spends all day around teenage boys. And this place
doesn't seem like it attracts women, so.

DELLA
Been awhile since I used my sexuality for anything.

DETECTIVE BERRY
Ok, we'll go with the badge.

They approach the empty stools on either side of Simpson,
who takes a sip of his whiskey.

SIMPSON
Ladies.

DETECTIVE BERRY
(shows her badge)
Buy a girl a drink?

Simpson gives them both a look.

SIMPSON
Sure.

Nods to the bartender.

DETECTIVE BERRY
Cranberry and seltzer.

DELLA
Two.

SIMPSON
(to Detective Berry)
My brother was a cop.

DETECTIVE BERRY
I know. I'm sorry.

SIMPSON
Everyone was so sure they'd catch the son-of-a-bitch who
ran him down.

DETECTIVE BERRY
We will.

SIMPSON
(snorts)
Hope I live long enough.

DETECTIVE BERRY
This is Della. She's a reporter for the Gazette.

Simpson raises his glass and nods.

The bartender sets down their drinks.

DELLA
We've met. I wrote the articles about Garden Lakes.

SIMPSON
(narrows his eyes)
Long time ago.

DELLA
I remember that day you were already there when the
parents got wind and rushed down to collect their children.

SIMPSON
Was a clusterfuck.

DELLA
I never understood how you got there so quickly.

Simpson drains his glass and motions to the bartender for another.

SIMPSON
Just doing my job.

DETECTIVE BERRY
Remarkable, though. Kid calls 911 and you show up.

SIMPSON
It was a scheduled visit. Check with Randolph.

DETECTIVE BERRY
No, I'm sure they'll say so.

DELLA
Your brother didn't tip you off?

SIMPSON
Who are you to talk to me about my brother?

Bartender sets his drink down and he sips it.

DELLA
No disrespect. It's just always bothered me.

SIMPSON
How about you write an article about how the cops can't seem to locate the asshole who killed my brother during a traffic stop. That's always bothered me.
They all drink their drinks.

Detective Berry produces the poster of the cold case victim.

DETECTIVE BERRY
We think this girl was with those kids at Garden Lakes.

SIMPSON
(looks at the picture)
So what if she was?

DETECTIVE BERRY
Are you saying she was?

SIMPSON
No.

DELLA
Was there a girl there?

Simpson eyes her.

DELLA (CONT'D)
Katie Sullivan?

DETECTIVE BERRY
We heard the teacher ran off with her.

SIMPSON
School says he moved to California to be closer to family.

DETECTIVE BERRY
This her?

She holds up the poster. Simpson doesn't look at it again.

SIMPSON
Dunno. Never met her.

DETECTIVE BERRY
But she was a student at St. Agnes?

Simpson nods.

DELLA
What happened?

SIMPSON
Guy drove off with her. Shit hit the fan. Teach got sent
packing.

DETECTIVE BERRY
But what happened to the girl?

Simpson shrugs.

EXT. TEMPE TOWN LAKE - DAY

A CROWD OF PEOPLE rim the man-made lake as they
watch a dragon boat race, sun glinting off the smooth
water. CHEERING can be heard as one dragon boat
overtakes another. At the edge of the crowd, Handley and
Figueroa are huddled with CASEY MURFIN, 23.

MURFIN
I don't know what you want me to do about it.

HANDLEY
Just giving you a head's up.

FIGUEROA
Can't have this thing come unraveled now.

MURFIN
Agree. Tell the others?

HANDLEY
Came to you first.

FIGUEROA
Roger is overseas, so that's solid.

MURFIN
What about Assburn? He's all over the radio. He could
blow it.

FIGUEROA
Took care of Assburn.

MURFIN
(gives a look)
What about Warren. That earnest little asshole could spill.

HANDLEY
He's in law school down in Tucson.

MURFIN
The sophomores are down there too. They all share a house
near campus.

HANDLEY
The reporter might track them down. She interviewed them
back in the day.

FIGUEROA
If everyone sticks to the story, we're in the clear.

MURFIN
I'll tell them.

The three walk off in different directions.

EXT. CENTRAL HIGH SCHOOL – PARKING LOT

Detective Berry waits in her car. The BELL RINGS and
students filter out of the buildings. She squints and smirks
as she spots Keith, but the smirk disappears when
REBECCA, 16, tags along behind him, followed by Nate.
The three laugh about something. Nate says something to

them and jogs over to the car while Keith and Rebecca wait.

DETECTIVE BERRY
Hey.

NATE
Hey. Is it all right if I go to Scottsdale Fashion Square?

DETECTIVE BERRY
How you getting there?

NATE
Rebecca said she'd drive us.

DETECTIVE BERRY
Who's us?

She looks over at Keith and Rebecca, who are chatting and laughing.

NATE
C'mon, Mom.

DETECTIVE BERRY
Doesn't Keith have his own car?

NATE
It's in the shop or something. I dunno. Can I go?

Detective Berry gives a half nod. She's not happy about it, but knows there's no point in saying anything.

NATE (CONT'D)
Great! Be home for dinner.

He runs back towards Keith and Rebecca. As the three

head towards Rebecca's car, Keith gives Detective Berry a glance and a smirk.

EXT. DESERT LEDGE HOUSING DEVELOPMENT - DAY

Della drives past the sign for "Desert Ledge: a McCloud Community" and parks near the lunch truck. Construction workers are spread around, sitting in what little shade there is, eating their food. Della approaches and the lunch truck owner, VIC, 60s, nods.

DELLA
Hey-ya, Vic.

VIC
(warily)
Lois Lane.

DELLA
Long time.

VIC
Yeah? The days all run together when there are no seasons.

He points to the sky.

DELLA
True, true.

VIC
You hungry or am I not that lucky?

DELLA
Hey, I kept your name out of the Garden Lakes stuff.

VIC

Yeah, but McCloud put us all through background checks thanks to you. Was real paranoid. Had me on probation for a couple of months, which killed the bottom line.

DELLA

Sorry about that.

VIC

(waving her off)
Just ask me what you want to ask me.

DELLA

Hear about that hit-and-run at Sunset Meridian. The little girl?

VIC

Yeah. Terrible.

DELLA

(nods at workers)
These guys talking about it?

VIC

(smiles)
I don't speak Spanish.

DELLA

But you understand it.

VIC

(gives her a look)
Poquito.
(quietly)
Yeah okay maybe one thing. There's a loudmouth on this crew who always buys jalapeno poppers--I get them from Jack-in-the-Box for him, the only kind he likes. Every day,

as many as I've got.

DELLA
Those are surprisingly good.

VIC
Seems like a bunch of the others are a little afraid of
Poppers, the way he's always loud and does whatever. You
can see it in their eyes.

DELLA
Which one is he?

VIC
That's the thing. Right around the time that little girl got
hit, Poppers disappeared. Haven't seen him since.

DELLA
Could be out sick.

VIC
Nothing can bring this S.O.B low.

DELLA
What then?

VIC
One of McCloud's foremen said Poppers took a company
vehicle without permission. Boss found out and sent him
back to Mexico.

EXT. RED ROCK TOURS PARKING LOT - DAY

Detective Berry leans against her car, sunglasses on against
the late afternoon sun, as a tour bus pulls into the parking
lot and glides toward the stucco depot. Casey Murfin is the
tour guide and as the bus shudders to a stop, he sees Berry

and then pretends like he doesn't. The bus door opens and tourists file out into the bright light.

MURFIN
(grandly)
Thank you all again for such a magnificent afternoon!

Detective Berry pushes off her car and moves in his direction and he purposefully takes the arm of a Tourist who doesn't really need his help.

TOURIST
Thank you, dear.

MURFIN
I hope you enjoyed yourself.

DETECTIVE BERRY
Excuse me, Smurf?

Murfin pretends to be startled.

DETECTIVE BERRY (CONT'D)
That's what they call you, right. Smurf?

The tourists continue to disembark and Murfin drifts away from them.

MURFIN
Only my friends call me that. You a friend?

DETECTIVE BERRY
(shows her badge)
Definitely not. But I'll bet your friends told you about me.

MURFIN
What do you want?

Detective Berry shows him the poster of the girl from the cold case.

MURFIN (CONT'D)
Seems like a nice girl.

DETECTIVE BERRY
Was she?

MURFIN
How would I know?

DETECTIVE BERRY
(motions to the empty parking lot)
The audience is gone, you can drop the act.

MURFIN
(patronizing)
Do you have a question for me?

DETECTIVE BERRY
Just trying to confirm that the girl in the photo is Katie Sullivan, the girl Mr. Malagon ran off with in the middle of the night.

She puts the photo in his face, but he flicks it away.

MURFIN
How did you find out about Malagon?

DETECTIVE BERRY
Want to see the badge again?

MURFIN
Man, I can't say anything about that.

DETECTIVE BERRY
Don't call me "man." Why not?

MURFIN
We all signed the papers.

DETECTIVE BERRY
What papers?

MURFIN
The school made us sign papers saying we wouldn't talk
about it.

DETECTIVE BERRY
What did they offer you in return?

MURFIN
(smartly)
The chance to graduate.

DETECTIVE BERRY
I can do them one better and offer you the chance to stay
out of jail.

MURFIN
Whoa. Why am I going to jail?

DETECTIVE BERRY
Tell me what you know about Katie Sullivan.

MURFIN
(considers, then:)
I don't know anything. Her parents sued the school. She
wasn't at St. Agnes anymore. Heard she changed her
name.

DETECTIVE BERRY
See, you can be helpful. Bet the school paid her parents
off. They pay off the construction guy, too. What's his
name. Baker?

MURFIN
Man, I cannot tell you these things.

DETECTIVE BERRY
What did I say about the "man" stuff?

MURFIN
Sorry, sorry. No offense meant.

DETECTIVE BERRY
The whole thing is offensive.

INT. WARREN'S APARTMENT - DAY

Handley and Figueroa are standing in Warren's kitchen
when Warren walks in. He is startled to see them.

WARREN
How did you get in?

HANDLEY
Amy let us in.

WARREN
(a little panicked)
Who's Amy?

FIGUEROA
Your girlfriend?

WARREN
Sarah.

He closes the door and tosses his keys on the counter.

FIGUEROA
Right, sorry.

HANDLEY
How've you been, Warren?

WARREN
Been better.

HANDLEY
Sorry to hear that.

They move to the living room and all sit around the coffee table.

WARREN
Assume you're here about the thing in the newspaper.

FIGUEROA
They come around to you yet?

Warren shakes his head no.

HANDLEY
They will.

WARREN
And you're here to tell me what to say? Cuz those days are over.

FIGUEROA
Cool it. We just want to make sure everyone is still on the same page.

HANDLEY
And keeping our promise to the school.

WARREN
Fuck them, and fuck the both of you. Maybe it's time we
come clean.

FIGUEROA
I'd think about that if I were you.

WARREN
(mocking)
Would you? This thing clearly isn't going to go away.

HANDLEY
It will. It has. This is a little tremor. The last one, likely.

WARREN
You can't know that.

FIGUEROA
You of all people should know that breaking the
confidentiality agreement we signed with Randolph would
be bad news.

WARREN
For them, too. Coercing a bunch of kids into signing it. We
were all minors anyway, so they're invalid.

HANDLEY
And then what? We all look like a bunch of liars?

Warren puts his head in his hands.

FIGUEROA
They might kick you out of law school, too.

Warren jolts to his feet and paces.

HANDLEY
We didn't come here to hassle you, really. We just have to
stick together a little longer on this. Everything has already
happened. It's done. All we do is keep nodding along.

FIGUEROA
Smurf says the cops think the picture of the girl they found
in the desert is Katie Sullivan.

WARREN
(his eyes widen)
He tell them that?

FIGUEROA
They assumed.

WARREN
So they're onto the Malagon story. Who gave them Katie
Sullivan's name?

HANDLEY
Assburn, probably.

WARREN
(moans)
Christ.

HANDLEY
Have you seen the sophomores?

WARREN
See them around. They live together on a house over on
Speedway.

FIGUEROA
Talk to them?

WARREN
Tried to once in a Taco Bell, but they bolted. They're
clearly still freaked.

FIGUEROA
But Randolph gave them all tuition waivers for their junior
and senior years, so that's a debt they have to honor.

WARREN
Or what?

EXT. WARREN'S APARTMENT COMPLEX -
MOMENTS LATER

Handley and Figueroa are getting into separate cars.

FIGUEROA
You didn't tell him whose picture the cops have.

HANDLEY
He didn't ask.

Gets in the car and SLAMS the door and drives away.
Figueroa looks up at Warren's apartment and sees Warren
in the window.

EXT. DESERT OUTSIDE GARDEN LAKES – DAY –
(FLASHBACK)

Young Warren James trudges away from Garden Lakes.

MOMENTS LATER:

Young Warren James is deeper into the desert. Garden

Lakes is no longer in view. He spies a migrant camp ahead. Migrants are on Break in various poses of relaxation. He spies a girl, AXIA, 19, from behind, busying herself with something can't see.

INT. DETECTIVE BERRY'S CONDO – MORNING

Detective Berry is at the kitchen table, drinking her morning coffee. Nate bounds down the stairs and grabs his backpack off the couch, searching through the bag to make sure he has everything.

DETECTIVE BERRY
You see the message from Keith?

NATE
(distracted)
Yeah.

DETECTIVE BERRY
What did he want?

NATE
Some homework thing?

He zips up his bag, satisfied that it's packed for the day.

DETECTIVE BERRY
You doing his homework for him?

NATE
(laughs)
Nah.

DETECTIVE BERRY
I guess the administration didn't find out about his bullying Rebecca, huh?

NATE
Why?

DETECTIVE BERRY
Because he didn't get suspended.

NATE
Bullying is a strong word.

DETECTIVE BERRY
Not strong enough if you ask me. I'm surprised Rebecca
isn't more upset.

NATE
(shrugs)
Just kid stuff.

DETECTIVE BERRY
Thought she was smarter than that. You too.

NATE
Me too what?

DETECTIVE BERRY
Too smart to hang out with the likes of Keith.

NATE
(slings his bag over his shoulder)
Not really hanging out with him. Just easier to get along,
know what I mean?

DETECTIVE BERRY
(likes this savvy answer)
Yeah, I guess I do.

NATE
Plus he's transferring to Randolph next year. Says he's

done slumming it in public school.

He grabs his sunglasses and doesn't see her anguished reaction to the comment.

NATE (CONT'D)
Ready?

INT. TIBURON BAR - LATE AFTERNOON

Della breezes in and finds George Simpson at his usual spot in the otherwise empty bar.

DELLA
You aren't hard to find.

SIMPSON
Not hidin'.

DELLA
Mind?

He shrugs. She pulls up a stool.

SIMPSON
You didn't bring the cop.

DELLA
(sassy)
We don't go everywhere together.

The bartender appears and Della points at Simpson's beer.

DELLA (CONT'D)
(to bartender)
Two more, please.

Bartender nods.

SIMPSON
Why you here?

DELLA
I did a little digging about your brother.

Simpson drains the last of his beer, the late afternoon sun shining through the empty glass end as he tilts it skyward. He sets the bottle down carefully and looks at her.

The bartender sets two fresh beers down and snatches the empty.

SIMPSON
Yeah?

DELLA
I'm working on a piece about the guy who car bombed my colleague--

SIMPSON
I read about that.

DELLA
He said he did it as a favor to Evan McCloud, but McCloud says he doesn't know the guy.

SIMPSON
Does he?

DELLA
Unclear. But I was out at one of McCloud's developments and a foreman told me that one of the day laborers borrowed a car without permission and was back in Mexico the next day.

SIMPSON
(interested)
Yeah?

Della nods.

SIMPSON (CONT'D)
You're wasting your time.

DELLA
What?

SIMPSON
McCloud's a dead end. He's untouchable.

DELLA
No one is untouchable.

SIMPSON
I seemed to remember him skating away from all the
Garden Lakes mess pretty easily.

DELLA
I made sure his name was mentioned in every article.

SIMPSON
Doesn't seem to have hurt his business.

Della gives a pained look.

DELLA
Speaking of. I've talked to most of the students who were
at Garden Lakes that summer. They're all clearly lying, but
hard to say about what exactly.

SIMPSON
I can't talk about the students. I'll lose my job.

DELLA
Not asking you to. Just making an observation.

SIMPSON
It's almost as if they have their stories straight, right?

Della eyes him.

DELLA
I'm not going to ask you if Randolph is covering up the
murder of a student by one of their teachers--

Simpson chokes on his beer.

SIMPSON
Jesus. What the fuck are you talking about?

DELLA
We know about Katie Sullivan and Malagon.

SIMPSON
(nonchalantly)
That's all taken care of.

DELLA
What do you mean?

SIMPSON
The I's have been dotted
(makes the Sign of the Cross)
And the T's have been crossed.

DELLA
So you're part of the cover-up?

SIMPSON
(shakes his head)

Nope. For the record, I don't know anything about it and I have no comment. Be sure to spell my name right.

DELLA
If you talk, I can put you on background. Not use your name.

Simpson finishes his beer and stands.

SIMPSON
Thanks, but no.

Della takes a long swig of her untouched beer.

DELLA
How complicated will your life become if I write a piece suggesting that Malagon killed Katie Sullivan and got away with it, and that you and everyone at Randolph are covering it up?

SIMPSON
(smirks)
Not as complicated as yours would become.

DELLA
That a threat?

SIMPSON
Katie Sullivan is alive and well.

EXT. GARDEN LAKES HOUSING DEVELOPMENT –
MALAGON'S HOUSE – NIGHT – (FLASHBACK)

Young Duane Handley and Young Jason Figueroa are peering through the lit window of a finished home. The girl Mr. Malagon is kissing, KATIE SULLIVAN, 17, turns her head towards the window. She's not the girl in the cold case poster. Mr. Malagon looks over her shoulder at the window too.

INT. TIBURON BAR – CONTINUOUS

SIMPSON
Her parents settled with the school and moved away. Got a new name, the whole shebang.

DELLA
Know the new name?

SIMPSON
Do yourself a favor and don't try to find out.

Simpson heads for the exit.

Della sits stunned, looking after him.

EXT. KEITH'S HOUSE - NIGHT

Detective Berry KNOCKS on the door. KEITH'S MOTHER, late 40s, answers. Detective Berry flashes her badge.

INT. KEITH'S HOUSE - MOMENTS LATER

Detective Berry is standing in the spacious tiled kitchen outfitted with expensive appliances. Keith's Mother stands with her arms crossed, a worried frown on her face. The front door OPENS AND CLOSES and the SOUND OF FOOTSTEPS approaching is heard. Keith freezes when he enters the kitchen and sees Detective Berry and the look on his mother's face.

KEITH
Now what?

KEITH'S MOTHER
She's with the police.

KEITH
Yeah, I know.

KEITH'S MOTHER
(alarmed)
You know?

DETECTIVE BERRY
I'm here because your car was spotted at a party where a
girl was victimized.

KEITH
(skeptical)
When?

DETECTIVE BERRY
Last weekend.

KEITH'S MOTHER
(impatiently)
Where you there. Did you see anything?

DETECTIVE BERRY
The girl's name is Rebecca. Know her?

Gives Keith a hard stare.

KEITH'S MOTHER
Answer her.

KEITH
I don't know anything.

DETECTIVE BERRY
(to Keith's Mother)
She's pretty traumatized but as soon as she's able, we'll hear what she has to say.

KEITH'S MOTHER
(to Keith)
I swear to God if you're involved in this--

KEITH
I'm not!

DETECTIVE BERRY
(calmly)
If you know anything, it would be helpful.

KEITH'S MOTHER
(throws up her hands)
Your father is going to have to deal with this. I'm done.

KEITH
No! Don't say anything to him!

He gives Detective Berry a pleading look.

DETECTIVE BERRY
I'd be happy to come back and speak with him.

KEITH'S MOTHER
He's out of town until next week.

DETECTIVE BERRY
I'll leave my card.

She smirks at Keith while his mother looks at the card.

INT. PHOENIX GAZETTE - BRENNAN'S OFFICE -
DAY

Della is across the desk from Brennan. The PHONE
RINGS but he doesn't make a move to answer it.

BRENNAN
I specifically warned you.

DELLA
But I said "suspected." That's playing by the rules.

BRENNAN
But it's only you who suspects McCloud's day laborer of
being the driver in the hit and run. Do the cops suspect
him?

Della is quiet.

BRENNAN (CONT'D)
We can't do what we do here if one of our reporters
compromises the paper's integrity. Think about that while
you're on suspension.

INT. HEMPEL'S ON MAIN RESTAURANT AND BAR
– MIDDAY

Hempel's is a warm, casual bar with brick walls and
leather couches. Della is seated at the horseshoe-shaped
bar when Detective Berry walks in.

INT. HEMPEL'S RESTAURANT AND BAR -
MOMENTS LATER

Detective Berry and Della have moved to a leather couch
with their drinks.

DETECTIVE BERRY
It'll blow over.

DELLA
Just as long as that asshole McCloud doesn't use it as a distraction from all his other shit.

They both sip their drinks.

DETECTIVE BERRY
I took a drive out to the Sonoran Desert Rehab place to see if I could get at Charlie Martens.

DELLA
And?

DETECTIVE BERRY
Buckley's got him locked away tight.

DELLA
How long is he in?

DETECTIVE BERRY
It's voluntary, so who knows.

DELLA
Who the fuck would voluntarily do something like that?

Detective Berry sets her drink down and leans in.

DETECTIVE BERRY
I wondered the same. Very weird. And then I got a tip from the overly chatty receptionist.

INT. SONORAN DESERT REHABILITATION CENTER - DAY - (FLASHBACK)

Detective Berry is in the reception area, which is a vast white space with a short marble counter, like a hotel. The receptionist, 20s, is a tall, lithe woman with an open face and bright eyes and her blonde hair pulled back tight. She wears a discreet metal name badge with the name TINA etched in cursive.

TINA
Oh, I almost forgot.

She reaches under the counter and hands over a bulky envelope. Detective Berry opens the envelope and finds a pair of sunglasses.

TINA (CONT'D)
Your colleague left these here this morning. Thought he might want them back.

Detective Berry gives her a look, processing the information.

DETECTIVE BERRY
Right, thanks.

TINA
Ask him to get you on the approved list. I feel bad!

DETECTIVE BERRY
He's sort of a pain in the ass about the details.

TINA
As long as he keeps bringing me presents from Miami. My brother's been but not me. He said it was awesome.

INT. HEMPEL'S ON MAIN RESTAURANT AND BAR - CONTINUOUS

Detective Berry smiles.

DETECTIVE BERRY
So I called around Miami Dade and tracked down said
colleague and it seems our man Charlie got himself into a
little trouble there.

Della stares at her intently over the rim of her highball
glass.

DETECTIVE BERRY (CONT'D)
Seems he ended up bartending at some dive where he had
an apartment upstairs.

DELLA
Ugh. I know those bars.

DETECTIVE BERRY
One night at closing time he invites a woman upstairs and
what happened next depends on who you ask.

DELLA
He rape her?

DETECTIVE BERRY
They never knew. She filed a complaint but then
disappeared. The whole thing was like a car crash on a
deserted road.

DELLA
They arrest him for anything?

DETECTIVE BERRY
Nope. Just suggested that he move on.

DELLA
Whose idea was the rehab place?

DETECTIVE BERRY
(sipping her drink)
Had to have been Buckley's.

DELLA
Why are they visiting him there, then?

DETECTIVE BERRY
Apparently, the girl turns up periodically screaming at them for not doing anything, so they take a flight and sit down with him.

DELLA
Surprised Buckley allows that.

DETECTIVE BERRY
He put up a fight, but he also wants to keep it out of the press, so.

DELLA
Charlie tell them anything new?

DETECTIVE BERRY
Sticking to his story.

DELLA
Did you tell Miami about Katie Sullivan?

DETECTIVE BERRY
Said he'd ask Charlie about it next time he has to come out.

DELLA
(dead-pan)
Great.

A beat passes between them.

DELLA (CONT'D)
How's Nate?

DETECTIVE BERRY
Wants to spend the summer with his father in California.

Della gives her a sympathetic look.

DELLA
What about the summer thing?

DETECTIVE BERRY
(shakes her head)
Didn't get it.

DELLA
Oh, sorry.

DETECTIVE BERRY
What's worse is he expected not to get it.

DELLA
Self-sabotage?

DETECTIVE BERRY
World weariness. After all the time shielding them from
the crappy realities, they suss it out for themselves.

DELLA
High school is good for that.

DETECTIVE BERRY
I guess. Still. You think those fucks at Randolph live in the
same world?

DELLA
Eh, their whole lives are lived in a bubble.

DETECTIVE BERRY
I'd like to pop it.

EXT. AIRPORT RUNWAY - DAY

Detective Berry looks out the window as the plane lands. A copy of the Phoenix Gazette is in her lap, a picture of the cold case above the fold.

Insert: headline "Police Seek Identity of Cold Case Victim"

STEWARDESS (V.O.)
Welcome to Lincoln, Nebraska. Current time is 1:15pm and the weather is sunny and 70. Thank you for flying with us...

INT. LINCOLN AIRPORT - MOMENTS LATER

Detective Berry deplanes and makes her way through the terminal.

MALE (V.O.)
Yeah, the girl in the paper? We picked her up on the freeway. It was our spring break and we were headed to Mexico. You know, fun in the sun.

DETECTIVE BERRY (V.O.)
Did she tell you her name?

MALE (V.O.)
Maybe. Can't recall. But I remember she said she was from Lincoln, Nebraska because someone in the car was from Iowa and he tried to pick a fight with her about whose football team was better. What was that dick's name?

Detective Berry gets into a cab and the cab pulls away from the airport.

EXT. RANCH HOUSE ON A QUIET STREET - LATE AFTERNOON

The cab idles in the driveway.

INT. RANCH HOUSE - CONTINUOUS

Detective Berry sits at a Formica table in a cluttered, dimly-lit kitchen across from DETECTIVE TURNBULL, 70s, who is staring at the poster of the cold case. They both have piping tea cups in front of them.

DETECTIVE TURNBULL
(quietly)
That's her. Definitely.

DETECTIVE BERRY
What's her name?

DETECTIVE TURNBULL
She had a couple. Her given name was Virginia, but the couple who adopted her, the Graysons, renamed her Lisa because the mother had an aunt named Virginia that she hated.

DETECTIVE BERRY
Wow.

DETECTIVE TURNBULL
(grimly)
It was a strict household. No TV, no friends over, just school and then home.

DETECTIVE BERRY
Religious?

DETECTIVE TURNBULL
Just strict. She found out she was adopted when she was
fourteen and it was like woosh! And then the trouble
started.

DETECTIVE BERRY
Like what?

Steeps her tea bag as the steam rises from the cup.

DETECTIVE TURNBULL
Typical teenage rebellion at first. Then the running away.

DETECTIVE BERRY
Where would she go?

DETECTIVE TURNBULL
Not far. Neighbors' houses.

DETECTIVE BERRY
How did her parents react?

DETECTIVE TURNBULL
Over-reacted at first. Then gave up.

DETECTIVE BERRY
(sipping her tea)
Any idea how she ended up in Arizona?

DETECTIVE TURNBULL
That's a story. Of course no one knew she'd gone to
Arizona. But everyone knew when she left.

DETECTIVE BERRY
Yeah?

DETECTIVE TURNBULL
It wasn't her fault.

DETECTIVE BERRY
Boyfriend?

DETECTIVE TURNBULL
You could say. You see all the Breck Oil signage around
town on your way in?

Detective Berry nods, sips her tea.

DETECTIVE TURNBULL (CONT'D)
Three generations of upstanding Brecks—or as upstanding
as oil barons can be—but the fourth was no good.
Everyone had problems with Truman.

DETECTIVE BERRY
Two troubled kids, then?

DETECTIVE TURNBULL
Truman was no kid. He was ten years older. And married.

Detective Berry reacts to this.

DETECTIVE TURNBULL (CONT'D)
His wife was from our other prominent family, the
Leonards. Bankers. Anyway, Truman was into all sorts of
things. You'd hear rumors down at the station, but nothing
you could prove.

DETECTIVE BERRY
Violence?

DETECTIVE TURNBULL
Sometimes. But bruises can't testify.

DETECTIVE BERRY
Know that story well.

DETECTIVE TURNBULL
Lisa had literary ambitions. Always talking about moving to New York to be a writer. So Truman gets her a job writing smut for an old oilman friend of his father's. Real sick stuff.

DETECTIVE BERRY
Her parents find out?

DETECTIVE TURNBULL
By then, Truman had left his wife and he and Lisa were shacked up in the Providence Hotel downtown. Ordering room service for every meal. By some accounts, not bathing regularly.

DETECTIVE BERRY
Wait, I know this story.

DETECTIVE TURNBULL
Know it made the national news. Truman gets her head all twisted around and convinces her to be in a suicide pact.

DETECTIVE BERRY
But after he shot himself, she didn't.

DETECTIVE TURNBULL
Correct. We think she was alone with the body for a day or two before she fled.

DETECTIVE BERRY
No one heard the shot?

DETECTIVE TURNBULL
They had the penthouse, which is the entire top floor. And it was a small caliber pistol.

DETECTIVE BERRY
What tipped the police?

DETECTIVE TURNBULL
Chambermaid. He was starting to stink.

DETECTIVE BERRY
And she vanished?

DETECTIVE TURNBULL
One of the papers started a rumor that maybe she was the one who pulled the trigger on him.

DETECTIVE BERRY
Fingerprints?

DETECTIVE TURNBULL
Gun was wiped clean. Found it in the pocket of his robe.

Pulls the cold case poster towards him and keeps his finger on it.

DETECTIVE TURNBULL (CONT'D)
The thing they don't tell you about retirement is that your mind continues to work the cases.

INT. UNIVERSITY OF ARIZONA LAW LIBRARY - DAY

Detective Berry enters and scans the quiet room full of Students studying at tables and cubicles. She spots Warren with his head buried in a book. He doesn't see her come up behind him and lay the cold case poster over his open book. Warren looks up, fearfully.

EXT. UNIVERSITY OF ARIZONA LAW LIBRARY - CONTINUOUS

Detective Berry and Warren stand in the blazing sunlight as Students scurry by.

DETECTIVE BERRY
I know you know her, Warren.

WARREN
Who says I do?

DETECTIVE BERRY
Not who, but what. The fact that you're all pretending not to.

She holds up the poster again. Warren looks away.

DETECTIVE BERRY (CONT'D)
(softly)
C'mon. You'll feel better. Help me put this all to rest.

WARREN
(exhales, then:)
She called herself Axia, but her real name was something else.

DETECTIVE BERRY
Lisa. She was from Lincoln, Nebraska. I just got back.

WARREN
(eyes widen)
If you know all of this, why are you bothering me?

DETECTIVE BERRY
Because I want to know what happened out there. It was you who found her in that camp, convinced her to join in the fun at Garden Lakes.

WARREN
Who says it was me?

DETECTIVE BERRY
Who says it wasn't?

Warren hesitates, then nods.

DETECTIVE BERRY (CONT'D)
Did something happen to her there?

WARREN
Nothing. She stayed for a few days and then took off.

DETECTIVE BERRY
That's what we call in the business bullshit, Warren.

WARREN
(defensive)
It's true!

DETECTIVE BERRY
Ok, so she was there and then she left. What aren't you telling me?

WARREN
What is it you want me to say. She stayed maybe three nights and then we woke up and she was gone. I tried to find her--

DETECTIVE BERRY
You tried to find her?

WARREN
I wanted her to know she could stay longer if she needed
to. She didn't have anywhere else to go.

DETECTIVE BERRY
But she didn't want to stay? Or was she getting perved?

WARREN
(annoyed)
Nothing like that. She probably just didn't dig all the chaos
that was going on.

DETECTIVE BERRY
Was Katie Sullivan there at the same time?

WARREN
(surprised but trying to play it off)
No.

DETECTIVE BERRY
There's one thing that doesn't make a lot of sense.

WARREN
(warily)
What?

DETECTIVE BERRY
Why cover it up. If she really left on her own, why are all
you douchebags pretending like it never happened?

Warren shuffles his feet and leans against the building.

DETECTIVE BERRY (CONT'D)
Maybe I'll leak to the press that you told me she was there
and now she's a rotted corpse. I remember how much you
and your friends like being in the news.

WARREN
Oh, God.

DETECTIVE BERRY
Give me a reason not to. Tell me why everyone is covering
it up.

WARREN
Because her arrival started everything that happened there.

DETECTIVE BERRY
What exactly happened?

Warren considers.

DETECTIVE BERRY (CONT'D)
(sternly)
What happened, Warren?

WARREN
I've told you the truth, but the answer to that question
affects more lives than my own, so I cannot tell you.

He starts to walk away.

DETECTIVE BERRY
(calling after him)
You'll make a hell of a lawyer.

WARREN
Thank you.

Opens the library door forcefully and disappears inside.

INT. SUPERMAX PRISON - WAITING AREA - DAY

Detective Berry and Della are emptying their personal

items into lockers while a PRISON MATRON, 30s, stands nearby.

DETECTIVE BERRY
Think he's trying to reduce his sentence?

DELLA
Nah, he's a lifer.

They shut their lockers.

PRISON MATRON
Earrings, too, please.

Della gives a quizzical look.

PRISON MATRON (CONT'D)
I've seen too many bloodied earlobes.

They remove their earrings.

SECURITY - CONTINUOUS

Detective Berry and Della move through metal detectors.

INTERVIEW ROOM - CONTINUOUS

Detective Berry and Della sit at a steel table in a spotless, windowless room.

DETECTIVE BERRY
Did the cellmate know about the car bomb?

DELLA
Said he didn't. Only confirmed that his old roommate was wacko, which plays if the guy really was a lone wolf.

DETECTIVE BERRY
You don't buy it, though?

DELLA
I can't tell anymore.

DETECTIVE BERRY
When will they let you back at work?

DELLA
Never if they find out I'm here.

The door CLICKS open and there's a long BUZZ and a
Prison Guard escorts an inmate, STANLEY JENKINS, 50s
to the table. Jenkins is shackled hands and feet and the
Prison Guard pulls the chair out for him. Jenkins sits and
the Prison Guard moves to the corner behind him.

DELLA (CONT'D)
Stanley, this is the detective I was telling you about.

JENKINS
You didn't tell me she was so pretty.

DETECTIVE BERRY
Maybe I'm not her type. I'm definitely not yours.

JENKINS
How you know?

DETECTIVE BERRY
I'm guessing at this stage in your life you're more into
men.

JENKINS
Next time I'm gonna close my eyes and think about you.

DELLA
We heard you know about the girl found in the desert.

JENKINS
I doubt it.

DELLA
You doubt we heard about it, or you don't know?

DETECTIVE BERRY
(to Della)
This feels like a waste of time.

DELLA
One shot, Stanley. When we leave, we don't come back.

JENKINS
So? No one asked you to come in the first place.

Detective Berry stands and the Prison Guard flinches, moves towards Jenkins.

DELLA
(desperately)
You said to bring someone who could help you. She can help.

Detective Berry and Jenkins eye each other. Jenkins breaks and nods for her to stay.

DELLA (CONT'D)
Did you tell your old cellmate about the girl in the desert?

JENKINS
Maybe.

DETECTIVE BERRY
Maybe doesn't make me want to stay.

DELLA
Did the kids at Garden Lakes hire you to do it?

Detective Berry looks at Della, but she's staring intently at
Jenkins, who stares back.

JENKINS
Maybe.

DETECTIVE BERRY
Maybe again?

JENKINS
What's in it for me?

DELLA
Depends on what you give us. How about a transfer to a
better facility?

JENKINS
Some funds in my prison account might help.

DETECTIVE BERRY
This guy sounds comfortable right where he is.

Jenkins looks at each of them, considering.

JENKINS
My memory isn't too good today. Lemme think on it.

EXT. RED ROCK TOURS - DAY

Casey Murfin is headed home after a long day. He opens
his car door and Detective Berry kicks it closed.

MURFIN
Hey!

DETECTIVE BERRY
Hey fuck you! You lied to me.

MURFIN
I did not.

DETECTIVE BERRY
(holds up the cold case poster)
You said this was Katie Sullivan.

MURFIN
You said it was Katie Sullivan.

DETECTIVE BERRY
(condescendingly)
How did such a sharp kid end up a tour guide for senior citizens. Maybe you could've been a lawyer like your buddy.

Murfin eyes her a little fearfully.

DETECTIVE BERRY (CONT'D)
Yeah, that's right. You know what Warren told me?

MURFIN
No.

DETECTIVE BERRY
Said he brought this girl into Garden Lakes when all you homos were out there doing what you were doing.

MURFIN
So?

DETECTIVE BERRY
I take it back. You're too dumb to be anything but a tour guide. Warren would know not to obstruct justice, like your dumbass is doing right now. He told me everything.

MURFIN
If he told you everything, you wouldn't be here.

DETECTIVE BERRY
(appraises him, then:)
Know a guy named Stanley Jenkins?

MURFIN
Should I?

DETECTIVE BERRY
Better hope for your sake that you haven't.

MURFIN
Can I go?

DETECTIVE BERRY
Don't go far.

She walks off.

MURFIN
(calling after her)
You dented my door!

Detective Berry smiles to herself.

EXT. CENTRAL HIGH SCHOOL – PARKING LOT – DAY

Keith pulls out of the parking lot, all of his windows down. A few blocks away, he looks in the rearview mirror and sees blue and red flashing lights. He eases to the side of the road, as does the cop car. A PATROLMAN gets out and approaches the driver's side.

PATROLMAN
License and registration, please.

KEITH
What did I do?

PATROLMAN
License and registration.

Keith leans over and opens his glovebox for his registration and a bag of cocaine falls out.

PATROLMAN (CONT'D)
Out of the car!

KEITH
That's not mine!

Patrolman yanks open the car door and forces Keith out.

EXT. I-10 FREEWAY - DAY

Casey Murfin is driving, his car door still dented. Duane Handley is in the passenger's seat and Dave Figueroa is in the back. The windows are down and the hot air is blowing all around them. All three are staring forward, lost in their thoughts.

MURFIN
What time did they say they'd be home?

HANDLEY
They didn't.

MURFIN
It's just a matter of time. They'll crack if that bitch cop gets to them.

FIGUEROA
We'll remind them what'll happen if they do.

Silence fills the car again.

EXT. APARTMENT COMPLEX ON EUCLID AVE - LATER

Murfin leans against the car while Handley and Figueroa KNOCK on the door of a ground floor apartment.
No one answers.

EXT. WARREN'S APARTMENT - A LITTLE LATER

Warren checks his mail and heads to his apartment. He finds Murfin, Handley, and Figueroa hanging out in the courtyard around a dry fountain.

MURFIN
You snitched.

WARREN
What?

MURFIN
You told the cop about the girl.

WARREN
Fuck you, she knew.

HANDLEY
How did she know?

WARREN
Don't know, but she just got back from Lincoln, Nebraska,
so...

FIGUEROA
What's in Lincoln, Nebraska?

HANDLEY
It's where she was from.

WARREN
Good recall. We done?

MURFIN
Nah. You told her something.

WARREN
Yeah, ok. I told her she was there, and then she was gone.
Simple as that.

FIGUEROA
You didn't tell her about all the shit she caused?

WARREN
That's not how I remember it.

MURFIN
But no one knows about all that shit and no one has to.

WARREN
Cuz we're heroes, right?

INT. SUPERMAX PRISON - VISITATION BOOTH -
DAY

Detective Berry sits in a chair in a booth. Next to her a
Woman is SPEAKING SPANISH quietly. There's a

BUZZ and a door on the other side of the glass opens.
Jenkins appears, his hulking presence suddenly filling the
booth as he sits. He picks up the receiver on the wall and
she does the same.

JENKINS
You again.

DETECTIVE BERRY
Me again.

JENKINS
Didn't think I'd see you again. You send-in? My account is
low and I owe, owe, owe.

Detective Berry shakes her head.

DETECTIVE BERRY
Sorry to hear that. You help me, maybe I can help you.

JENKINS
Ah, that's bullshit. You just want to use me.

DETECTIVE BERRY
You sure it's me who is using you. Not the other way
around?

JENKINS
Meaning?

DETECTIVE BERRY
I know you don't know anything about this case. Maybe
you read about it in the newspaper. If you can even read.
Maybe you just heard about it and wanted to be a big man.

JENKINS
I am a big man.

DETECTIVE BERRY
Only in your mind. You're a punk lifer.

Jenkins gives her a sadistic smile.

DETECTIVE BERRY (CONT'D)
So a reporter shows up and she hears that you've been bragging about killing the girl and that makes me have to come down here. And then you start asking for favors.

JENKINS
I might know more than you think.

DETECTIVE BERRY
(disinterested)
You probably know less.

JENKINS
(trying to call her bluff)
If you don't want the juice, I won't give it to you.

DETECTIVE BERRY
(dismissive)
Nothing you can tell me will make a difference in what I know.

JENKINS
What you think you know?

DETECTIVE BERRY
Bunch of spoiled kids fucked off for the summer, not working like most kids do, like my kid does. Not these kids, no. It isn't enough they go to private school—same elementary schools, same middle schools. Only know their own kind.

Camera shows the events as Detective Berry imagines they

happened:

SCENE: School bus outside Randolph Prep is loaded. The bus driver looks in the mirror and sees rows and rows of young male faces, all staring straight ahead.
MR. HANCOCK, 60s, strolls up the aisle, checking each seat for anything improper.

DETECTIVE BERRY (V.O.)
A group of the chosen are chosen again, to be part of an exclusive summer fellowship, one they'll use on college applications and resumes for years to come to vault ahead of other just-as-worthy candidates.

SCENE: Mr. Hancock stands near his car in the parking lot of Garden Lakes with Mr. Malagon, deep in discussion.

DETECTIVE BERRY (V.O.) (CONT'D)
But right away there's a small hiccup: one of the teachers, Mr. Hancock, has to take a personal leave. Mr. Malagon will have to hold down the fort, but only for a day or two.

SCENE: Mr. Malagon and Katie Sullivan on the couch in his house.

DETECTIVE BERRY (V.O.) (CONT'D)
Which is all he needs to sneak his teenage girlfriend in, a student at Randolph's sister school.

INT. SUPERMAX PRISON – VISITATION BOOTH – CONTINUOUS

Jenkins is momentarily gone from Detective Berry's thoughts as she puts the narrative together.

SCENE: Back at Garden Lakes, the previous flashback of Young Duane Handley and Young Jason Figueroa peering through the lit window while Mr. Malagon kisses a teenage girl plays again.

DETECTIVE BERRY (V.O.)
Or maybe she came out on her own. Teenage girls are sometimes like that. Putting others' best interests ahead of their own.

QUICK CUT: Keith and Rebecca together in the Central High parking lot.

QUICK CUT: Back to Young Duane Handley and Young Jason Figueroa outside Mr. Malagon's window. The flashback completes when the girl hears something and turns her head towards the window. It's Katie Sullivan. Mr. Malagon peers over her shoulder towards the window.

DETECTIVE BERRY (V.O.) (CONT'D)
Once exposed, Malagon would know instinctively that he's in a shitload of trouble.

SCENE: Mr. Malagon and Katie getting in Malagon's Jeep in the middle of the night.

DETECTIVE BERRY (V.O.) (CONT'D)
So he'd have to bolt.

SCENE: Jeep takes off, braking at the entrance to Garden Lakes before turning left and disappearing into the night.

DETECTIVE BERRY (V.O.) (CONT'D)
He'd lose his job, maybe his reputation, but Mr. Hancock is set to return in the morning, so the boys will be fine. Boys like them are always going to be fine.

SCENE: Day breaks over Garden Lakes, the boys waking in their various houses. Young Duane Handley, Young

Jason Figueroa, and Young Warren James are seated at a long table in the Garden Lakes cafeteria, Young Duane Handley standing and speaking to the other juniors, who are at their tables, eating breakfast.

DETECTIVE BERRY (V.O.) (CONT'D)
But Mr. Hancock doesn't return. And due to some internal...snafu, a replacement isn't sent.

QUICK CUT: Shot of empty Randolph Prep campus.

DETECTIVE BERRY (V.O.) (CONT'D)
It's summer after all and Randolph's administrators would be taking their hard-earned vacations.

SCENE: Young Duane Handley and Young Jason Figueroa coming out of Mr. Malagon's house in the morning, closing the door behind them as some juniors approach.

DETECTIVE BERRY (V.O.) (CONT'D)
Maybe everyone was in on the plan to stay quiet and soldier on.

SCENE: Young Duane Handley and Young Jason Figueroa sign for a food delivery from a driver, gesticulating and
shrugging.

DETECTIVE BERRY (V.O.) (CONT'D)
Or maybe they claimed Mr. Malagon was ill, if only to buy more time.

QUICK CUT: Young Jason Figueroa doubles over in a vomiting gesture, to the driver's amusement.

SCENE: Shots of juniors at Garden Lakes: self-studying in the classroom, working in shifts on the construction project, relaxing by playing cards in the living room of one of the houses.

DETECTIVE BERRY (V.O.) (CONT'D)
A few days go by and everyone is feeling sure they'll get away with everything. The idea of getting caught never occurs to them because all their lives their actions have never had consequences. (beat) They make it a week or so.

INT. SUPERMAX PRISON – VISITATION BOOTH – CONTINUOUS

Detective Berry opens her eyes. Jenkins is rapt by the narrative.

DETECTIVE BERRY
And then this other girl shows up.

She spreads her hands, to say "as if by magic."

QUICK CUT: Replay flashback of Young Warren James in the desert, stumbling across the migrant camp. Axia turns around and sees Young Warren James. She's the girl from the cold case poster.

QUICK CUT: Axia wandering into the midst of Garden Lakes with Young Warren James. The boys all stop and look.

DETECTIVE BERRY (CONT'D)
Everything turns on its head. Maybe she likes the attention, maybe not. But it doesn't matter, because the new leaders decide she can't stay.

SCENE: Replay of flashback from Garden Lakes showing

Young Warren James, Young Duane Handley, and Young Jason Figueroa huddled together deciding if Axia can stay or not.

DETECTIVE BERRY (V.O.)
But then something happens—probably an accident knowing these pussies—

QUICK CUT: Axia falling off a ladder, everyone rushing around her.

QUICK CUT: Axia playing soccer, is tripped, hits her head on a rock.

DETECTIVE BERRY (V.O.) (CONT'D)
And they bury her in the desert.

INSERT: Young Duane Handley and Young Jason Figueroa supervising the digging of a hole in the desert.

DETECTIVE BERRY (V.O.) (CONT'D)
Everything is chaos now. Those who didn't witness her death have heard rumors. Enter Mr. Baker, the construction overseer.

SCENE: Mr. Baker pulls up in his Statewide Construction pickup. He gets out and looks around, confused at the absence of order. A couple of juniors grab him.

QUICK CUT: Mr. Baker's mouth, arms, and legs are duct-taped as he sits in an empty room of one of the finished houses. He wriggles loose and gets to his truck.

DETECTIVE BERRY (V.O.) (CONT'D)
He finds the emergency channel on his CB, which is scanned by the police.

QUICK CUT: OFFICER SIMPSON, 40s, listening to the CB channel back at the police station. He picks up the phone.

DETECTIVE BERRY (V.O.) (CONT'D)
The call is intercepted and Randolph sends in their cleaner.

QUICK CUT: George Simpson answers the phone in his office at Randolph, listens, and runs out.

QUICK CUT: George Simpson speeding along the freeway, rushing through the gates of Garden Lakes.

DETECTIVE BERRY (V.O.) (CONT'D)
And by the time the police arrive, everyone's singing the same song.

QUICK CUT: George Simpson greets the police as they pull into Garden Lakes, their sirens not flashing. Simpson waves as they come to a stop, smiles.

DETECTIVE BERRY (V.O.) (CONT'D)
Randolph buys off Baker.

QUICK CUT: Mr. Baker relaxing in his infinity pool.

DETECTIVE BERRY (V.O.) (CONT'D)
And the lies become official, burying the truth along with that poor girl's body in a shallow desert grave.

INT. SUPERMAX PRISON – VISITATION BOOTH – CONTINUOUS

Detective Berry is gripping the prison phone tightly, her face contorted in anger and rage.

DETECTIVE BERRY
Most of life is people like them doing as they please,
usually at the expense of everyone else. Ordinary people
with ordinary lives don't count with them. We're the ones
they laugh about with each other. And you know the worst
part?

JENKINS
What?

DETECTIVE BERRY
(angrily)
They feed us a horseshit line about how with a little elbow
grease and luck anyone can be them. Fuck that! People like
you and me know. Save all those American Dream
horseshit speeches. The watchful eyes of the few can live
with the incremental movement of some, but they like the
rest of us right where they've got us.

Detective Berry's anger has given way to exhaustion. She
goes to replace the receive on the wall as the prison guard
moves behind Jenkins. Jenkins motions for her to put the
receiver back to her ear.

JENKINS
She said nothing happened when she was there. I found her
wandering near the freeway.

QUICK CUT: Axia climbing into Jenkins's pickup truck.

JENKINS (V.O.)
She said there was another girl. Ran off with one of the
teachers.

INT. SUPERMAX PRISON – VISITATION BOOTH –
CONTINUOUS

JENKINS
Her name was Katie. Right?

Detective Berry slumps in her chair as relief and sorrow overcome her.

EXT. APARTMENT COMPLEX ON EUCLID AVE - DAY

Della is standing in front of the ground floor apartment. She knocks on the door and one of the sophomores from Garden Lakes, now a MAN IN HIS EARLY 20s, answers, a look on his face.

INT. PHOENIX POLICE DEPARTMENT - VIEWING ROOM - DAY

An EYEWITNESS, a woman in her 30s, is seated at a table. A POLICE OFFICER sits next to her. Beyond the one-way glass, there's a line-up of FOUR WHITE MEN IN THEIR 20s. The Eyewitness looks at each man carefully.

POLICE OFFICER
Take your time.

HALLWAY – CONTINUOUS

Detective Kennard is watching through a window in the viewing room door. A POLICE SERGEANT, 50s, walks by.

POLICE SERGEANT
Whatcha got?

DETECTIVE KENNARD
Eyewitness to that hit-and-run.

POLICE SERGEANT
No shit?

DETECTIVE KENNARD
She was out walking her dog. Saw our man panic and drive
away.

POLICE SERGEANT
How'd'ya find her?

DETECTIVE KENNARD
Neighborhood canvas. She gave us the license plate and
the computer did the rest.

VIEWING ROOM - CONTINUOUS

The police officer is growing impatient.

EYEWITNESS
I'm sorry, but I'm not sure. It was dark.

The police officer glances back through the window at
Detective Kennard, exasperated.

HALLWAY – CONTINUOUS

Detective Berry passes by, distracted.

DETECTIVE KENNARD
Hey-ya, Berry. Captain is looking for you.

Detective Berry nods, moves down the hallway, passing a
WOMAN, 60s, who is sitting quietly on a chair outside the
captain's office.

Detective Berry enters the captain's office and the woman
watches as the captain tells Detective Berry to close the

door, which she does. The captain motions for her to sit down and she does. The captain's face is tense and the woman watches the exchange. Detective Berry's expression turns to alarm as the captain speaks.

EXT. KEITH'S HOUSE – DAY – (FLASHBACK)

Detective Berry opens the passenger's side of Keith's car, opens the glovebox, and stuffs the bag of cocaine inside. What she doesn't see is the woman watching through the window from across the street.

HALLWAY – CONTINUOUS

The woman looks nervous as Detective Berry stands and places her badge and gun on the captain's desk. She averts her eyes when Detective Berry walks out.

POLICE STATION RESTROOM – CONTINUOUS

Detective Berry enters a stall and locks it. She starts flailing and punching the walls.

EXT. PHOENIX POLICE DEPARTMENT - PARKING LOT - A LITTLE LATER

The Eyewitness steps out of the station and puts on her sunglasses. She peers around and then walks with purpose towards a car parked under a shade tree. Della TURNS DOWN THE RADIO as the Eyewitness approaches.

DELLA
How'd it go?

EYEWITNESS
It's done.

Della hands her an envelope, which she tucks into her purse. The Eyewitness adjusts her sunglasses.

EYEWITNESS (CONT'D)
Why?

DELLA
(looks off into the distance, thinking)
To keep the heat on the one who needs to pay.

The Eyewitness stares at her for a moment and then walks away, her heels CLICKING against the pavement. Della watches her go.

EXT. RANDOLPH COLLEGE PREP PARKING LOT – DAY – (FLASHBACK)

A hulking red and white school bus with "Randolph College Preparatory" stenciled on the side idles out front. Expensive luxury cars pull into the parking lot one at a time, dropping students with bags. It's early and some of the students move slowly.

Mr. Hancock stands at the door of the bus, stern-faced. As the boys board, they avert their eyes deferentially to Mr. Hancock, who nods at each of them.

Mr. Malagon bounds out of the bus.
MR. MALAGON
Let's go, boys! Chop, chop!

He high fives one of the boys as he passes.

INT. SCHOOL BUS – MOMENTS LATER

The bus is loaded. The bus driver looks in the rearview mirror and sees rows and rows of young male faces, all staring straight ahead. Mr. Hancock strolls up the aisle, checking each seat for anything improper.

The bus driver opens the door for a straggler, and a YOUNG CHARLIE MARTENS, 17, steps inside.

Mr. Hancock gives Charlie a look and then continues his inspection.

MR. MALAGON (CONT'D)
Welcome, Master Martens.

MR. HANCOCK (O.S.)
Seatbelt, young man.

MR. MALAGON
Just like camping, right boys?

An EXCITED MURMUR fills the bus.

Mr. Malagon picks up the clipboard from the dashboard.

MR. MALAGON (CONT'D)
(reading from the clipboard)
Handley?

YOUNG DUANE HANDLEY
Here.

MR. MALAGON
Warren?

YOUNG WARREN JAMES
Here!

MR. MALAGON
Figs?

Mr. Hancock shoots a look.

YOUNG DAVE FIGUEROA
Here!

MR. MALAGON
Assburn?

MR. HANCOCK
(objecting; sternly)
Mr. Malagon.

YOUNG VINCE GLASSBURN
Here.

EXT. RANDOLPH COLLEGE PREP PARKING LOT –
CONTINUOUS

The bus slowly pulls out onto Central Avenue, the fresh
faces glancing out the window at the ornate school
building. As the bus passes a local bank, the electronic
time and temperature sign flashes 101.

EXT. FREEWAY – A LITTLE LATER

The bus travels along, desert on both sides as they leave
the city behind them.

EXT. GARDEN LAKES HOUSING DEVELOPMENT –
LATER

The bus pulls through the gates of the abandoned, half-
built housing development, a palm tree-studded median
separating the channels that allow cars in and out. From
above, Garden Lakes looks like a sophisticated crop circle,
composed of two paved roads—an outer and inner loop—
with a wide river of dirt flowing between the loops, the

brick community center bridging the two loops at their southernmost convex. The dry manmade lake at the center of the development yawns like an open mouth with only its top teeth, the twelve finished houses, six on either side of the community center.

The bus pulls up to the community center and stops. The door opens and the boys file out, taking in the scenery.

A banner draped over the door of the community center reads: "The Randolph Mothers' Guild Welcomes You to Garden Lakes!" Several women appear from inside the community center to greet the boys.

MOTHER #1
(to Mother #2)
They're here.

MOTHER #2
Oh, don't they just look terrific?

MOTHER #1
(calling out)
This way, gentleman.

The boys follow her directions and file into the community center.

Mr. Hancock and Mr. Malagon bring up the rear.

The community center doors close behind them.

The bus RATTLES TO LIFE and slowly pulls away, back out the front gates.

THE END

WE'RE SO FAMOUS

INTRODUCTION

I love movies. Good movies, bad movies, mediocre ones—
doesn't matter. As a novelist, I find it as instructive when a
truly great movie hits all the highs—acting, writing,
directing—as when a film strives for greatness but falls
short, or just plain stinks. Even the worst movies have
perfect scenes, but all-too-often the seams show, and
within the cacophony of false notes and missteps the
aspiring screenwriter can learn what makes a movie work
and what does not.

When a Hollywood producer showed interest in my
first novel, *We're So Famous*, and asked if I'd be
interested in adapting the novel for the screen, I readily
agreed. The novel's premise—three talentless girls hungry
for fame—seemed like a strong enough hook to build a
movie around. Based on the experimental nature of the
novel—some of it written as a screenplay, some as a series
of letters, etc.—I understood that while I would be
borrowing the characters and the arc of the narrative from
the novel, I would be starting from scratch in terms of
dramatization.

And then I was visited again by an early problem
from when I attempted the first draft of the novel: how to
wrangle my absolute disgust with the fame culture into a
fun plot with likable characters. In my biased opinion, the
novel more successfully conveys this notion than the
adaptation herein. But I had fun trying. The finished
version is the fourth revision, and hours were spent on the
phone going over notes on the previous versions, all in an
effort to tell a story moviegoers might be interested in
seeing.

The fate of *We're So Famous*: *The Movie* is perhaps Hollywood's most well-known narrative: the excitement of drawing up the list of actors and directors to solicit, whispers of interest from still other actors and directors, the script finding its way into the hands of some famous names. Any moment the phone could ring with news. But it didn't, and then no one spoke of the screenplay, much like family members avoiding talk about a relative deceased under dubious circumstances. No one ever said they weren't interested. No one ever said anything. The producer eventually left Hollywood, and I went back to writing novels.

Re-reading the screenplay more than a decade after it was written, I see some moves I borrowed from favorite movies, and some inside jokes from the novel found their way into the script. But mostly it remains an exercise in enthusiasm for a mode of storytelling I continue to admire.

--Jaime Clarke (2007)

BLACK SCREEN

DAISY (V.O.)
If you haven't heard of us, your friends probably have. You might have a copy of our album, We're Mary Jane Lane. But there are a lot of bad rumors and gossip about us and how we became famous and what happened, so this is for the record.

INSERT: Home movies of Gert and Daisy growing up through the years, play-acting, singing for the camera, playing dress-up, signing autographs for their fans (their parents).

DAISY (V.O.)
The most untrue thing said about us is that we're just lucky, which makes me and Gertrude so mad we can't talk. We resent that. Anyone who's ever done anything knows it takes a lot of hard work and always a little luck, and when someone is an overnight sensation, they've really been at it for years.

INSERT: Home video of adolescent Gert and Daisy as they preen and goof around for the camera in a girl's bedroom. They take turns holding up a magazine cover featuring Madonna. A poster for the movie Desperately Seeking Susan hangs above the bed.

DAISY (V.O.)
Me and Gert fantasized how it was to be famous, which was having nice cars, wearing really nice clothes, living in a nice neighborhood, and basically just having the things you wanted. And people would give you things. In magazines and on TV it never looked like any celebrity was hurting for anything. We couldn't imagine Madonna eating a hot dog, or waiting in line for tickets to a movie.

Not that she <u>couldn't</u> do those things if she wanted to, but Madonna wanting a hot dog wasn't the same thing as me and Gert wanting a hot dog.

INSERT: Video of Gert and Daisy lip-synching at the talent show at their high school in Phoenix.

DAISY (V.O.)
We liked to dress outlandish like rock stars, which is what we wanted to be. We modeled ourselves on our favorite band, probably the best band in the world: Bananarama. They're way better than any of the hyper-ironic shite you hear now. People want music that's fun. Me and Gert do like some new stuff, but most of it isn't fun.

INSERT: Video of Gert and Daisy and Stella working in a recording studio.

DAISY (V.O.)
A little-known fact about Mary Jane Lane is that we made a single when it was the three of us, long before We're Mary Jane Lane. Stella's father loaned us the money to do it, and we paid some studio guys to come up with the song, which was called "What the--, Who the--, Hey!" I think between me, Gert, Stella, and Stella's father we still have the five hundred copies we paid for. But we weren't down about our singing career. It doesn't happen overnight.

INSERT: Video of Stella graduating while Gert and Daisy watch from the gymnasium bleachers, getting a new car for graduation, driving off to California.

DAISY (V.O.)
Stella was like an advance scout, surveying the landscape in Hollywood for us until me and Gert could graduate and join her. She called us every day with stories about the celebrities she'd met.

INSERT: Still pictures of Stella with various celebrities.

DAISY (V.O.)
Me and Gert waited breathlessly for Stella's calls, but soon she didn't call as much, and me and Gert settled for rushing to the mailbox for the occasional letters from Stella.

INSERT: Still pictures of Stella auditioning for acting roles.

DAISY (V.O.)
Stella never said it outright, but her decision to become an actress would cut into the time she could give to Mary Jane Lane, and me and Gert never said too much about that.

INT. GERT'S BEDROOM – PRESENT DAY

GERT, a blonde in her late teens, and DAISY, her brunette counterpart, are spread out on the floor, heads bent down over paper, markers in their hands. They are working on the artwork for the cover of their as-yet-unrecorded album.

DAISY (V.O.)
We wished Stella the best—even after her letters stopped coming and me and Gert realized we were on our own.

Daisy holds up a crude drawing of three girls on a stage with a crowd of hands reaching out to them. Gert takes the drawing and exes out one of the figures.

DAISY (V.O.)
We didn't even tell Stella about when we got a local DJ to put our song on the radio.

INSERT: Still photograph of Gert and Daisy being interviewed in the radio station's studio.

DAISY (V.O.)
When the DJ asked us about Stella, we told him it was just like how Bananarama started out with three members but ended up with two.

INSERT: Gert and Daisy reading Stella's letter.

DAISY (V.O.)
We got one last letter from Stella after she heard about the radio interview, but we couldn't read the whole thing because we didn't want Stella's angry words burned into our brains forever.

EXT. DESERT – DAY
Gert and Daisy drive through the desert.

DAISY (V.O.)
Maybe we were sorry we cut Stella out of Mary Jane Lane, but if we were, me and Gert never talked about it. It didn't even come up when we saw the plastic-fantastic news about how Madonna was going to pick the winning band from a talent showcase in L.A. to open up for her concert at the Hollywood Bowl.

EXT. LOS ANGELES - DAY

Gert and Daisy drive through the streets of Los Angeles, consulting a map to Stella's apartment. They drive past various L.A. landmarks, pointing excitedly: Grauman's Chinese Theatre, the Capitol Records Building, the corner of Hollywood and Vine, the Hollywood sign.

DAISY (V.O.)
Even when we decided to go to L.A., we weren't sure we were going to visit Stella.

INT. TALENT SHOWCASE – DAY

Gert and Daisy sing their song while a panel of
unimpressed judges looks on.

DAISY (V.O.)
But when those talent judges, who wouldn't know talent if
it snuck up behind them and tapped them on the shoulder,
told us we didn't win a spot in the showcase, Gert said,
"Why not call up Stella?" Sometimes Gert just has to
speak her mind. So that's what we did.

EXT. LOS ANGELES – DAY

Gert and Daisy pull into the parking lot of a dilapidated
motel-style apartment complex, all the units huddled
around a swimming pool that hasn't been used in ages.
They take in the complex as they get out of the car, clearly
expecting something more glamorous.

GERT
What number?

Daisy looks at the address scribbled on the map.

DAISY
Twelve.

The girls follow the numbered doors up a staircase to the
second level, finding themselves in front of Stella's
apartment. Gert leans her forehead against the curtained
window but can't see inside. She raises her fist and
KNOCKS. They wait, but no one answers. Gert KNOCKS
again.

GERT
You sure it's twelve?

DAISY
She said twelve.

Gert KNOCKS again and the door falls open. The girls
look at each other. Daisy shakes her head no, but Gert
takes a step inside.

GERT
(calling out)
Stella?

STELLA (O.S.)
In the bedroom.

INT. STELLA'S APARTMENT – CONTINUOUS

The dark apartment is littered with empty takeout food
containers. The front-room television is tuned to the E!
channel, the volume on low. By the light of the television
Gert and Daisy make their way to the back bedroom.

BEDROOM

STELLA, a dark-haired girl in her early twenties, stares at
her computer screen. She's dressed in sweatpants and a T-
shirt, and her hair is up. Her white face reflects the light
from the computer screen. The bedroom walls are covered
with magazine clippings, photos, and a framed poster of
Ryan Metro, a rock star in his twenties.

GERT
(to Stella)
What are you doing?

Stella continues to stare at the computer screen.

STELLA
Trying to see if this guy on IM is bullshitting me or not.

GERT
(beat)
Aren't you going to say hello?

Stella looks over at Gert and Daisy, seeing them for the first time.

STELLA
I knew you'd make it eventually.
(turns back to computer)
What do you think of L.A.?

GERT
(looks at the walls)
What is all this?

STELLA
That's Ryan Metro. The rock star?

GERT
(mildly insulted)
I know. Why is he on your wall?

Stella stops typing and looks up.

STELLA
Don't you guys read the paper?

GERT
Not really.

STELLA
He's missing. Or dead.

DAISY
Where did he go?

Stella turns her attention to the computer again.

STELLA
That's what I'm trying to find out.

DAISY
Is he that gross guy who bites animals onstage?

STELLA
(indignantly)
That's his less talented brother.

Daisy notices a thick notebook at her feet, the words
"Murder Book" spelled out in cut-out newspaper letters
glued to the cover. She bends down and picks up the
notebook.

DAISY
What's this?

STELLA
It's for my dead pool.

DAISY
(eyes wide)
Dead pool?

Daisy flips through the book and sees articles and pictures
devoted to particularly notorious celebrity murders: John
Lennon, Bob Crane, O.J. Simpson's wife and her friend,
etc.

STELLA
A bunch of us at the Starion pool money and try to guess

which celebrity is going to kick over next.

Daisy closes the book as if it's infected and gently sets it back down.

STELLA (CONT'D)
(looks at her watch)
Shit, we're going to be late.

INT. STARION RESTAURANT – NIGHT

The Starion is a 50s-style restaurant that has seen better days. The meager audience of Patrons are seated at tables scattered in front of the obviously makeshift stage. Candlelight from the tables illuminates the Patrons and Waitresses serving the tables. Gert and Daisy and Stella are seated at a table near the stage.

STELLA
It was my idea to do celebrity deaths. This place used to be a morgue, after all.

DAISY
Gross. Really?

STELLA
(ignores her)
Monday night we do the murder of Lana Turner's mobster boyfriend, Wednesday is the drowning of Natalie Wood, Friday is a medley of automobile deaths: James Dean, Isadora Duncan, and Jayne Mansfield. I suggested adding the murder of Bob Crane and a couple of celebrity suicides, but management didn't think the crowd would want snapped necks or bashed brains with their linguine and clam sauce.

DAISY
I can see their point.

STELLA
There's a scavenger hunt later. Did I tell you? You'll be on my team. Everyone wants to be on my team because I have a list of killer addresses.

GERT
Like a star map?

STELLA
(snorts)
Please.

DAISY
Do you have the address to Madonna's house?

STELLA
Not sure. Maybe.
(looks around)
Hunter better hurry his ass up.

GERT
Who's Hunter?

STELLA
My acting class buddy. You'll dig him. He's not a boyfriend or anything. Just a friend.

Two guys in their late twenties, ELLIOT and HUNTER, join their table.

HUNTER
(kisses Stella on the cheek)
Not a boyfriend yet, anyway.

STELLA
About time.

ELLIOT
Who are your friends?

STELLA
That's Gert and Daisy.
(points to Elliot and Hunter)
That's Elliot and Hunter.

Hellos all around.

ELLIOT
(to Gert and Daisy)
You in the show?

DAISY
We're not actors.

ELLIOT
I thought everyone in L.A. was an actor.

GERT
We're in a band.

Daisy nervously looks from Gert to Stella to gauge Stella's
reaction. There is none.

ELLIOT
What's the name of your band?

GERT
Mary Jane Lane.

HUNTER
We're not really actors either. We're trying to start a

record company.

STELLA
(to Elliot and Hunter, jokingly)
You should sign Mary Jane Lane.

ELLIOT
We've got a full studio at our house in Silver Lake. You
should come out.

DAISY
That sounds awesome.

The lights on the stage dim, and Stella and Hunter get up
from the table.

STELLA
Show time.

Stella and Hunter disappear behind a stage curtain.

ELLIOT
Are you a Lana Turner fan?

DAISY
We only know her from the Madonna song.

Elliot gives a funny look as Gert and Daisy watch the stage
with anticipation. Hunter's voice comes over the loud
speaker.

HUNTER (O.S.)
Ladies and Gentlemen, welcome to Monday night at the
Starion. Now that the waitstaff have your orders, please
stay seated and silent. Our presentation lasts a half an hour,
and we expect to hold you spellbound for that half hour.

BACKSTAGE

Hunter covers the microphone and takes a deep breath.

HUNTER
(into the microphone)
On a rainy April night in 1958, the police were summoned
to 730 North Bedford Drive in Beverly Hills...the home of
screen star Lana Turner.

AUDIENCE

The stage lights up on a gorgeous pink bedroom.
Stella/Lana is folding laundry on the bed.

HUNTER (O.S.)
Johnny Stompanato, a former mob bodyguard, had fallen
in love with the glamorous movie star. Theirs was a
passionate affair, but when Lana learned of her boyfriend's
underworld connections, she wouldn't let him accompany
her to the Oscars.

BACKSTAGE

The ACTOR playing Stompanato stands next to Hunter,
clenching his fists, trying to get into character.

HUNTER (O.S.) (CONT'D)
So he beat her within an inch of her life. The tension
increased, as Lana would phone Stompanato continually,
telling him how much she missed and loved and wanted
him, but wouldn't meet him anywhere in public.
Finally...the lies and confusion came to a head.

Hunter makes a stage KNOCK.

AUDIENCE

Stella/Lana freezes.

STELLA/LANA
I don't want to talk to you.

ACTOR/STOMPANATO
C'mon, baby. It's me.

STELLA/LANA
We're through. Go away!

THREE LOUD KNOCKS are heard. Stella/Lana hurries to the door and unlocks it.

STELLA/LANA (CONT'D)
We're through, can't you understand that?

ACTOR/STOMPANATO
You'll never get away from me.

He enters the room and closes the door behind him.

ACTOR/STOMPANATO (CONT'D)
I'll cut you good, baby. No one will ever look at that pretty face again.

INT. STARION RESTAURANT – LATER

Gert and Daisy stand in line for the ladies' room.

DAISY
What did you think?

GERT
(shrugs)

I thought it sucked.

DAISY
No, I mean about Stella. Did you look at her Murder
Book? It was gruesome.

Gert shrugs again as Hunter approaches.

HUNTER
What'd ya think of the show?

GERT
The blood looked fake.

HUNTER
(earnestly)
It is. It's ketchup and corn syrup. Stinks like hell.
(beat)
So do you guys want to come out to Silver Lake?

DAISY
Maybe.

A Woman exits the bathroom, and Daisy and Gert push
through the door.

INT. STARION RESTAURANT - BATHROOM –
CONTINUOUS

DAISY
You shouldn't have said that about the blood.

GERT
Why not?

DAISY
You don't always have to say what you think.

GERT
Why, you want to go with them?

DAISY
Could be our big break. Those guys might know someone
important.

GERT
They seem a little...shady.

DAISY
Hunter's kinda cute.

GERT
It would be pretty cool to have our own demo.

DAISY
Gets us out of the scavenger hunt too.

GERT
Done.

INT. STARION RESTAURANT – CONTINUOUS

Gert and Daisy find Elliot, Hunter, and Stella backstage.
Gert picks up the knife bloodied with fake blood and
makes a stabbing motion. Stella surprises her by taking her
picture with a Polaroid camera. She shakes the picture as it
develops.

STELLA
Good one.
(to Gert and Daisy)
Just give me a couple of minutes to get changed.

GERT
Actually, we're going to go over to Hunter and Elliot's.

Stella pauses, clearly miffed.

HUNTER
Cool.

STELLA
I'll probably be out late. How will you get home?

ELLIOT
We can get you back.

Stella pretends to busy herself with removing her costume
to hide her anger.

EXT./INT. HUNTER AND ELLIOT'S HOUSE IN
SILVER LAKE – LATER THAT NIGHT

Headlights sweep across a Mediterranean-style house as
Gert and Daisy pull in behind Elliot and Hunter.

The house is sparsely decorated, a real bachelor pad. The
walls are white, and assorted sporting equipment lies
about. The kitchen is littered with dirty dishes and pizza
boxes.

ELLIOT
What are some of your songs?

GERT
We need some new material, actually.

The four make their way into the living room, which is
crowded with recording equipment, various keyboards and
guitars on stands, and a black leather couch.

DAISY
Wow.

HUNTER
What kind of music do you like?

GERT
Fun stuff. Eighties. Whatever.

HUNTER
Elliot's a huge Wham! fan.

ELLIOT
Fuck off.

DAISY
Do you like Bananarama?

HUNTER
Which ones are they?

DAISY
(mock-impatiently)
"Cruel Summer," "Robert DeNiro's Waiting," "Venus." C'mon.

ELLIOT
Yeah, from the shampoo commercial, right?

DAISY
Yeah, from the shampoo commercial.

She smiles at Hunter and rolls her eyes.

HUNTER
We've got a song we're trying to find the right voices for. To start our label with. Maybe you want to give it a shot.

GERT
You guys are starting a label?

ELLIOT
Trying to. Repeat Records. You like it?

Elliot hands Gert and Daisy a postcard designed like a
cassette tape that features the name and logo of their label.

GERT
Can I keep this?

HUNTER
Sure. We've got plenty.

GERT
What's the song?

ELLIOT
"World Gone Water." It's a pop tune. You two look perfect
for it.

Awkwardness descends as Gert and Daisy consider Elliot's
remark.

HUNTER
What my jackass partner means is that we've been
searching for the right look to go with the song, and you
two are exactly what we've been looking for.

Gert and Daisy are flattered, relax.

ELLIOT
Yeah, that's what I meant.

DAISY
Awesome. Me and Gert would love to be on your label.
We want to be as big as Madonna.

GERT
Bigger.

HUNTER
Hey, if we do this right, Madonna will be singing your
songs.

DAISY
(gasps)
Oh my God. That would be awesome.

EXT. HUNTER AND ELLIOT'S HOUSE -
CONTINUOUS

Stella slows as she drives by the house. Her Jeep is full
of Scavenger Hunters busy looking at a map.

SCAVENGER HUNTER #1
I think we're lost.

Stella doesn't hear, though, as she peers intently at the
house.

INT. HUNTER AND ELLIOT'S HOUSE - LIVING
ROOM – LATER

The living room is enveloped in cigarette smoke. A city of
beer bottles has been erected on the coffee table. Everyone
is huddled around the equipment while the song plays.
Gert and Daisy are grooving to the song. Their voices
aren't great, but they don't realize it, and Elliot and Hunter
don't say anything.

GERT
I dig this song.

ELLIOT
Top of the charts, man. Top of the charts.

Elliot stops the CD and pops it out, then puts it in a plastic case.

HUNTER
Just have to make copies.

Daisy takes the CD, opens the case, and draws a heart on it with a red marker. She proudly hands it back to Elliot, and as Elliot goes to file it away, he drunkenly knocks over a pile of CD cases.

HUNTER
Good one, d-bag.

ELLIOT
(mimics him)
Good one, d-bag.

DAISY
Hey, will you make one for us?

Daisy looks at Gert.

DAISY (CONT'D)
Maybe we can send it in to the talent showcase judges.

HUNTER
You guys should try out for the showcase. You're good.

GERT
Actually, we got an audition--

DAISY
Yeah, maybe we will.

Gert smirks and rolls her eyes at Daisy.

A LOUD KNOCK on the front door reverberates through the room.

ELLIOT
I thought your mom was going to quit coming around late at night.

Hunter makes a face, as if to say "Good one" and Gert's and Daisy's eyes follow Elliot as he disappears down the long hallway to the front door.

HUNTER
Who's up for some Taco Bell?

DAISY
I'm starvin', Marvin.

SUDDEN SHOUTING is heard at the front door, a WOMAN'S VOICE rising to drown out Elliot, all of it muffled.

HUNTER
(trying to relieve the tension)
Maybe that is my mom.

The front door SLAMS shut and Elliot reappears, a little chagrined.

ELLIOT
(laughs)
Imagine. Bible salesmen. At this hour.

Gert and Daisy LAUGH at the joke, but Hunter eyes Elliot.

ELLIOT (CONT'D)
Did I hear someone say something about Taco Bell?

INT. STELLA'S APARTMENT – EARLY MORNING

The apartment is empty. Gert notices a flashing light on the answering machine and plays the message.

STELLA (V.O.)
Got a big lead on you-know-who and am checking it out.
Be back soon.
(beat)
Hope you had fun with Elliot and Hunter.

The machine BEEPS twice and then stops.

GERT
Christ, she's a scatterbrain.

INT. STELLA'S APARTMENT – A LITTLE LATER

Gert and Daisy mindlessly flip through the channels on the television, exhausted but still buzzing.

GERT
Didn't you think Hunter was sort of cute?

DAISY
Yeah.
(beat)
Did you ever think it would be this easy? I mean, to just fall into a big break like this?

Gert shrugs.

DAISY (CONT'D)
(almost to herself)

The key was coming to LA. It makes sense that we had to come to L.A. to get famous.

Daisy continues to flip through the channels. Gert reaches for Stella's Murder Book and casually fans through the pages.

DAISY
That'll give you nightmares.

Gert yawns.

INT. HUNTER AND ELLIOT'S HOUSE – MORNING

The living room is a hive of activity, COPS everywhere, carefully dancing around the bodies of Hunter and Elliot, who lie dead on the floor. In the middle of it all is DETECTIVE BOUCHER, a middle-aged woman with a confident yet inquisitive look on her face as she takes in the scene. An OFFICER approaches.

OFFICER
West Hollywood got a hold of a busboy who says they were with a couple of girls. Or one girl. It's hard to tell. The guy didn't really speak English. A...

He consults his notebook. Detective Boucher listens but continues to scan the room.

OFFICER (CONT'D)
Mary Jane Lane.

Detective Boucher nods as if to say "Thank you" and the Officer moves on with his duties.

INT. STELLA'S APARTMENT – LATE MORNING

The sun pours in through the curtains. Gert and Daisy are on the couch, looking at Stella's star map. The television is on low.

GERT
(skeptically)
How can he live here? And here? And here? It doesn't make any sense.

Daisy SHRIEKS.

GERT (CONT'D)
What?

Daisy points at the television, and they both see a picture of Elliot and Hunter on the screen under the caption "Double Murder."

ANCHORWOMAN
(on the television)
...were murdered early this morning in their Silver Lake home. Police are searching for a duo of singers calling themselves Mary Jane Lane, who may be the last to have seen the two men alive. Police are seeking help in locating the members of Mary Jane Lane for questioning. In other news..."

Gert and Daisy are stunned into silence.

INT. STELLA'S APARTMENT – A LITTLE LATER

Gert and Daisy have shuttered themselves inside the apartment, having pushed the couch against the front door. They've also unplugged the apartment phone. The television flickers on their sleeping faces, the channel tuned to CNN, the volume down. A KNOCK on the door jolts them awake.

DAISY
(whispers)
What was that?

GERT
(whispers)
I think someone knocked.

Gert sneaks over to the blinds and tries to look through without opening them.

DAISY
(whispers)
Don't let them see you!

Another KNOCK.

DAISY (CONT'D)
(whispers)
Is it Stella?

GERT
It's two guys. One has a camera.

VOICE (O.S.)
(through the door)
We're from the L.A. Times. Will you talk to us?

DAISY
(whispers)
How did they find us?

VOICE (O.S.)
If you let us in, I'll tell you.

GERT
Damn it.

Gert moves the couch away from the door. Daisy scatters toward the hallway. Gert opens the door on the pair from the Times: a reporter, MEYERS, and a photographer named BUTTREY.

MEYERS
(respectfully)
My name is Meyers and this is Buttrey. May we come in?

DAISY
We didn't do anything. We don't know anything. So go away.

MEYERS
(holds up his hands)
I just want to ask you a couple of questions. That's it.
Gert and Daisy look at each other. Daisy mouths "No."

GERT
Like what?

MEYERS
(opens his notebook to write)
When did you last see Mr. Ryan and Mr. Roberts?

GERT
Why?

MEYERS
They were helping you record a demo for your band, Mary Jane Lane.

GERT
Right. And they were alive when we left.

MEYERS
Did you see any guns in the house?

GERT
No.

MEYERS
See any drugs? Or did anyone deliver a package while you
were there?

GERT
No.

MEYERS
Did you overhear either Mr. Ryan or Mr. Roberts talking
about something or someone called...
(flips through his notebook)
...Boudinot.

Gert and Daisy exchange glances and Gert shakes her head
no.

BUTTREY
Excuse me, but I have to get to another shoot, so do you
mind if I take your picture now?

DAISY
For the paper?

BUTTREY
(a little annoyed)
Yeah, for the paper.

GERT
But you're going to say we're innocent, right?

MEYERS
Right.

DAISY
Okay, but give us a minute.

Daisy grabs Gert and whisks her down the hall.

INT. STELLA'S BEDROOM – CONTINUOUS

Daisy still has Gert by the arm.

GERT
You're not really going to let them take our picture, are you?

DAISY
This could be good for the band.

Gert looks at her skeptically.

DAISY (CONT'D)
Think about it. Our picture in the Los Angeles Times, talking about Mary Jane Lane.

GERT
(frustrated)
Yeah, the band that murdered Hunter and Elliot.

DAISY
But they're going to say we didn't have anything to do with it. They'll clear it up. And we'll get some free publicity. Maybe the showcase judges will give us another shot.

GERT
(angrily)
So we're going to use Elliot and Hunter to get publicity? Where does it end with you? They were nice guys.

DAISY
(softly)
They were nice guys. They didn't deserve what happened
to them.
(beat)
But what can we do about that?

Gert looks at her, understands.

DAISY (CONT'D)
Hunter and Elliot would think it was funny to see our
picture in the paper, don't you think?

GERT
(laughs despite herself)
If they weren't dead.

FRONT ROOM

Meyers and Buttrey are looking at all the pictures of Ryan
Metro taped up on Stella's wall. Gert and Daisy re-enter,
dressed up in their rock star outfits, their hair redone.
Buttrey gives Meyers a look, and Meyers motions for him
to take their picture.

DAISY
Where do you want us?

BUTTREY
How about sitting on the couch?

Gert and Daisy sit together on the couch, leaning into each
other as if posing for the cover of a rock magazine. Buttrey
SNAPS the picture.

BUTTREY (CONT'D)
Got it.

DAISY
You want one of us standing? We could do it outside if
that's better.

Buttrey gives Meyers a look.

MEYERS
Thanks, Buttrey. I'll catch up with you later.

BUTTREY
Okay, yeah. I'll leave it on your desk.

Buttrey heads for the door.

DAISY
Nice to meet you.

Buttrey waves awkwardly and is gone.

GERT
(a little bitterly)
A man of few words.

MEYERS
He's just doing his job.

He takes out his notebook again.

MEYERS (CONT'D)
I want to ask you if any of these names mean anything to
you.

GERT
We really don't know anything. I mean, we hardly knew
them. They seemed like nice guys.

DAISY
(insistently)
They were nice guys.

Meyers considers this, then puts his notepad away.

MEYERS
Can I make a suggestion?

Gert nods.

MEYERS (CONT'D)
You should go to the police.

GERT
(coolly)
Why?

MEYERS
Because they want to talk to you. They'll find you sooner
or later, and it's better if you go in on your own.

DAISY
Will you come with us?

The request catches Meyers off-guard.

MEYERS
Yeah, sure. I'll drive you, if you want.

INT. MEYERS'S CAR – CONTINUOUS

Meyers drives Gert and Daisy to the police station. Daisy
is riding up front and Gert is in back. The radio is playing.

D.J. (V.O.)
(through the radio)

Okay, kids. Got a WLAZ exclusive for you: a cut from
Mary Jane Lane, the hot new wanted-for-murder all-girl
band from right here in La-La Land.

The music starts and Meyers turns up the radio.

MEYERS
Sing along if you know the words.

Gert and Daisy both recognize the song, and Daisy turns
around and looks at Gert. Meyers bobs his head a little to
the music.

MEYERS (CONT'D)
Not bad.

DAISY
(trying not to be pleased)
Wonder how the radio station got a hold of it.

MEYERS
They probably bribed the cops.

EXT. POLICE STATION PARKING LOT -
CONTINUOUS

Meyers pulls into a parking space out front.

INT. MEYERS'S CAR - CONTINUOUS

MEYERS
Wait here. I'll go to the desk and explain everything, and
then they'll come get you. Otherwise, it'll be a mad scene.

Meyers starts to get out of the car, then hesitates.

GERT
What?

MEYERS
I wonder...I shouldn't ask you this, but I wonder if you could promise not to talk to any other reporters. Until after I file my story, I mean.

DAISY
(hopefully)
Will there be reporters?

MEYERS
There are usually a couple hanging around. Maybe not. But I just thought.

GERT
Yeah, sure.

Meyers smiles, knowing they are not out of it yet.

MEYERS
Also, my card.

Meyers takes out a card and scribbles on it.

MEYERS (CONT'D)
This is my home address and number, too. In case you think of anything else.

Meyers hands the card to Daisy.

DAISY
Okay, thanks.

MEYERS
Be right back.

Meyers disappears and Daisy watches him walk away.

GERT
Who do you think put our song on the radio?

DAISY
Yeah, that's what I was thinking. You don't think it's the cops?

GERT
No way. Not that fast. I think it was someone who was there before the cops.

DAISY
Like who?

GERT
Did you hear any of that fight at the door?

DAISY
Not really. I saw the woman, though. She stuck her head in the door to get a look at us.

GERT
What did she look like?

DAISY
You'll laugh.

GERT
C'mon.

Gert sees Meyers through the rear window, walking toward the car with a POLICEMAN.

DAISY
Remember Heather McNamara? The one who transferred

junior year?

GERT
Who? Pippi Longstocking?

DAISY
Yeah, except without the pigtails. She was wearing a
baseball hat.
(beat)
Why would she put our song on the radio?

GERT
To frame us, obviously.

DAISY
Should we tell the police about her?

GERT
I'll do the talking.

Meyers and the Policeman reach the car, and Meyers opens
the door. Gert looks at Daisy and Daisy, understands that
they aren't going to say anything.

INT. DETECTIVE BOUCHER'S OFFICE -
CONTINUOUS

Detective Boucher is on the phone with the door closed.

DETECTIVE BOUCHER
(into the phone)
Yep...Yes...Uh-huh.

A POLICEWOMAN gives a SHORT KNOCK and pokes
her head in, motioning.

DETECTIVE BOUCHER (CONT'D)
Okay, gotta go. Yep. Sounds good. About a half an hour.

INT. POLICE STATION – INTERROGATION ROOM –
MOMENTS LATER

Gert and Daisy sit on one side of the table, across from
Detective Boucher. The room is painted white and is
extremely bright.

DETECTIVE BOUCHER
You wouldn't believe the morning I've had.

Gert and Daisy don't take the bait.

DETECTIVE BOUCHER (CONT'D)
I probably shouldn't tell you this, but we processed a
famous actress this morning for biting her boyfriend's face.

Daisy wants to ask who the actress is and is barely able to
refrain. The detective notices this and pushes on.

DETECTIVE BOUCHER (CONT'D)
I guess after a while you get used to all the celebrities that
pass through here. If they're not being charged, they want
to ride along to research a part in a movie.

DAISY
Like what are some of the celebrities you've met?

Gert gives Daisy a look, but Gert is interested in the
answer too.

DETECTIVE BOUCHER
Well, I can't say any names, but you know the big action
movie that just came out?

Daisy gasps.

DAISY
What did he get arrested for?

DETECTIVE BOUCHER
It wasn't him, it was the boy that played his son. Him and a friend had some fun burning down a neighbor's fence.

GERT
Who else?

DETECTIVE BOUCHER
Let's see. A month or so ago we had a pretty famous singer in here, but that was just possession. Caught him at the airport with a bag full of marijuana.
(laughs)
These people, right? They make a lot of money and think the laws don't apply to them. Can you imagine trying to take a bag of pot on an airplane?

Daisy giggles.

DETECTIVE BOUCHER (CONT'D)
So I understand you were smoking a little pot with Elliot and Hunter the night they were killed.

DAISY
(abruptly)
That's a lie.

GERT
(to Daisy)
She knows it's a lie.
(to Detective Boucher)
Right?

DETECTIVE BOUCHER
I don't know anything until you tell me something.

GERT
You know we didn't have anything to do with it.

DETECTIVE BOUCHER
You didn't?

GERT
(trying to act cooler than she is)
No.

DETECTIVE BOUCHER
I got two dead guys out in Silver Lake and you're the last
to see them alive.
(sarcastic)
Guess that's another coincidence, eh?

DAISY
What do you mean, "another coincidence"?

DETECTIVE BOUCHER
Like your song playing on the radio a couple of hours after
we find these guys. Do you want to see how we found
them?

She slides a folder across the table. Gert slides it back.

GERT
Why don't you ask your friends who bribed them to put
our song on the radio?

Detective Boucher gets a confused look on her face and is
about to ask Daisy what she's talking about, but doesn't.

DETECTIVE BOUCHER
We found a set of tire tracks we can't identify. Do you mind if we check them against your car?

GERT
Go ahead. They're not ours.

DETECTIVE BOUCHER
I'll tell you the truth: I'm set to retire next week. They already got the cake, it's in the shape of a police badge with gun-metal-gray frosting that's probably going to taste like Crisco, but I'm not going to be able to enjoy that cake until I can get this case off my desk. So I am going to check the tires on your car and everything else I can about last night. Okay?

GERT
We'd like to make our one phone call, please.

DETECTIVE BOUCHER
You can have as many calls as you want. You came to me, remember?

Detective Boucher stands up and Daisy and Gert follow her out, staying a few steps behind.

INT. POLICE STATION HALLWAY – CONTINUOUS

Gert waits with the phone in her hand while Daisy fishes out her address book.

DAISY
(opens address book, flips a few pages)
Here.

Gert dials Stella's number. Daisy stands close to Gert while it rings and rings and rings. Finally Gert slams down the phone.

GERT
Shit.

ALAN (O.S.)
Excuse me.

Gert and Daisy look in the direction of the voice and see
ALAN HOOD, a short man with a high forehead.

ALAN
My name is Alan Hood. I'd like to talk to you about your
song.

Gert and Daisy look at him skeptically.

ALAN (CONT'D)
If you're not interested, I'll leave right now. I promise.

GERT
(suspicious)
How did you know where we were?

ALAN
(obviously lying)
I, uh, had to come down and pay a parking ticket and, uh,
noticed you. I heard your song. It's really good. You've
got a great look.

DAISY
We might be interested.

ALAN
Have you heard of the talent showcase at the Viper Room?

Gert and Daisy look at each other.

GERT
Not interested.

ALAN
Why not?

DAISY
What she means is they're not interested in us. We already
auditioned.

ALAN
What if I told you I got them to change their minds? That I
talked them into giving you a shot?

DAISY
You'd do that?

ALAN
Already did. They're friends of mine and they want Mary
Jane Lane on the bill.

GERT
How much will they pay us?

ALAN
(awkwardly)
Well, you wouldn't be paid for the showcase, but I've got a
friend at Ocean Records here in town, and they'd be
interested in maybe doing an album with you. I could talk
to them for you.

Daisy lets out a YIP. Gert plays it cool.

ALAN (CONT'D)
If you want, we could talk about it at the Viper Room.
Have you ever been there?

EXT. BEVERLY HILLS HOTEL – DAY

Stella enters the lobby.

INT. BEVERLY HILLS HOTEL – CONTINUOUS

Stella approaches the registration desk. An UPTIGHT
WOMAN, 20s, is working the counter.

STELLA
(breezily)
Ryan Metro, please.

UPTIGHT WOMAN
Room number?

STELLA
Don't you know it?

UPTIGHT WOMAN
I'm sorry, ma'am, but we can't connect you by name. Only
by room number.

STELLA
Actually, I'm not sure that he didn't check out already.
Can you tell me if he's even still here?

UPTIGHT WOMAN
I'm sorry. I can't give out any information about our
guests.

STELLA
(snaps her fingers)
I just remembered. It's room six.

UPTIGHT WOMAN
(unamused)

There is no room six here.

STELLA
I said room sixty. Six-oh.

UPTIGHT WOMAN
Goodbye.

EXT. PHONE BOOTH – MOMENTS LATER

Stella dials a number.

UPTIGHT WOMAN (O.S.)
Beverly Hills Hotel.

STELLA
(into the phone)
Room 2132, please.

UPTIGHT WOMAN (O.S.)
Thank you.

Beat. Stella waits while the phone RINGS.

MAN (O.S.)
Hello?

STELLA
Ryan?

MAN (O.S.)
Oh, I'm afraid they've rung the wrong number.

STELLA
I'm very sorry. I hope I didn't disturb you. While I have
you on the line, though, may I ask you a question?

MAN (O.S.)
Well, I really don't know. Who are you calling for?

STELLA
That's what I want to ask you about. Do you know if Ryan
Metro is staying there? I mean, have you seen him around?
Maybe in the hotel bar?

MAN (O.S.)
Who's Ryan Metro?

STELLA
The rock star. You know, "Big Noise," "The Vegetable
King." I'm his cousin from South Dakota, and I was
supposed to meet him, but I can't remember which room
he's in.

MAN (O.S.)
Did you ask the front desk?

STELLA
They were unhelpful.

MAN (O.S.)
Well, I don't know who he is, so I don't know if he's here.
Sorry.

Stella is about to hang up when the man continues.

MAN (O.S.) (CONT'D)
I did see Alex Trebek by the pool yesterday.

STELLA
Oh?

MAN (O.S.)
Yeah, he's not as smart as he thinks he is. I asked him the

four states whose capital shares the same first letter as the name of the state. He was stumped. Do you know that one?

STELLA
I guess I don't.

MAN (O.S.)
Maybe I should go on Jeopardy! What do you think?

STELLA
Go for it.

MAN (O.S.)
Maybe I will.

STELLA
Anyway, thanks a lot.

MAN (O.S.)
You're welcome. Good luck finding your friend.

Stella hangs up the phone.

EXT. VIPER ROOM - LATER

Tourists slow down as they walk under the famous marquee.

INT. VIPER ROOM - CONTINUOUS

Gert and Daisy admire the 30s-style jazz club setting, checking out the various memorabilia, while Alan hovers behind them.

GERT
Are there always so many people out front when it isn't open?

ALAN
Mostly tourists. And gawkers. A town full of gawkers,
right?

GERT
What's upstairs?

ALAN
A dance floor. Wanna see it?

Gert shakes her head no. They all take a seat at a booth.

ALAN (CONT'D)
The showcase is going to be on both floors.

Daisy whispers something into Gert's ear, and Alan gives a
curious look.

GERT
Do you know Johnny Depp?

ALAN
(caught off-guard)
Yeah. I mean, no. I mean I used to know him.

DAISY
Really?

ALAN
I used to represent one of his ex-girlfriends. An actress
from Sausalito. She stuck with me for quite a while.

GERT
What do you mean?

ALAN
(earnestly)

Sometimes you're up and sometimes you're down, that's all.
(beat; then hopefully)
The showcase is all part of the upswing.

Gert and Daisy exchange looks.

DAISY
We'd need to rehearse a little before the showcase.

Alan pulls a card out of his pocket and writes something on it.

ALAN
Why don't you meet me at Ocean Records later this week and we'll talk to them, set up a rehearsal schedule.
(beat)
And if anything else comes up, any other offers, you can just refer them to me and I'll handle them for you.

GERT
So you're, like, our agent?

ALAN
(carefully)
Or a manager. I mean, I'd love to be your manager. If you want one.

Nobody says anything.

DAISY
Yeah, sure. Why not?

ALAN
(smiles, relieved)
Terrific. I think you girls can be anything you want to be.

DAISY
Can we help design the poster?

ALAN
Great idea. We should get on the poster right away.

He takes out a second card and writes on it.

ALAN (CONT'D)
Meet me at this address tomorrow, and we'll shoot some photos for the poster. Everyone's probably dying to see what you look like.

DAISY
Should we bring some outfits?

ALAN
Wear whatever you like.

EXT./INT. CEDARS-SINAI – DAY

Stella approaches the admitting counter in the emergency room. A NURSE is manning the station.

STELLA
Excuse me.

NURSE
How can I help you, honey?

STELLA
I'm trying to find out if Ryan Metro has been admitted.

NURSE
Are you family?

STELLA
Just a fan.

NURSE
I'm sorry, sweetie, but I really can't give that information
out.

STELLA
Oh.

NURSE
Are you a reporter?

STELLA
Uh, no, not really.

NURSE
What do you mean, "not really"?

STELLA
Well, you're not allowed to talk to reporters, right?

NURSE
Not on the record, no.

STELLA
Are you saying you can say something off the record?

NURSE
(looks around)
I might be persuaded. But you can't use my name.

STELLA
I don't know your name.

NURSE
Right.

STELLA
So, has Ryan Metro been admitted?

NURSE
No. But we did admit someone today.

STELLA
Yeah? Who?

NURSE
Someone pretty famous.

STELLA
Who?

NURSE
Guess.

STELLA
Uh, give me a hint. Is it someone who knows Ryan Metro?

NURSE
Forget Ryan Metro, honey. He isn't here.

STELLA
Would Ryan Metro know who this person is?

NURSE
I would hope so.

STELLA
Is this person famous just in Hollywood or all over the world?

NURSE
How can anyone just be famous in Hollywood?

She spots her supervisor.

NURSE (CONT'D)
Here comes my boss. Shoo.

Stella fades away from the desk.

EXT. HUNTER AND ELLIOT'S HOUSE - DAY

Gert and Daisy park down the block from Elliot and Hunter's. A lone police car is stationed in front of the house. The front yard is covered in yellow police tape.

EXT. BACK OF HUNTER AND ELLIOT'S HOUSE - CONTINUOUS

Gert and Daisy sneak around back. They try the back door, but it's locked. Gert leans in to peek through the window, and the screen pops out and CRASHES on the living room floor. Gert and Daisy freeze momentarily. The coast is clear. Daisy hoists Gert up.

INT. HUNTER AND ELLIOT'S HOUSE – CONTINUOUS

The floor near the couch is splattered with blood, and Daisy turns away.

DAISY
(whispers)
Let's get out of here.

Gert grabs Daisy's arm and steers them away from the scene of the crime. They slink down the hall and look into the empty bedrooms, which are cluttered with Elliot's and Hunter's stuff.

DAISY (CONT'D)
I don't even know what we're looking for.

GERT
Me, neither.

DAISY
(loud whisper)
Look!

Daisy points to a framed photo of Elliot and a red-haired woman smiling for the camera at what looks like a movie premiere.

GERT
Is that her?

Daisy shrugs. LOUD VOICES erupt from the front of the house, and Gert and Daisy look for a place to hide. They open the nearest door, a closet.

HALL CLOSET – CONTINUOUS

Gert and Daisy cower in the closet.

GERT
(whispers)
Can you move over?

DAISY
(whispers)
There's no room!

They open the closet door a crack and see Detective Boucher talking to the DUTY OFFICER who was staked out front.

DUTY OFFICER (O.S.)
You think they're good for it?

DETECTIVE BOUCHER (O.S.)
They were the last to see them alive, their prints are all
over. You tell me. I'll bet you my star on the Walk of
Fame that we'll find their bloody fingerprints all over the
murder weapon when we find it.

Gert's and Daisy's eyes bug out. They wait and listen until
all is quiet again. Gert carefully opens the closet door, and
they unpack themselves from the crammed closet. A pair
of skis start to fall from the closet, but Gert catches them.

GERT
We gotta get out of here. Did you hear what she said?
We're just putting more of our fingerprints all over.

DAISY
Should we go back to Phoenix?

GERT
We can't go back now. That'll make us look more guilty.

DAISY
What's that?

She points to a small cabinet door at the back of the closet.

GERT
Open it.

Daisy bends down and pushes on the small cabinet door.
Nothing happens.

DAISY
It won't open.

GERT
Is there a knob or something?

DAISY
No.

She feels around for a hinge or a knob, and in the process slides the panel back, revealing a plastic toolbox.

GERT
What is it?

Daisy lifts the toolbox out and sets it on the hall floor. She snaps open the lid, and they both see that the box is filled with what look like blank CDs, all in same-colored plastic cases. The plastic cases are all labeled with names. Gert lifts out a handful of CDs.

GERT
Must be demos.

DAISY
Maybe Pippi wanted her demo back.

The skis slide down the wall and CLACK against the floor. Gert and Daisy grab the toolbox full of CDs and bolt back out the way they came.

EXT. HUNTER AND ELLIOT'S HOUSE - CONTINUOUS

Gert and Daisy sneak back to their car, but Detective Boucher spots them, watches them drive away.

INT. STELLA'S APARTMENT – LATER

Gert and Daisy walk through the door and put the toolbox

on the kitchen table. The answering machine is beeping, and they play the message.

STELLA (O.S.)
(voice through the answering machine)
Hey. I'm out in Palm Springs. Help yourselves to whatever you need. I'll be home soon.

The answering machine BEEPS again, the message over.

DAISY
What do you think Stella would say?

Gert shrugs.

DAISY (CONT'D)
I wonder if they're playing our song on the radio in Palm Springs. But maybe not. She didn't mention it.

GERT
She might not have mentioned it on purpose.

Gert opens the toolbox and pulls out a fistful of CDs and sets them on the table. Daisy reaches into the toolbox and pulls out a single CD. She puts the CD into the stereo and hits play. Nothing happens.

DAISY
Blank.

GERT
Track through.

Daisy tries to advance through the CD, but nothing. She stops the stereo and puts the CD back in its case.

GERT (CONT'D)
Try this one.

She hands Daisy another CD, but the CD is the same as the last. Gert reaches for the toolbox and accidentally knocks it over. A strip of paper falls out in the avalanche of CDs. She picks it up and holds it between her fingers.

DAISY
What's that?

GERT
(matter-of-factly)
A ticket stub.

DAISY
For what?

GERT
Something called Imagistic Photo.

DAISY
C'mon. We can stop on the way to the photoshoot.

EXT. IMAGISTIC PHOTO - DAY

Gert and Daisy pull into the parking lot of the small, freestanding building.

INT. IMAGISTIC PHOTO - CONTINUOUS

Gert and Daisy wait at the counter while the PHOTO

TECH
flips through a bin of photos.

PHOTO TECH
When did you say you brought these in?

DAISY
A couple of days ago.

GERT
(looks at Daisy)
A few days. It was a few days.

DAISY
Yeah, a few days.

PHOTO TECH
They're not here.

The Photo Technician looks at ticket again.

PHOTO TECH (CONT'D)
Oh. You're in the wrong place. This is for our West
Hollywood location. Do you want me to call over there for
you?

Gert snatches the ticket back.

GERT
That's okay. We gotta go.

PHOTO TECH
(suddenly)
Hey, aren't you in that band? The one that killed all those
people?

Gert makes a gun with her hand and points it at the Photo
Tech.

DAISY
You want our autograph?

PHOTO TECH
Yeah!

Photo Tech grabs the nearest piece of paper.

PHOTO TECH (CONT'D)
Make it out to Tedd. Two Ds.

Gert and Daisy autograph the piece of paper.

GERT
We're going to be late.

DAISY
(to Tedd)
We've got a big photo shoot. You coming to the
showcase?

TEDD
I have to work.

DAISY
You're going to miss all the fun.
(to Gert)
Let's scram.

Gert and Daisy move toward the door. Tedd looks at the
piece of paper.

TEDD
(disappointed)
You forgot the second d!

But Gert and Daisy are gone.

EXT. FOREST LAWN CEMETERY OFFICE – DAY

Stella walks into the office.

INT. FOREST LAWN CEMETERY OFFICE - CONTINOUS

A CLERK, 20s, is pounding on the computer keyboard in exasperation. He looks up when Stella walks in.

CLERK
Can I help you?

STELLA
I have sort of an odd question.

CLERK
It's a cemetery, honey. You won't offend anyone here.

STELLA
Is Ryan Metro buried here?

CLERK
Metro...Metro. Is he that silent-film star?

STELLA
(shaking her head)
Rock star.

CLERK
Maybe. When did he die?

STELLA
I'm not sure he did.

CLERK
Tell you the truth, I'm new here and I don't know. And the

computer is down. If you want to leave your number, I can look it up later and call you.

STELLA
That's okay. Don't worry about it.

Stella walks out.

EXT. POOL SOMEWHERE IN THE HOLLYWOOD HILLS - DAY

Gert and Daisy arrive, each with a suitcase. Alan and a Photographer are huddled together. Alan looks up and sees them.

ALAN
You made it.

DAISY
The gate code wouldn't work the first time. Whose house is this?

Gert and Daisy survey the landscape and are clearly impressed.

ALAN
You ever see Wall Street?

GERT
No way.

ALAN
Yeah, Charlie's a friend of mine.
(points to the Photographer)
This is Max. Max Q. Best photographer in L.A.

MAX Q.
(still fiddling with his camera)
Hey.

ALAN
(points)
There's a cabana behind the lilac grove.

DAISY
(disappointed)
We can't change in the house?

ALAN
(laughs nervously)
Afraid not. Sorry.

GERT
(hopefully)
Is Charlie home?

ALAN
He's filming. Somewhere in Tanzania. I'll get you his
autograph, though.

DAISY
Cool.
(to Gert)
Should we get one for Stella, too?

GERT
I don't know. He's not dead.

DAISY
(to Alan)
Will you get one for us, and one for Stella?

ALAN
(bemused, but nervous)
Yeah, sure. Should we get started?

EXT. POOL SOMEWHERE IN THE HOLLYWOOD
HILLS – A LITTLE LATER

Gert and Daisy are in the pool, fully-dressed. Max Q. is in
the pool too, while Alan watches from a chaise lounge.

MAX Q.
On three.
(beat)
One. Two. Three

Gert and Daisy and Max Q. all submerge in the pool. Gert
and Daisy strike a pose and stare at the camera, and Max
Q. snaps the picture, flashing them a thumbs-up, and they
all surface, Gert and Daisy gasping for breath.

ALAN
(to Max Q.)
Got it?

MAX Q.
Got it.

Alan claps his hands together while Gert and Daisy catch
their breath. Alan shades his eyes as Detective Boucher
makes her way into the pool area.

ALAN
Who are you?

DETECTIVE BOUCHER
(flashes her badge)
Police.

ALAN
We have permission to be here.

DETECTIVE BOUCHER
(to Gert and Daisy)
I need to talk to you for a minute.

Gert and Daisy shade their eyes and look up at Detective Boucher.

EXT. FRONT OF HOUSE IN HOLLYWOOD HILLS –
MINUTES LATER

Gert and Daisy are wrapped in towels, their drenched clothes still on underneath. Detective Boucher reaches into her car and pulls out a large envelope. She spreads the contents on the hood of her car, and Gert and Daisy lean in for a look. They see a series of typed love letters between Daisy and Hunter.

GERT
What is this?

DETECTIVE BOUCHER
You tell me.

DAISY
I've never seen these before in my life.

DETECTIVE BOUCHER
I thought you said you just met them that night?

DAISY
Are you saying you think these are from me?

DETECTIVE BOUCHER
Are you denying you wrote them?

Gert picks up a letter and starts reading it.

DAISY
I didn't write them.

GERT
It's true. You don't know how to spell "occasion." It's spelled right here.

Alan walks up.

ALAN
What's the story?

GERT
Someone is framing us for a murder we didn't commit.

Daisy looks at Gert. Gert shakes her head no.

DAISY
There was someone else there that night. The night of the murder.

DETECTIVE BOUCHER
(crossing her arms)
Really? Who?

DAISY
A woman with red hair came to the door and had a fight with Elliot.

DETECTIVE BOUCHER
Why didn't you mention this before?

DAISY
We remembered it after we left the police station.

DETECTIVE BOUCHER
Can you describe this woman?

GERT
We told you, she has red hair.

DETECTIVE BOUCHER
So do I between dye jobs. Need a better description than that.

GERT
(pretending to remember)
There was a picture of her in their living room.

Detective Boucher looks at them askance.

DETECTIVE BOUCHER
That's Elliot's sister. But nice try.

ALAN
(to Detective Boucher)
I'm their manager, and I don't want them to say anything more without a lawyer.

DETECTIVE BOUCHER
They don't need a lawyer. Yet.
(to Gert and Daisy)
You girls better get out of those wet clothes. You'll catch a cold.

Detective Boucher gathers up the letters and gets back in her car.

EXT. CHATEAU MARMONT POOL – CONTINUOUS

Stella spies around the corner on RYAN METRO, who is laid out in jeans and a T-shirt on a chaise lounge, the sunlight reflected in his mirrored sunglasses. The pool area is otherwise empty. Stella walks stealthily toward Ryan, finally blocking out his sun.

RYAN
What's up, man? You're in my sun.

STELLA
(in awe, almost whispering)
I thought you were dead.

Ryan looks mildly alarmed. He half-sits up and raises his sunglasses but then sees he's in no danger and lies back down.

RYAN
It's L.A., man. Everyone here is dead.

STELLA
Are you hiding out from someone?

RYAN
You ask a lot of questions for a cabana boy, er, girl.

STELLA
I don't work here.

RYAN
Are you a reporter?

Stella sits down tentatively in the chair next to Ryan's, as if he's a mirage that may disappear.

STELLA
No.

RYAN
Cool, man.

STELLA
Why did you cancel those shows in Japan?

RYAN
Why do you want to know?

STELLA
(thinks)
I guess it really doesn't matter now.

RYAN
(ignoring her)
Fuckin' Chinks.

STELLA
I don't think Japanese people are called Chinks. Those are the Chinese.

RYAN
Whatever, man. Fuckin' Japs, then. Okay?

STELLA
Why did you say you would play shows in Japan if you hate the Japanese?

RYAN
I don't hate them, man. They hate me.

STELLA
You mean like the maid at the Hilton who said you--

RYAN
Next question.

Stella goes to the edge of the pool and kicks off her
sandals, then touches her toes to the water.

RYAN (CONT'D)
Wanna go to a party?

INT. WEST HOLLYWOOD IMAGISTIC PHOTO - DAY

Gert and Daisy wait at the counter. They're in obvious
disguises—sunglasses, hats, and scarves--and keep looking
over their shoulders whenever anyone walks in. The
manager, a girl named MARY, hands them a packet of
photos.

MARY
Lucky. These were in the discard bin.

DAISY
Thanks. We were out of town, touring.

Mary gives them a queer look, but Gert and Daisy don't
explain and rush out with the pictures in hand.

EXT. PARKING LOT - CONTINUOUS

Gert and Daisy sit in their car, Gert passing the pictures to
Daisy one at a time.

GERT
What are these?

DAISY
(holds up a picture of a woman on a Jet Ski)
Maybe it's Jet Ski Girl.

GERT
Here's one of someone's dog.

(flips to another picture)
Here's one of a half-empty beer bottle.

Gert hands all the pictures to Daisy.

DAISY
What if I gave the police a description, so they'd have someone else to look for?

GERT
You mean make it up?

Daisy nods.

GERT (CONT'D)
That idea is about as bad as us thinking we could find this chick on our own. She keeps typing letters and we're going to end up in prison.

A cop car pulls up next to them. The COP in the driver's seat looks over, and Gert and Daisy adjust their disguises. Gert starts the car and they pull out of the parking lot.

EXT. STREETS OF LOS ANGELES – DAY

Gert and Daisy drive down the street, slowing when they see a bank of their poster, the underwater shot of them standing on the bottom of the pool, fully clothed, papering a wall. Gert slows the car, and Daisy gets out and rips a couple down as keepsakes.

INT. CAR - CONTINUOUS

Daisy hands a poster to Gert.

GERT
Cool.

DAISY
This would make a great album cover.

EXT. OCEAN RECORDS - DAY

A car is broken down in front of a nondescript southwestern-style building that looks like it used to be a fast-food restaurant. There is no sign, and Gert and Daisy grab the front door like they don't expect it to open, but it opens easily and they move tentatively inside.

INT. OCEAN RECORDS LOBBY – CONTINUOUS

A rock ballad BLASTS from the recording studio. Gert and Daisy peer in and see an all-male metal band rehearsing. They see Alan, too, listening and swaying to the ballad. Alan is moved by the music, his face contorting to the emotion of the lyrics. Alan sees them and waves. He steps out of the recording studio and into the lobby.

GERT
Who's that?

ALAN
Flight Recorder. They're playing the showcase too.

DAISY
(peers in again)
Cute.

GERT
I thought we were rehearsing today.

ALAN
They'll be done soon. Meantime, let me introduce you to Ian Black.

He directs them through a door.

INT. IAN'S OFFICE - CONTINUOUS

The office is nothing to speak of: a cluttered desk, bare walls, and a fluorescent light. IAN BLACK, 50s, looks up from his desk when they walk in.

ALAN
Girls, this is Ian, owner and operator of Ocean Records. A legend in the recording world. Ian, meet Mary Jane Lane.

IAN
The band that needs no introduction.
(looks them over)
Wow, what a terrific look.

He gets up and comes around the desk to shake their hands.

ALAN
Take good care of them, Ian. Otherwise they won't remember you when they get to the top.

IAN
Hopefully, we'll all get there together.

ALAN
(to Gert and Daisy)
I gotta take off. Oh, and before I forget. Wanna go to a party tonight? It's at Shampu. I'll throw in a limo.

GERT
Well, if there's going to be a limo, how can we say no?

ALAN
Good. It'll pick you up at seven.

Gert and Daisy nod, and Alan leaves.

IAN
Shall we?

Ian leads Gert and Daisy down a narrow hall and into a backroom, which is outfitted with some recording equipment and a sound booth. JAMMIN' JAY JASPER, a blond in his late thirties, sits at the control panel, a guitar in his lap.

IAN
Jammin' Jay is Ocean Records' lead studio musician. Been playin' by ear since he was five.

DAISY
Wow.

JAMMIN' JAY
(to Ian)
I think I've got it.

IAN
(to Gert and Daisy)
See what I mean?

Jammin' Jay fiddles with the control panel and the instrumental for "World Gone Water" BLASTS over the speakers.

IAN (CONT'D)
What do you think? Want to give it a try?

Daisy pulls on Gert's shirt a little as Gert heads for the mic, but follows Gert's lead. Gert and Daisy huddle around the mic as the MUSIC STARTS. They SING into the microphone. Ian mans the control panel and nods his head to the beat of the drum machine. Gert's voice warbles, and Jammin' Jay looks back at Ian skeptically, but Ian continues to bob his head. Daisy struggles with a lyric and then waves off the music. Ian cuts the music.

DAISY
(worried she's ruined the song)
I'm a little nervous. I need to write down the lyrics.

IAN
Okay, we'll write them down next rehearsal.
You looked great. Fantastic.

GERT
Want us to do it again?

IAN
That's enough for today. Let's head over to my office. Alan and I would also like you to record a message for your fans.

GERT
What kind of message?

IAN
I've opened an 800 number so that fans can hear your voices, to get them psyched for the showcase. 1-800-MARYJANELANE.

DAISY
(counts on her fingers)
That's too many letters.

IAN
(smiles)
The number just corresponds to the first seven digits, then it starts to ring, so that by the time you put the phone to

your ear...
(mimics a phone call with his hand)
...they hear you right away.

DAISY
Cool. What should we say?

IAN
Say whatever you want. Just be sure to mention the
showcase, to remind people.

DAISY
Awesome idea.

IAN
Great. Phone's in my office.

INT. SHAMPU – NIGHT

Ryan and Stella are stuffed in a booth with FAMOUS
ACTORS AND ACTRESSES from popular film and
television. Everyone is chain-smoking and TALKING
RAPIDLY. The MUSIC IS UP LOUD and people have to
scream to be heard. Ryan offers Stella a cigarette, and even
though she doesn't smoke, she takes one. The FAMOUS
ACTOR sitting across from her lights it, and Stella blows
smoke across the table.

RYAN
(yelling)
--so I told them to fuck off. Right, man?

FAMOUS FILM ACTOR #1
(yelling)
That's fuckin' right. Scumbags.

FAMOUS T.V. ACTRESS #1
(yelling)
Ryan, where've you been? We haven't seen you in, like,
forever.

RYAN
(yelling)
Camped out. Stella here got me out.

Stella waves awkwardly to the table. Someone has
complained about the music and it NOTCHES DOWN to a
decent level.

FAMOUS FILM ACTRESS #1
Are you in the business?

STELLA
Yeah, sort of. Trying to be.

FAMOUS T.V. ACTRESS #1
What have you done?

STELLA
Mostly I do theater.

No one says anything.

INT. STELLA'S APARTMENT – BATHROOM - NIGHT

Gert and Daisy are busy getting ready for the party. Daisy
is blow-drying her hair while Gert fixes her make-up.
Daisy kills the blow-dryer and tosses her hair in the mirror.

FRONT ROOM – MOMENTS LATER

Gert and Daisy are ready to go.

DAISY
Which shoes?

Daisy holds up a pair of pink tennis shoes and a pair of black flats.

GERT
The flats.
(beat)
Did the phone ring? There's a message.

Gert points to the blinking light on the answering machine. Daisy presses the button and plays the message.

DAISY
Maybe it's Stella.

MARY (O.S.)
Hi. This is Mary from the photo lab. We forgot to include the photo CD with your pictures. I'll set it aside for you, and you can pick it up anytime during our business hours. Thanks.

Gert looks at Daisy.

DAISY
What?

GERT
Hand me the CD.

Daisy opens Hunter and Elliot's toolbox and she hands a CD with a star on it to Gert. Gert turns on the TV and slides the CD into the DVD player. The screen stays black for a few seconds and Gert and Daisy are about to give up on the idea until Hunter's smiling face fills the screen. Gert and Daisy recoil at the close-up. On-screen they see Hunter

move behind the camera to reveal a WOMAN and Elliot
sitting on the couch together, both holding scripts.

ELLIOT
(on the TV)
Ready?

WOMAN
(on the TV)
Ready.

DAISY
Oh my God. Is that Stella?

GERT
(leaning into the screen)
I don't think so.
(beat)
No, it's not.

ELLIOT
(on the TV)
You sure your husband isn't coming back?

WOMAN
(on the TV)
He won't be home for hours.

ELLIOT
(on the TV)
I hope not.

The image cuts violently and Gert's and Daisy's faces
contort as we hear PANTING AND MOANING coming
through the TV, along with Hunter's exhortations spurring
Elliot on. Daisy reaches up and switches off the DVD.
Neither knows what to say.

There's a KNOCK at the door. Daisy hides the toolbox and Gert opens the door to find Alan standing in the doorway in his best suit.

ALAN
Ready?

Gert and Daisy look past Alan at the black limo idling in the parking lot.

DAISY
Ready.

ALAN
Time to show you off to L.A.

GERT
Let's do it.

The three head out.

ALAN
(suddenly)
Oh, can I use your bathroom? Just be a sec.

DAISY
Can we wait for you in the limo?

ALAN
(smiles)
Sure. How do I lock the front door?

GERT
Just lock it and pull it shut behind you.

ALAN
Got it.

INT. BLACK LIMO – MOMENTS LATER

Gert and Daisy are playing with the moon roof when they hear a LOUD THUD, the sound of the trunk slamming shut. The door opens and Alan jumps in.

ALAN
What do you think?

DAISY
Plastic fantastic.

EXT. STREETS OF LOS ANGELES - NIGHT

The black limo navigates the streets.

The sound of a PHONE RINGING, then a BEEP.

GERT (V.O.)
Hello, superfans. This is Gert.

DAISY (V.O)
And this is Daisy.

GERT AND DAISY (V.O.)
We're Mary Jane Lane!

GERT (V.O.)
We're looking forward to seeing you at the Viper Room.

DAISY (V.O.)
So come out and bring your friends. And make sure you say hello.
(to Gert)
Should we say where the Viper Room is?

GERT (V.O.)
(to Daisy)
I think everyone knows where the Viper Room is.

DAISY (V.O.)
(to Gert)
Okay. What else?

GERT (V.O.)
Buy our album!

DAISY (V.O.)
(giggles)
When it comes out!

EXT. SHAMPU - NIGHT

The black limo pulls up to the club, which is swarming
with activity. A white limo in front of theirs begins to pull
away.

EXT. STREETS OF LOS ANGELES – NIGHT

The white limo turns a corner, and Stella sticks her head
out of the window and pukes. Ryan alternately laughs and
tries to remember the words to "Billie Jean" by Michael
Jackson.

RYAN
(drunkenly singing)
She was more like a beauty queen…than popped-cherry
ice cream…

Stella pulls her head inside the car.

STELLA
(nauseous)

Maybe the driver should pull over. There's puke all down the side of the car.

RYAN
(continues to sing)
I told her my name was Super Queen...and she said...

STELLA
(head down, eyes closed)
Ryan.

RYAN
(singing loudly)
I said I am the one, but that's not my gun...

Stella bolts her head out the window again and pukes. Ryan reaches over as if to steady her, but gropes her instead.

RYAN
(high-pitched voice)
Hee, hee, hee.

EXT. SHAMPU – NIGHT - CONTINUOUS

The Driver opens the limo door, and Alan pops out. The Bouncer removes the velvet rope, and Alan helps Gert and Daisy out of the limo. Gert and Daisy look around at the Pedestrians on the sidewalk, who are in turn staring at Gert and Daisy. Suddenly a CRAZED WOMAN appears at their side.

CRAZED WOMAN
(yelling)
Shame! Shame! Shame!

Pedestrians stop to watch the confrontation.

CRAZED WOMAN (CONT'D)
Shame on you for capitalizing on those murders! Their
blood is on your hands!

Alan pushes the Crazed Woman away from Gert and
Daisy.

CRAZED WOMAN (CONT'D)
Their blood is on your hands!

The crowd swallows the Crazed Woman, and Alan pulls a
stunned Gert and Daisy through the club entrance.

INT. SHAMPU - NIGHT

The party is in full swing, beautiful People and Celebrities
packed into the hip club. The volume of the conversations
increases as Mary Jane Lane walk in, Gert and Daisy each
looping their arms through Alan's. They pass by a wall-
size poster of Sarah McLachlan on the cover of R*O*C*K
magazine.

DAISY
(shaken)
That woman looked like she wanted to kill us.

GERT
She was crazy enough to do it.

ALAN
Gotta shrug it off, girls. Everyone's watching.

Gert and Daisy scan the crowd and see that what Alan said
is only half true.

GERT
(poking Daisy)
Look.

Gert nods at Sarah McLachlan as she walks by the giant
poster.

DAISY
Weird.

Silver and gold confetti litters the floor, and Gert's
sneakers are caked in it by the time she and Daisy make
their way to one of the plush sofas at a table in the back.

ALAN
I'll get us some drinks.

Gert and Daisy continue to gawk at the crowd, some of
whom wave to them. Daisy waves back tentatively. Gert
cranes her neck to search the crowd and sees Detective
Boucher, who is dressed in her party clothes. The detective
waves at her.

GERT
Shite.

DAISY
What?

Detective Boucher saunters over to their table.

DETECTIVE BOUCHER
Enjoying the party?

DAISY
(nods her head without making eye contact)
Uh-huh.

Alan returns to the table with drinks. He sets the drinks on the table but remains standing.

ALAN
(to Detective Boucher)
Working undercover?

DETECTIVE BOUCHER
(laughs)
Heavens, no. I'm a consultant for Angel Vice. I'm here with some of the producers.

ALAN
I love that show.

DETECTIVE BOUCHER
Yeah, it's fun. My job is to make it as realistic as possible.

Detective Boucher looks at Gert and Daisy.

DETECTIVE BOUCHER (CONT'D)
Of course, it has to be entertaining. They don't really show how it is, what really happens when someone is arrested and booked for murder. It's not as exciting as it looks on the little screen.

GERT
(coolly)
Interesting.

Detective Boucher and Gert lock eyes.

DETECTIVE BOUCHER
So. What are you going to say to Madonna when you meet her?

Gert and Daisy don't say anything, too afraid to speak.

DELIVERYMAN (O.S.)
Excuse me.

Alan and Detective Boucher glance up and see a
DELIVERYMAN holding a package wrapped in pink with
an elaborate white bow.

DELIVERYMAN (CONT'D)
Is one of you Detective Boucher?

DETECTIVE BOUCHER
(suspiciously)
That's me.

DELIVERYMAN
Sign here, please.

He puts a clipboard in front of Detective Boucher and sets
the package on the table, looking around at the wild party.

DETECTIVE BOUCHER
Who's it from?

DELIVERYMAN
(shrugs)
Don't know. My last delivery of the day. You think I could
hang around here?

Detective Boucher signs the clipboard and gives it back.

DETECTIVE BOUCHER
Make sure you try the little bacon things.

The Deliveryman tips his hat and saunters through the
crowd.

ALAN
Is it your birthday?

Detective Boucher gives him a look. She takes up the
package and holds it to judge its weight. She looks the
package up and down.

DETECTIVE BOUCHER
It doesn't seem to be ticking.

She shakes the box and a THUMPING SOUND is heard.

ALAN
Not fragile, either.

GERT
Which way to the bathroom?

Alan points in the direction of the bathroom.

DETECTIVE BOUCHER
You must get presents like this every day. You're not even
curious. Must be nice.

Detective Boucher carefully rips the wrapping paper and
opens the box. She looks into the box and furrows her
brow.

ALAN
What is it?

As Gert and Daisy move away from the table, Detective
Boucher reaches into the box and hoists out a girl's pink
tennis shoe, the sole lacquered with dried blood. Gert's and
Daisy's eyes get wide, and they dart through the crowd for
the limo.

EXT. SHAMPU - CONTINUOUS

Gert and Daisy jump into the limo. The Crazed Woman
from earlier suddenly slaps the hood and presses her face
against the window. The limo pulls away as Detective
Boucher and Alan make it through the crowded club, the
Crazed Woman screaming after Gert and Daisy. They all
watch the limo drive off.

EXT. MEYERS'S APARTMENT BUILDING - NIGHT

The limo pulls up in front of Meyers's apartment building,
a pink stucco affair studded with withering palm trees.

INT. MEYERS'S APARTMENT – A LITTLE LATER

Gert and Daisy and Meyers are sitting in Meyers's kitchen,
which has an unintended retro feel.

MEYERS
And it was yours, for sure?

DAISY
I was going to wear them tonight.

MEYERS
How do you think this woman got into your apartment?

GERT
The lock on the front window is busted. That's probably
how.

MEYERS
I wonder…

GERT
What?

MEYERS
I got something strange in the mail.

GERT
Strange like how?

MEYERS
I got a typed note that said you guys knew Elliot and
Hunter going back years, so that you were lying when you
said you'd just met them. It was typed like the letters you
say the police had.

DAISY
What? No way.

MEYERS
Swear to God.

GERT
Give it to us.

MEYERS
I tossed it. Figured it was some crank that saw you on TV.
Or saw your posters. Cool poster, by the way.

DAISY
Thanks.

MEYERS
Maybe you should stay here with me. It might not be safe
at Stella's.

DAISY
You really think so?

Meyers shrugs.

MEYERS
It's nothing great, but I have an extra room. You could
bunk there until the showcase. Congratulations on that, too.
It's all over the radio.

DAISY
Are you going to come?

Meyers hadn't planned on it, but:

MEYERS
Yeah, sure. Wouldn't miss it.
(beat)
Just, you know, be careful.

Gert and Daisy wonder what he means.

MEYERS (CONT'D)
(lightens up)
Just don't believe everything you see. A lot of it is
just...fairy dust.

He pretends to sprinkle the air with dust.

INT. STELLA'S APARTMENT – BEDROOM -
MIDNIGHT

Gert and Daisy are packing up their stuff for the move to
Meyers's.

GERT
Is this your lotion?

DAISY
Give it.

Gert throws the bottle of lotion a little too hard, and Daisy lunges to catch it, knocking into the wall. The framed poster of Ryan Metro slips off the wall and lands on the floor.

GERT
Lucky for you it didn't break.

DAISY
Why doesn't she like real music? She probably never even really liked Madonna.

Daisy picks the frame up off the floor.

DAISY (CONT'D)
(mock relief)
It's plastic. Whew!

Daisy inspects the back of the frame.

DAISY (CONT'D)
Look at this.

Daisy turns the frame and shows Gert the CD in a plastic case taped to the back of the framed poster.

INT. STELLA'S APARTMENT - FRONT ROOM - CONTINUOUS

Gert and Daisy slip the CD into the stereo and press play. The familiar strains of "World Gone Water" start, and the hear Stella's voice singing the lyrics.

DAISY
Oh my God.

GERT
I thought she said she met Elliot and Hunter in acting class.

DAISY
Oh my God, Oh my God. Now it makes sense.

She opens Stella's Murder Book and flips to the back.

DAISY (CONT'D)
I was flipping through this the other day and found this.

She hands Gert the Polaroid of Gert holding the knife at the Starion.

GERT
So?

DAISY
This book is full of people who are dead. Or who are going to be dead.

GERT
That's crazy. You think Stella wants to kill us? Are you still drunk?

DAISY
Not kill us. Frame us. Some crazed fan could kill us. She's just trying to make sure we get famous.

GERT
Yeah, right.

DAISY
(excitedly)
She could've given our CD to the radio station.

INSERT: Stella dressed in disguise, handing the CD to the Radio DJ

DAISY (CONT'D)
And she could've told Meyers where to find us.

INSERT: Stella dressed in a second disguise, approaching Meyers.

DAISY (CONT'D)
And given him the typed letter.

INSERT: Stella dressed in a third disguise, typing on a typewriter.

DAISY (CONT'D)
And she could've told Alan we were at the police station.

INSERT: Stella dressed in a fourth disguise, calling Alan on the phone.

Gert rushes over to the stereo and rips it out of the wall, throwing it across the room. She continues to trash the front room while Daisy looks on fearfully.

DAISY
(yelling)
Stop! Stop!

Daisy grabs ahold of Gert, who is out of breath.

DAISY (CONT'D)
I'm as scared as you are, but you're scaring me more. Let's just go back to Phoenix. Stella can't hurt us if we leave.

GERT
(still breathless)
No. No way. I'm not letting her run us out of town. We're going to win that showcase, and she can come see us open for Madonna from the back row, for all I care.

Gert stomps off into the bedroom, leaving Daisy in the middle of the junked front room.

INT. RYAN METRO'S SUITE AT THE CHATEAU MARMONT – DAY

Ryan and Stella are in bed, awake. The floor is littered with pornographic magazines. The night table is heaped high with bloody Kleenexes. The phone is off the hook. Next to an unopened bottle of warm champagne are needles, a rubber hose, and a small balloon of heroin.

STELLA
I'm going for a swim.

RYAN
Another?

STELLA
I didn't go today.

RYAN
Yes you did.

STELLA
That was yesterday.

RYAN
(unsure)
Was it?

STELLA
(firmly, as if trying to convince him)
It was yesterday. I haven't been out of this room all day.

EXT. STREETS OF LOS ANGELES - DAY

Gert and Daisy are driving down the street.

DAISY
I still think we should go to Meyers's.

GERT
What for? We can handle Stella. Just wait until I get my
hands--

They catch sight of a WOMAN, obviously wearing a wig,
stapling something to a wall of Mary Jane Lane posters.

GERT (CONT'D)
(yells out)
Hey!

The Woman freezes. When she sees Gert and Daisy, she
runs. Gert and Daisy chase after her, but the Woman gets
into her car and drives off. The windows are down and a
pile of paper blows off the dashboard and hits the sidewalk
in the car's wake. Gert and Daisy look down at the paper
and see that it's a wad of color copies of the photo of Gert
holding the bloody knife from the Starion, blown up to full
size.

DAISY
I told you! I told you it was her!
(on the verge of tears)
Why is she doing this? Is she that jealous?

Gert scoops up the pictures and folds them in half.

GERT
C'mon.

They walk back to their car, pulling down the photos the
Woman stapled to their posters.

DAISY
Where are we going?

INT. STARION RESTAURANT – A LITTLE LATER

The restaurant is closed, with minimal Waitstaff setting up
for the evening. Gert and Daisy walk through the
restaurant but are stopped by the MANAGER, 40s.

MANAGER
We don't open until six.

GERT
We're friends of Stella's.

MANAGER
(annoyed)
You just missed her. I told her to clean out her locker.
Ingrate. You tell her for me that she'll never make it in this
town with her work ethic. I had to cancel a week's worth
of shows.

GERT
Stella was just here?

The Manager recognizes Gert and Daisy from the paper.

MANAGER
You're the two from the paper. Say, you interested in
acting? We could do a variety hour--singing, dancing, all
that crap.

GERT
Thanks, but no. Did Stella say where she was going?

MANAGER
Straight to hell, if you ask me.

INT. BOUCHER'S OFFICE – DAY

Detective Boucher is at her desk, studying a color copy of
the Polaroid of Gert with the knife. There's a KNOCK on
the door, and Detective Boucher folds the color copy and
puts it in her drawer.

DETECTIVE BOUCHER
Come in.

The door swings open and the entire Police Force is
standing there, with her retirement cake in hand. The room
ERUPTS in congratulations.

INT. SPAGO – NIGHT

Gert and Daisy are seated at a table with Alan and Ian.

ALAN
The Oscar party here last year was out of hand. You'll
probably get invited this year.
(takes a deep breath)
I've got some big news. I got you an interview with
R*O*C*K magazine.

DAISY
(covers her mouth)
You...are...kidding!

GERT
Plastic fantastic.

ALAN
I'm trying to talk them into making you the cover. But first
thing's first. They want you to show up tomorrow at the
Chateau Marmont at noon.

IAN
If they don't give you the cover now, they said they might when your album comes out.

DAISY
Mondo cool. Madonna was on the cover for Like a Virgin.

GERT
And for Who's That Girl.

A MUSIC EXEC, 50s, walks up to their table.

MUSIC EXEC
I'm sorry to interrupt, but I wanted to introduce myself. I'm John Keyes. I'm in A&R at—

IAN
(coldly)
I know who you are.

JOHN KEYES
Well, just wanted to say hello.
(to Gert and Daisy)
I'm looking forward to the showcase.

DAISY
Thanks.

GERT
Yeah, thanks.

John Keyes walks away.

IAN
That guy's a snake.

GERT
He seemed okay.

ALAN
I want you two to promise me you won't talk to him
without me present.

DAISY
Why?

ALAN
You'll just have to trust me. This town is full of nuts who
will try to take advantage of you.

DAISY
We want to ask you a question, but you can't get mad.

ALAN
Uh-oh.

GERT
Who told you how to find us at the police station?

Alan and Ian exchange glances.

ALAN
(relieved)
Oh, that. Someone called me.

DAISY
Who?

ALAN
They didn't say. They just left a message with my service
that said where you were and that you were looking for
representation.

GERT
Man or a woman?

ALAN
I can't remember. A woman, I think.

A MAN, 30s, obviously drunk, presses up against the glass and screams something at Daisy, who SCREAMS and recoils.

MAN
(muffled, through the glass)
I can't believe it!
(to Daisy, through the glass)
Can I get your autograph?

The DOORMAN suddenly appears and escorts the drunken Man away.

EXT. SPAGO PARKING LOT - LATER

As Gert and Daisy pull out, they see Detective Boucher pulling in.

DAISY
Go!

Gert punches it and they peel out.

INT. SPAGO - CONTINUOUS

Detective Boucher walks up to Alan and Ian's table. Alan and Ian look up from their coffee.

DETECTIVE BOUCHER
Good. You're both here.

Detective Boucher pulls out a chair to join them at the table.

INT. STELLA'S APARTMENT - NIGHT

Gert and Daisy sit silently in the dark, watching the TV with the sound off. They hear FOOTSTEPS, and Daisy clicks off the TV.

EXT. STELLA'S APARTMENT - CONTINUOUS

Detective Boucher KNOCKS on the door.

INT. STELLA'S APARTMENT - CONTINUOUS

Gert and Daisy freeze. Daisy closes her eyes as Detective Boucher KNOCKS again. Finally they hear FOOTSTEPS RECEDING as Detective Boucher leaves.

EXT. CHATEAU MARMONT – GARDEN TERRACE - DAY

Gert and Daisy sit at a table, sipping iced tea.

DAISY
(motioning and whispering)
Is that someone?

Gert sneaks a peek and shakes her head no.

GERT
(impatiently)
Where is this chick?

Daisy pulls out the clipping of their picture from the L.A. Times and unfolds it, spreading it out to look at it again. She hopes the WAITER will recognize it as he approaches.

WAITER
Another iced tea?

DAISY
Yes. Two, please.

The Waiter nods and walks away without noticing the picture.

Daisy admires the photo again and then folds the clipping back up, stopping when she notices a small item.
INSERT: Headline: "Ryan Metro Arrested in London Nightclub Brawl."

DAISY (CONT'D)
Look.

She thrusts article toward Gert, who scans it.

GERT
Palm Springs, my ass.

A young, hip woman is suddenly standing in front of their table. She is the INTERVIEWER from R*O*C*K magazine.

INTERVIEWER
Mary Jane Lane, right?

Gert holds up the clipping and smirks.

INT. CHATEAU MARMONT – LOBBY – A LITTLE LATER

Gert and Daisy are on a velvet couch in the corner, while the Interviewer perches on a chair across from them, a tape recorder between them. The Interviewer is also taking notes.

INTERVIEWER
And what about some of your influences?

GERT
(grandly)
Well, let's see. Madonna, certainly.

DAISY
And Bananarama.

GERT
We're Bananarama fans going all the way back. We also dig Motley Crue.

Daisy looks at Gert quizzically, but the interviewer doesn't catch it. Gert just smiles.

GERT (CONT'D)
I would say we're fans of pretty much any Brit-pop band as well as all the American hair bands.

INTERVIEWER
(skeptically)
Even Twisted Sister?

DAISY
(picking up on the game)
Those guys are the best. They took us to Vegas a couple of weekends ago. In their limo. Gert threw up out the moon roof.

GERT
(riffing)
It hit a cop car that was following us, but he didn't do anything. That's how famous Twisted Sister is.

DAISY
The best was Duran Duran's party at the airport. It was in a whadyacallit…

GERT
A hangar.

DAISY
Yeah, a hangar. They had a live alligator.

INTERVIEWER
An alligator?

DAISY
Coulda been a croc, I guess. Not sure. But it just chilled. I petted it.

GERT
What about the thing at that guy's stables?

DAISY
Stables?

GERT
(to Interviewer)
This guy we met had this limo, and he took us to his house way out…
(motions with her arm)
…and he had all these horses and stuff, and it was a party because one horse was doing it with another horse. Insemination Celebration, that's what it was called. I saw Magic Johnson there with his wife. And that guy who has all those chicken restaurants.

DAISY
Ryan Metro was there too.

INTERVIEWER
Oh? I'm interviewing him tomorrow before I head over to
the showcase.

GERT
Really?

INTERVIEWER
Right here in the lobby of the Chateau.

DAISY
Ha! How about that?

Gert and Daisy exchange looks.

INT. STELLA'S APARTMENT - DAY

The apartment is empty. The phone RINGS and the
answering machine answers.

STELLA (O.S.)
Hey, ladies. Very excited about the showcase. I'm back in
L.A. and will be in the crowd. I'll try to meet you
backstage before to wish you luck. See you then.

EXT. STREETS OF LOS ANGELES – DAY

Gert and Daisy are on their way to the showcase. Daisy
concentrates on driving while Gert stares out the window
from the passenger seat. Both are sullen and silent.

GERT
God, I'm starving. Can we stop and get something to eat?

DAISY
We have to be there an hour before we go on. Did you
have oatmeal for breakfast like I told you?

GERT
(irritated)
No, I didn't have oatmeal for breakfast like you told me.

Daisy shoots her a look but doesn't say anything.

DAISY
What are we going to say to her?

GERT
We're going to make her go to the cops and tell them that
she was behind the whole thing.
(beat)
God, I feel sick to my stomach.
(beat)
None of this would've happened if you wouldn't have
kicked her out of the band.

DAISY
(shocked)
What? I did not kick her out.

GERT
That's not what you told the DJ in Phoenix. Did you really
think she wasn't going to find out about that?

DAISY
What about all the times we called her and she didn't call
us back? For all I knew, she quit the band.

GERT
You still shouldn't have said it. You're always making up
shite, telling people what they want to hear. Just to try to
make it.

DAISY
(angry)

What about you? You're always pissing people off with
your mouth.

GERT
(yelling)
That's it. I've had it. Pull over.

DAISY
I'm not pulling over.

GERT
(yelling)
If you don't pull over, I'll jump out.

Daisy pulls over and Gert gets out.

GERT
(yelling)
See how you do without my mouth.

Gert slams the door and takes off.

Daisy rolls down the window.

DAISY
(yelling)
Gert!

EXT. MEYERS'S APARTMENT – A LITTLE LATER

A cab pulls up and Gert gets out. She approaches Meyers's
door and lifts her hand to knock, when the door swings
open. Meyers is startled to see her.

MEYERS
What are you doing here? I was just on my way to the
showcase. The paper wants me to do a little feature on

Mary Jane Lane's performance. A sort of post-mortem.

Gert winces.
MEYERS (CONT'D)
I know. Bad pun.

GERT
Mary Jane Lane just broke up.

MEYERS
What? When?

GERT
We got into a fight and I left.

MEYERS
But what about the chance to open for Madonna? You want it to be somebody else?

GERT
It's not worth it. I'm sick of it.

MEYERS
So you drove here from Phoenix, got mixed up in a double murder, got hounded by the police and press, and now you're just going to quit?

Gert crosses her arms and looks at Meyers.

EXT./INT. VIPER ROOM – LATE AFTERNOON

The showcase is jammed with Hipsters of all ages.

INT. VIPER ROOM - BACKSTAGE - CONTINUOUS

Daisy is peering out at the crowd while the band Flight Recorder is performing, to the delight of the audience.

GERT (O.S.)
Looking for someone?

Daisy whips around and is surprised to see Gert.

GERT (CONT'D)
Where's Ian?

DAISY
(shrugs)
I don't know. Alan isn't here either.

GERT
Listen, I'm sorry about what I said.

DAISY
(smiles)
That's okay. You were right. I shouldn't have said that
about Stella. I knew it when I said it, but I guess I thought
someone important might be listening to that interview and
I didn't want them to think Mary Jane Lane was falling
apart.
(beat)
Anyway, it was stupid.

They hug.

GERT
See Stella?

DAISY
(anxiously)
No, did you?

Gert shakes her head no. They both look out at the
audience.

MALE VOICE (O.S.)
(through the sound system)
That was Flight Recorder. Give it up.

The audience APPLAUDS.

MALE VOICE (O.S.)
(through the sound system)
Are you ready?

The crowd ROARS.

MALE VOICE (O.S.) (CONT'D)
I said, are you ready?

The crowd ROARS LOUDER.

MALE VOICE (O.S.) (CONT'D)
Let's hear it for Hollywood's very own, Mary...
(beat)
Jane...
(beat)
Lane!

The crowd GOES BERSERK, some waving Mary Jane
Lane posters in the air.

Gert and Daisy look at each other and take a deep breath.
They step toward the stage and Gert reaches back to grab
Daisy's hand and pull her up on stage, but they are both
pulled back by two PLAIN-CLOTHES POLICE
OFFICERS, who flash their badges.

PLAIN-CLOTHES OFFICER #1
You're under arrest for first-degree murder. It's my duty to
inform you that you have the right to remain silent--

The Officer is drowned out by the crowd, who start to chant.

CROWD (O.S.)
(chanting)
We. Want. Mary. Jane. Lane.
We. Want. Mary. Jane. Lane.

Gert and Daisy are stunned and don't resist when the Officers handcuff them and lead them out, to the amazement of everyone around them. Gert spots Meyers in a crowd of people, but Meyers is focused on the stage.

GERT
(yelling)
Meyers!

But Meyers can't hear her over the crowd.

INT. UNMARKED CAR – MOMENTS LATER

Gert and Daisy are in the backseat, driven by the two Plain-clothes Officers.

DAISY
(in tears)
You have to believe us.

PLAIN-CLOTHES OFFICER #2
Save it.

EXT. CHATEAU MARMONT – MOMENTS LATER

The unmarked car pulls up to the Chateau.

INT. UNMARKED CAR - CONTINUOUS

Gert nudges Daisy, who has her head against the window, her eyes closed.

GERT
What are we doing here?

INT. CHATEAU MARMONT – HALLWAY – A MINUTE LATER

The two Plains-clothes Officers lead Gert and Daisy toward the suite at the end of the hallway. They stop at the door and KNOCK. Detective Boucher answers the door.

DETECTIVE BOUCHER
Nice work, boys.

DAISY
We're innocent. Our friend was framing us.

Detective Boucher smiles.

DETECTIVE BOUCHER
(to the Officers)
Thanks, David. Pete. Appreciate it.

PLAIN-CLOTHES OFFICER #1
No problem, Christine. Consider it a retirement present.

PLAIN-CLOTHES OFFICER #2
Yeah, stay in touch, okay?

DETECTIVE BOUCHER
(touched)
I will.

The two Officers exit, and Detective Boucher opens the suite door all the way, revealing Alan Hood and Ian Black, who are relaxing on the sofa. Out on the patio the drunk Man from Spago is smoking cigarettes with the Deliveryman and the Crazed Woman from Shampu.

GERT
What's going on?

DETECTIVE BOUCHER
Come in.

ALAN
It's okay. Come in.

Gert and Daisy enter the suite.

INT. CHATEAU MARMONT - SUITE - CONTINUOUS

The TV BLARES a commercial, and Alan reaches for the remote and hits mute.

ALAN
You just missed yourself on TV.

IAN
(excitedly)
The crowd overtook the Viper Room, and the cops showed up. The real cops, I mean.

ALAN
Better than we hoped.

DAISY
(confused)
What do you mean?

DETECTIVE BOUCHER
The only thing worse than being talked about is not being

talked about. You've probably heard that one before.

GERT
You mean--

ALAN
C'mon! Let's celebrate.
(to Ian)
Call down for some champagne. On me.

Ian picks up the phone.

DAISY
(to Detective Boucher)
You mean we're not under arrest?

DETECTIVE BOUCHER
Hey, I'm retired. I'm just a publicist for an up-and-coming band now. I couldn't arrest a jaywalker.

ALAN
Well, it's sort of like this: In Hollywood, everything is about illusion and expectation. How many bands do you think want to make it?
(beat)
Too many. And let's face it—I'm not the biggest manager in town. I'm a has-been. That's what people say about me, you should know. But I believe in second chances. Everyone who needs one should get one. Including you two. Somehow you got mixed up in this murder--

GERT
But we really didn't have anything to do with it.

ALAN
Well, people think you're mixed up in it...

DAISY
Thanks to you!

ALAN
(ignoring her)
So the only thing that can launch this second chance is to
get as many people as we can to want you to have a second
chance. And everyone in this room wants you to have that
chance. Does that come close to making sense?

IAN
Mary Jane Lane can write its own ticket now. Anything
you want.

DAISY
(angry)
We wanted to open for Madonna. Remember? That's what
we wanted.

GERT
(angry)
All this shit. It's just fairy dust. You made us turn on our
friend. Fuck all of you.
(to Daisy)
C'mon.

INT. CHATEAU MARMONT – HALLWAY –
CONTINUOUS

Gert and Daisy stomp down the hall.

ALAN (O.S.)
Girls. Wait!

DETECTIVE BOUCHER (O.S.)
They'll come back. Don't chase after them like they're
nine.

IAN (O.S.)
They're out of champagne.

Gert pulls up abruptly and stops Daisy, pointing at a figure with an ice bucket, walking like a zombie toward them. It's Stella.

DAISY
Stella.

Stella stops but leans against the wall. She doesn't seem to recognize them. When she does, she smiles.

STELLA
Hey.

GERT
Where are you going?

STELLA
Ryan needs some ice.

INT. CHATEAU MARMONT – VENDING ROOM – MOMENTS LATER

Gert and Daisy help a weakened Stella fill the ice bucket.

GERT
And you've been here for a week?

STELLA
Feels like a month.

DAISY
We thought--

But Gert shoots her a look.

STELLA
How did the showcase go? Did you meet Madonna?

DAISY
No, we didn't.

STELLA
I'm sorry I didn't make it. I wanted to. I was just too...
(beat)
...embarrassed. Not just about Ryan.
(beat)
You know how when you look forward to something for so
long that you can't believe it when it happens? It was like
that. At first I was...I don't know, in disbelief. But then I
started hanging out with him and he was...just normal. All
that stuff I knew about him before I met him was...fake.
(beat)
I was embarrassed, too, because you guys are following
your dream. The band, everything. You never gave up. I
gave up a long time ago.

DAISY
Don't say that.

STELLA
It's true. Remember I was going to come out here and get
us hooked up? But then I started going on auditions, and
then...I ended up at the Starion. And here.

DAISY
We're sorry.

GERT
Really sorry.

STELLA
I'm sorry too. I shouldn't have gotten mad at you about

that stupid radio interview. It was childish. But the more I
failed out here, the more it hurt.
(beat)
So, do you want to meet Ryan?

Gert and Daisy shrug.

INT. CHATEAU MARMONT – HALLWAY –
CONTINUOUS

Gert, Daisy, and Stella head back to Ryan's suite but are
stopped by John Keyes.

JOHN KEYES
Hello.

Gert and Daisy recognize the man, but can't place him.

JOHN KEYES
(points at himself)
John Keyes. We met at Spago.

Gert and Daisy remember.

JOHN KEYES (CONT'D)
Anyway, I'm sorry that I missed you at the showcase.

GERT
That's okay.

DAISY
It didn't go so well.

JOHN KEYES
Oh? Sorry to hear it.

DAISY
We're not really what we seem.

JOHN KEYES
(laughs)
Who is?
(beat)
The reason I didn't make it to your show is that I quit my job. I'm going out on my own. Going to start my own label.

DAISY
Cool.

JOHN KEYES
You interested?

This catches Gert and Daisy off-guard.

DAISY
(automatically)
Yeah, of course.

GERT
We're not really singers, though.
(looks at Daisy)
But we want to be.

JOHN KEYES
Can you sing at all?

DAISY
Some.

GERT
Yeah, some.

Daisy grabs Stella.

DAISY
This is Stella, she's the third member of Mary Jane Lane.

Stella is pleasantly surprised by this gesture.

JOHN KEYES
Well, I'm willing to do the work if you are.

DAISY (V.O.)
Someone splashed in the pool outside, and it reminded me of a long time ago, when it was the three of us, out by Stella's parents' pool, leafing through magazines of celebrities at parties and movie premieres, celebrities smiling out at you in a way that let you know that their life was just fantastic, that every day was like their birthday and that their worst day was nothing like your worst day. We spent hours by the pool talking "what if," which over time became "when," but I don't think we had any idea of what it would take to have a life where every day was like your birthday. What would you say if someone offered you a chance like that?

BLACK SCREEN

DAISY (V.O.) (CONT'D)
And so I guess you probably know what we said.

THE END